MW00476734

about the author

Zachary Dillon studied creative writing under T.C. Boyle at the
University of Southern California. His first published book was
People With Problems, a collection of diverse flash fiction stories
illustrated by artists he admires.

I Hear You Watching is his first novel.

For more info, visit ZacharyDillon.com

also by Zachary Dillon

People With Problems: illustrated stories

I HEAR YOU WATCHING

ZACHARY DILLON

z

ISBN (paperback): 978-2-9583843-2-6

ISBN (ebook): 978-2-9583843-3-3

Work cited:

Bierstedt, Robert. "Chapter 3: Charles Horton Cooley." *American Sociological Theory: A Critical History*, Academic Press, a Subsidary of Harcourt Brace Jovanovich, Publishers, New York, NY, 1981, p. 98.

Cover art by Eliott Blue
eliott-blue-draws.blogspot.com

For Louise, ma seule

I HEAR YOU
WATCHING

I am not what I think I am;
I am not what you think I am;
I am what I think you think I am.

- Charles Horton Cooley
as summarized by Robert Bierstedt

A MONTH FROM NOW, I'll try not to worry whether anyone thinks I'm a good person. I'll move from my one-bedroom apartment into something called a "micro-studio," and see it as an upgrade. I'll get a job at a pet food store, which will force me to speak to people on a daily basis, and I'll frame it as immersion therapy.

Someone will buy four cans of dog food, and when I ask if he wants a bag he'll smile and say, "No, thanks, I'll eat it on the way home!" It'll be the third time I've heard that joke that day, but the small kindness of his smile will move me almost to tears.

An hour later, while "Margaritaville" plays from the ceiling speakers, I'll cling white-knuckled to the memory of that smile when I hear a voice in the next aisle say they poisoned my sandwich at lunch. It'll help me doubt another voice that says they're going to show up after closing and throw me in the trunk of a car.

I'll walk to work each morning, and home every night, refusing to look over my shoulder, with my heart in my chest like a leaf about to fall.

I'll have been a target of the universe. A searing pinpoint of light under the vast lens of the all-seeing Eye.

I'll have died many times, at hands that were mostly my own.

Once buried alive and shot into space.

Once like a pig drained of blood.

Once torn to smaller and smaller pieces by millions of tinier lives.

I'll have become a multiple murderer, despite my innocence. My victims will grow easier to kill and harder to ignore.

But that's all a month away.

Right now I'm sitting on the couch in my one-bedroom apartment with my pants around my ankles, blissfully unaware that these are my last few minutes of freedom.

I've found a porn clip I like. Nothing rough. The man is out of frame except his legs. The woman isn't pretending to be someone's cousin, sister, or stepdaughter. She smiles in the moments her mouth is free, and takes her time.

My right hand starts to cramp up, so I change to my left, and a voice outside my window says, "The stranger..."

I know "the stranger" is what it's called when someone masturbates with their non-dominant hand, because it feels like someone else.

The blinds are closed, no one can see me. Someone talking outside happened to say the words "the stranger" at the exact moment I switched hands. Synchronicity has told a perfect joke.

But it's too perfect.

I shrink like an untied balloon, and my hand stays in my lap like a circle of protection. My apartment is on the second floor, so it would take a ladder or X-ray vision to see me—unless the onlooker is in the house next door, which has a window facing mine. I bend, seeking a line of sight beneath my blinds to my crotch, but there isn't one.

Someone outside laughs.

I pull my boxers up and creep to the window. A look through my blinds proves the neighbor's blinds are also closed. As is their window. No one in the alley or carport below.

I slide my window shut and lock it.

Then I close the laptop and finish quickly in the bathroom. It's perfunctory and unsatisfying, because I can't shake the voice.

***

The stranger is a grain of sand in my shell.

Grit, lodged in a tender fold.

I don't know how it got in. Maybe it was always here, unfelt until now.

I'll turn and worry it in my mind, and soon it will thicken into something altogether different. Something iridescent.

This is how it begins.

A FEW HOURS AFTER hearing the stranger outside my window, it's midnight and I'm at work. The office is modern, with brick walls and exposed I beams painted dark gray. The main room has twenty workstations with just seven of us spread among them on the night shift. The only lights on are in this room and the kitchen down the hall. The only sound is the clatter of our keyboards like a constant hailstorm. Everything else is dark and quiet.

Tonight I'm captioning an episode of a reality game show called *All By Myself*. On my computer screen is a view from the ceiling of a small, closed room. The walls are bright orange. Near one wall is a table with jigsaw puzzle pieces on it. In the center of the room is a pudgy man in a purple jumpsuit with a number 8 on the back, spinning in a swivel chair and counting out loud.

I type his counting into onscreen captions, *Forty-eight... Forty-nine... Fifty.*

He stands, takes a step toward the puzzle table, sways like a sapling in the wind, vomits on himself and sits back in the chair.

He's struggling to get back up when a computerized voice speaks, and I type, *Number Eight, you have not assembled your puzzle, and your body has given up. This is your second strike.*

The man screams, and I type, *I don't give up! I'm still in!*

A splashy neon frame appears around the image with the words "coming up..."

The man paces, shouts, *I'm not [bleep] disqualified!*

The computerized narrator says, *Number Eight doesn't know when to quit. But his body is telling him time's up.*

A shot of the man leaning against the wall magnifies to the point of pixilation. He punches the wall and vomits again.

Can Number Eight's mind and body work together to win my $50,000? Analysis pending on All By Myself.

The image wipes to black and the timecode flickers by.

I look at the nighttime window near my desk, and my reflection stares back. The quiet in my headphones makes my coworkers' keyboards louder.

I forget what Number Eight said his name was in the first episode. Ron, or something. At this point he's been in his "chamber" for a week. No windows. His meals are served through a slot in the wall. His every action is recorded, edited, and when I'm finished with the closed-captioning, broadcast for millions to see.

I think of the stranger who laughed at me earlier tonight and wonder, does Number Eight think about being watched, or does his awareness end at the walls of his chamber?

I've noticed he tends to rub his nose when he thinks. Does he make sure to face a camera when he does, so viewers can't accuse him of picking his nose? Is the editor tempted to choose another angle to make it look like he's picking his nose? Is Number Eight embarrassed or proud of his depiction on the show, or does he even care? Does he think of himself as being a smart person? a strong person? a good person?

According to the episode's intro, Number Eight has been in this room for three weeks. When he lies on his retractable cot to sleep, does he stare at the close orange walls and think about everyone else? Does he miss anyone?

Does he have anyone to miss?

A siren goes off in my ears and neon smears across the screen.

The narrator says, *Number Eight's body has just earned him a second strike. Let's see if—*

I stop the video, rewind, create a new caption, timestamp it at the start of the segment, and type: *[siren wails]*

***

At 4 a.m. I'm halfway through the episode but can't keep my eyes open.

I remove my headphones to let the ringing in my ears fade, and go to the front of the office where it's dark and empty. I sit on the couch in the lobby and stare out the window at the Department of Water and Power across the street. I lose myself in plumes of steam lit purple-orange by the streetlights and bulging into the sky like great, wrinkling worms.

Later, my eyes open to the silhouette of my supervisor standing in the dark hallway, calling my name. "Alex... Alex..."

I stop by the kitchen and pour a cup from a pot of burnt coffee.

Back at my desk I check my email. Gavin sent Eli and me a map of the trail to Sulphur Springs, our campsite for the weekend. I met Gavin and Eli in college, and we go camping together once a month. These trips are my only escape from the city.

I think I might tell them about the coincidence with the stranger. Maybe they've had similar experiences. Maybe we'll laugh about it.

GAVIN SHUCKS STRIPS OF bark from his walking stick with his folding knife. "So your neighbor's a perv."

"But you couldn't see him." Eli vaults himself to sit on a fallen tree.

"I didn't see anybody."

"Huh." Eli thumps his bootheels against the trunk. "I've never had anything like that happen."

"Me neither." Gavin finds a rough spot on his stick and slices it away.

Eli says, "I'm pretty careful about that stuff."

I swirl my metal mug. "So am I."

"Eh, not careful enough." His eyebrows raise at me.

The blinds were closed, the laptop's volume was turned down—what else could I have done?

My black tea is gritty, bitter with iodine, and full of invisible corpses. Bean-shaped giardia, tentacled hydra, cluster-eyed daphnia, amoebas, and who knows what else. "I read about a woman who swam in a creek and got water in her nose. Two weeks later an amoeba had eaten most of her brain." I close my eyes and watch the sun and branches flicker red through my eyelids. "She was in a coma for a month before she died."

"So..." Eli says, "your point is, just because you can't see something doesn't mean it isn't there."

"I was changing the subject."

"You brought it up."

"It's a funny story, that's all. Just a coincidence." The shadows move through my eyelids. "If people still lived out here in the open instead of in little boxes stacked up in the city, we'd probably see each other jerk off all the time. Wouldn't be a big deal."

"Heh. Could be," Gavin says.

Eli says, "I think I prefer jerking off in my little box, thanks."

Gavin unbuttons the floppy brim of his hat against the sun. "Given the choice, I prefer sex with a real person, to be fair."

"I don't have that choice at the moment," I say.

"You're over what's-her-face, right?"

"We slept together twice, it wasn't a relationship. At least not to her."

"So talk to some girls."

I smile and run a hand through my hair. "Hi there, ladies. My name's Alex. I work five nights a week typing what people say on TV. Maybe someday I'll *manage* the people who type what people say on TV. How 'bout we go to my shitty one-bedroom apartment and get to know each other?"

Eli kicks his dangling legs. "I'd fuck you."

Gavin says, "My brother just got on a new dating app. Fire, or something?"

"Tinder," says Eli.

"There's dating apps now?" I ask.

"Full of loner creeps." Eli tucks his knees against his chest, perched like a vulture.

Gavin closes his knife. "No, really, they're becoming a thing. I thought of signing up myself."

"If you wanna meet a fifty-year-old married man." Eli's heel slips on the log, but he catches himself.

I raise my arms. "I'll just flap my wings and puff my throat sac."

"The internet's a big place." Gavin draws a slow squiggle with his walking stick. "Lot of people out there in the same boat."

Another sarcastic joke rises in my throat, but I swallow it back to let the subject die.

For a while before our day hike to the hot springs, Gavin and Eli strut around making whoosh-whoosh sounds in their convertible hiking pants, consulting their altimeters and compasses, trading 48-hour predictions about the weather.

I think of contestant Number Eight on *All By Myself* and how complete his isolation must've felt despite knowing so many people were watching. Or maybe he felt alone *because* they were watching.

***

Sulphur Springs is about an hour's walk from our campsite. Five small pools step down a rocky hill, their edges built up with stones and clay to hold the warm, rotten-egg-smelling water trickling from pool to pool on its way to the bottom where it finally spreads shining across a cracked rock plane to join the river.

Most of the pools are only big enough for two or three people. Among them are an older couple with floppy hats and zinc oxide on their faces, a set of college-age hikers split vertically between two pools (guys in the upper splashing girls in the lower), and some parents who've wheeled a cooler next to the pool they're sitting in. They drink beer and tell their kids playing on the wet rock below not to slip.

A bald man with his eyes closed sits alone in the large pool at the bottom. Water from above splashes around the fleshy stone of his head. He opens his eyes, sees us, and scoots to the end, his underwater body foreshortened and jiggling.

I sit next to him and nod a thank-you. He closes his eyes again.

Our faces hover close to the water and the sulfur smell is strong. My fingers slip through wisps of green algae. I look out the corner of my eye at the man, who's sitting so still he looks like a decoy to attract other humans.

I have to pee.

If I get out now, I'll have to explain myself within earshot of the man and everyone else. Then I'll try to find a secluded spot, but all these strangers will know I'm peeing.

I observe the expanse of the canyon. Oak leaves shiver in the sunlight, the creek glitters, and the children stomp in the water flowing across the rock floor. The water is so warm, I wonder how many of the people above us have peed into the stream filling our basin. Maybe none, maybe all of them.

I release a little urine and sneak a look down to see if it's visible. The sulfur water is cloudy, so no. I release the rest in small, carefully spaced bursts, and I look at Gavin and Eli and say, "Pretty good," using it like magician's patter to distract them from suspicion.

Gavin says, "Yup."

Would they be angry at me if they knew? Secretly peeing on people is the kind of thing a "loner creep" would do.

My relief turns to shame.

***

The grain of sand scrapes in my shell.

I squirm.

***

Later we leave the pool and walk to the river. It's cold and clear. We duck under and undulate like otters, and the sulfur water slips from our skin and rushes away in the current. The change from hot to cold makes me have to pee again.

Eli says, "You guys know about that fish that can swim up your urethra?"

Gavin says, "If you pee, it swims up the stream, right?"

"Yeah, and it's got barbs that lodge it in there."

Are they saying this because they're peeing now, or because they know I did?

"Good thing those're only in South America," Eli says, looking at me, and he lets out an exaggerated moan.

AT HOME, GAVIN'S WORDS echo in my mind—*the internet's a big place. Lot of people in the same boat.*

Los Angeles is a gigantic boat, carrying four million passengers. I can't be the only lonely person among them.

They're all fifty-year-old married men, butts in imaginary Eli.

Looking up dating sites, I think, *this isn't what normal people do—especially not people in their mid-20s—search the internet for a partner.* I feel like a creep in a sea of creeps.

I remember the stranger's laugh out my window.

Between me doing something in my own home, and my neighbor watching me do it, who is the real creep?

Imaginary Gavin says, *Your neighbor's a perv.*

But I was the one masturbating. If I'd just been cooking dinner or reading a book while they watched, the question of "which one of us is the perv" wouldn't come up at all.

I once watched a clip of a woman on a couch having sex with a standing man, and I couldn't stop staring at his legs. I masturbated in the opportune intervals: closeups of the penetration, faces and sounds she made in time with the movements, the way her breasts bounced and her nipples traced circles like the eyes of a cartoon character after a blow to the head. Then I'd see a wide shot of him standing there. His belly didn't bulge but clearly gathered at the bottom. His thighs were round like hairy hog backs, and his calves curved like fish bellies to the shifting egg sacs of his ankles. His feet settled flat on the floor like fistfuls of dough.

These visions triggered words: homunculus, hominid, biped, organism...

His legs tensed, almost breathed, muscles and tendons boiling as he pumped fertilizer into the receptive female, and I imagined the narration of an old science newsreel: *Behold man's strongest link to the rest of the animal kingdom, Porno erectus. Here we see a specimen in the act of procreation.*

The thing pulled itself out of the woman, and its genital wand bobbed the way a parade horse's does when it pisses on the street. Then it squished its doughy pads on the hardwood floor to position itself at the other end of the couch and held the woman's head. The tendons moving in its hands looked like bat wings, and I stopped the video.

Most people don't see it this way.

I am not a "porno erectus," I'm just human. My desire for sex doesn't make me gross or a pervert or a bad person. Everybody pees. Everyone masturbates. Why am I ashamed of these things?

I thought of signing up myself, imaginary Gavin says. He's my age, and this is something people our age are doing now.

But I need to find a place where sexual interest is stated up front, so I can get out of my head and meet someone eye-to-eye.

Where are all the open, honest people on the internet?

After more research and hesitation, I choose AdultXXXPlaydate.com. The membership fee is discounted for the first six months with a money-back guarantee: "If you don't get laid, we don't get paid!" I don't bother to read the fine print on how they handle those claims.

A popup asks if I'm 18. Then I enter my email address—one I created for use on this site—and another popup interrupts to tell me "Sherri" is waiting for me on her webcam and is "lonely and ready to party," along with a video image of a woman using a green vibrator that I don't watch long enough to know if it's an animated GIF, prerecorded, or piped in from somewhere else.

Maybe Sherri's really there, but she definitely isn't waiting for *me*.

Login opens a welcome marquee, followed by two banner ads for "sexy singles in the area" and a website for discounted sex toys—the image is a whip on display behind multicolored butt plugs lined up in a rainbow.

Below that is the real content: rows and rows of profiles and a number of ways to filter, categorize, and search. It's a gridwork wilderness of fanning feathers, distending vocal sacs, poses and dances, the human animal expressing its completely natural desire for physical companionship.

Some profiles are just a photo of breasts bubbling from a wet tank top and sprinkled with glitter. Many are body shots in varying levels of nakedness—bikini, nothing at all, open robe, electrical tape Xes on nipples, mix-and-matched pieces of cheap Halloween costumes. One woman with full sleeve tattoos taped leaves to herself and poses like a statue in a small yard with a Weber grill behind her.

Most of the photos were taken in fluorescent-lit bathroom mirrors, or yellow bedroom light through murky lo-fi webcams. A few are grainy, ghostly faces or breasts in dark rooms, dusted with the chalky blue glow of the computer screen.

One woman fills her lingerie like sandbags stacked for a flash flood and her smile burns with confidence.

I open an older couple's profile. In the first photo the man is just a pair of thick, pasty legs the woman straddles. In the next he's a large gut and droopy knees edging into frame behind her while she arches her back, her own gut nearly grazing the rumpled floral-print comforter like a milk-full udder.

I marvel at their boldness.

In another profile a woman pushes things into herself while seated on her apartment balcony. I wonder if her neighbors saw her. And I wonder if she knew.

All the couples I see are heterosexual (or labeled bisexual, but the photos are invariably of a man and woman). I wonder whether lesbians were driven away by messages from guys requesting threesomes or offering to "turn them straight."

Conversely, when I toggle the filter there's an avalanche of gay men. Pages upon pages of sculpted pecs and abs, erect penises both shaven and bushy, selfies on motorcycles or sailboats, on black leather couches in boxer briefs, older men with bodies like bruised pears, young men with shy smiles aimed next to or below their webcams. Some photos have the faces blurred out.

Whether heterosexual or homosexual, almost all of the men who show small penises look to be over fifty, and are either rail-thin or buddha-round.

But despite all this apparent honesty, I now realize there must be as many lies here as on a regular dating site. The pretty, girl-next-door-looking women feel like catfish profiles created by older men.

Lots of profiles make a point of specifying that the person is "clean." If a woman shows her vagina in a photo, why do I assume she's more or less likely to have an STD? Sure, the pose implies heightened promiscuity and therefore a higher possibility of having contracted a disease, but if a woman holds her breasts, or is fully clothed and smiling, or smooches at the camera, couldn't she be hiding visible indications of disease? It's easy to take a photo between outbreaks. Some diseases are invisible.

The more I look at these people—*into* these people—the less I know about them.

After an hour and a half looking at photos of naked people reflected in smudgy mirrors, opening their legs on unmade beds, standing in apartments with time-stained walls or stacks of boxes in the corner or a cat tree with torn carpet and sisal cord unraveling from its pillars, a lethargy comes like hot molasses behind my eyes.

My mind buzzes from the sheer amount of work on display: the putting forth of one's assets to attract a sexual partner, the effort to wear something revealing or titillating, the care taken to arrange oneself, to set the timer on the camera and pose quickly, or to have someone else take the photo.

Paradoxically, there's a complete lack of awareness about dried toothpaste specks on the mirror, half-empty plastic bottles of cloudy liquid standing around the sink, clumps of hair trailing from a brush in a puddle on the bathroom counter. These are human animals in all their glory, captured in their various caves and hovels. Brazen.

I can learn from them.

In my desk chair next to my unmade bed, wearing only a T-shirt and boxers, I examine my own cave. The walls are the typical off-white of low-rent apartments, and they're bare, which makes the room feel small. Then there are the sheets of aluminum foil I put over the bedroom window to help me sleep during the day. They crackle now in the breeze, as if acknowledging my attention. The intermittent whir of a tool from the nearby auto body shop seeps through the foil, trailed by the smell of hot rubber.

I'm heavy in my chair. I feel lived-in.

***

My username is "ZekeJones1986"—fake name, real birth year—and my profile has three photos.

1: I stand in my living room smiling. Pomade in my hair for the first time in a while, parted on the right but mussed to avoid looking too square. I have a two-week beard, the edges of which I trimmed on my cheeks and neck. I clipped the nose hair curling out my nostrils. I'm wearing my glasses. I have contacts, but I haven't used them since I started working nights, so wearing them in a profile photo would feel dishonest.

I'm only slightly sucking in my stomach.

I'm wearing my favorite T-shirt—a pen-and-ink portrait by the cartoonist Robert Crumb of the blues musician Robert Johnson holding his guitar, a cigarette at a slant in his mouth.

Visible on the shelf behind me were dusty books from college—*East Asian Ethical Thought, L.A. the Fiction, The Foundations of Screenwriting, Beowulf*, etc.—not the collection of a real reader, so I switched them around with my eyes closed to keep from consciously forcing an agenda. Kafka and Vonnegut wound up next to each other, which I worried might look pretentious or cliché, but I left them that way to avoid overthinking it.

I hope I appear kind, respectable, and intelligent, with eclectic interests.

I was careful to turn my vertical blinds to let in ambient light but block the neighbors' view of me taking pictures of myself. The site's emphasis on "singles in your area" means there's a small chance the stranger who saw me masturbating could have a profile on here too, and could recognize me.

2: Next is a shot I took while camping. I'm sitting against a tree. My jeans have holes in the knees, my black T-shirt is lightly sweat-dampened, and my floppy hat hangs on the back of my neck. There's no pomade in my hair, but repeated force and natural oils provide my right-handed part. The canopy behind me is mottled green with bursts of light.

I hope I look like someone who exercises, enjoys escaping into nature, and doesn't buy into the 24-hour preening vanity of L.A.

3: The third photo is intended to round out my presentation of self.

I'm in the driveway at Eli's birthday party wearing an orange-and-brown plaid collared shirt with the sleeves rolled up. Pomade in my hair. The side of Eli's house is light blue behind me, so I look like a maple tree on a clear fall day. Eli's arm reaches into frame as if to snatch the beer bottle nearing my mouth. I don't see this because I'm raising an eyebrow at the camera.

I hope people see a guy with a silly side, who likes drinks with friends.

That night at work I draft my bio. When I get home in the morning and read it a few more times it says:

Hello!

I'm new to this kind of thing. The site, I mean—haha. Interested in meeting people and seeing what happens. Feel free to send me a message.

I am 100% clean, always use protection.

You can see I like hiking and reading. I work nights, so I'm available during the day and on weekends.

I look forward to meeting you!

When that long-ago fish grew legs and crawled from the sludge, did it have any inkling of this moment? Was there a twinkle in the patch of photosensitive cells on its head that saw its descendant millions of years in the future, hunched and sweating in front of an electronic screen, transmitting black-and-white squiggles to negotiate sexual congress with other members of the species?

I have no idea what I'm doing.

A MESSAGE ARRIVES FROM "VanessaBabeNY83." It says, *hey wanna fuck all night?* And then, *u can cum on my tits. im not shy :)*

This message is only the fourth I've received on the site after a prostitute offering a discount if I paid cash, an older couple inviting me to break in their new sex swing, and a woman in Madagascar seeking a husband.

"VanessaBabe's" profile says she lives in New York City, and her posted age indicates that 83 is her birth year. Three years older than me, if true.

Her profile pic shows a pretty twentysomething brunette with round eyes and a long jaw. She's in a T-shirt, leggings, and chunky white sneakers, sitting on a folding chair at a backyard fire pit. In the second photo she's in a dim bar, a cigarette near her mouth, a lowball glass sweating in her hand—something clear with a slice of lime. In the third she's lying on a beach in a bikini, shading her eyes from the sun. She's got sunglasses on, but I can tell it's her because the left canine tooth slants inward a little, which is also visible near the cigarette in the bar photo. Her shaped brown eyebrows at the bar match those under the ridge of her beanie in the fire pit photo.

These are all the same woman.

Her eyes are sleepy and sultry, which is alluring, but I wonder how many shots it took to get "the right look."

And those messages? No, she's definitely not shy. She may be a veteran on the site.

A green dot appears next to her name with the words "ONLINE NOW."

So I respond, *Hey, thanks for the message. I'm available. Are you in LA?*

An ellipsis appears as she types. The back of my neck tightens. Blood shifts in my groin.

She writes back, *im in ny / but we can fuck rn if u want*

Disappointment. But part of me is relieved that my first encounter from the site won't be in person. If I embarrass myself, she's all the way in New York and I'll never see her again. I write, *Sure, I'd love that.*

we can fuck on skype / whats ur name?

Oh, my real name is Alex. Nice to meet you. Your name's Vanessa?

no i mean ur skype name / yeah im vanessa / hi alex :)

Seeing her write my name, transcribed by her fingers with a lowercase "a," I feel a familiar tingle. Like chatting with a middle school crush late at night on AOL Instant Messenger. That intoxicating squirt of dopamine when the response dings in the window.

I tell her, *My Skype ID is noleafclover55. I know, it's goofy. I basically used the first email address I ever had, which I got in middle school. I was really into Metallica then.*

i <3 metallica

Yeah? I was obsessed with the S&M album when it came out.

She says, *do u like s+m? / ;)*

Is this put-on sexy talk, or am I about to learn something new? How might S&M work over video chat? Would she just shout orders, like a deranged Simon Says? *I can't say I've ever tried it, actually. / I'm on Skype. Are you?*

I watch the cursor blink in our chat window. After a couple minutes her green dot turns orange and "ONLINE NOW" changes to "IDLE."

I write, *Vanessa, you there?*

The video call notification appears, ringing, from "ivny713." Maybe it stands for "I, Vanessa, New York"? I can't figure out the 713. But 7 + 1 = 8, so 83. I answer the call.

"Hello?"

Silence. The video shows me sitting at my desk.

"Vanessa? Your camera's not on. Or the sound."

A chat line appears. *hey babe / mic doesnt work / we can type on here :)*

I write, *Your video's not working either. I just see myself.*

one sec

It occurs to me that I've seen so many naked pictures of other people, and now it's my turn. Live.

My image blinks out and she appears.

Her camera is set up as a wide shot of the room, so I can see the full length of her from the side, lying on her stomach on a bed with her feet up behind her, staring at an open laptop. She's in a T-shirt and panties with her hair in a ponytail. There's a nightstand next to the bed with a lamp, an ashtray, and an orange pill bottle on it. When I took antidepressants in college they came in the same orange bottle. And now when I buy weed from the dispensary it comes in the same orange bottle. She could have anything in there.

From the side I can't see her face well enough to compare to the photos, but the hair color matches. She's a real person. And the webcam setup shows she's done this before.

Now I'm not sure what to say. *You're really beautiful.*

She types.

thx / get naked for me

Of course. You too!

I remove my T-shirt and watch her watch me on her screen.

Eventually she leans on an elbow and pulls her shirt over her head. Small breasts spring out from under the T-shirt, which she tosses aside before lying back down and typing: *come on babe lets see it / i wanna suck your cock*

I'd like that, I write. *It's too bad you're in New York.*

I realize if I stay seated, her view of my paunch is less than ideal. It might be easier to ignore that stuff in person than on a computer screen.

show me

I stand, push my boxers to my knees and let them drop to the floor. I'm naked in front of a stranger on the internet for the first time. Seeing my half-erect penis in the thumbnail view of my room I feel the same chill as my first time being naked with someone. My nerves are hypersensitive to the sudden absence of concealment and security. I'm grateful the feeling doesn't weaken my erection but encourages it. My hand goes to it like a master reassuring a dog in strange company.

I think of the bat-handed, hairy-hog-legged "P. erectus," and can't imagine what anyone thinks when they see me naked.

My body doesn't seem to deter Vanessa.

stroke it for me

I follow instructions, watching for her to do something, but she just stares at her screen. Her feet kick slowly in the air. She might as well be scrolling through her Twitter feed.

She writes, *stroke it hard*

I stop and type, *Are you going to join me?*

Her legs lower, and she types. Then the video cuts out. The call stays connected but shows a camera icon with a slash through it.

I type, *Your video cut out.*

I wait. My penis bobs with my heartbeat, now eager for this stranger's stare.

Vanessa?

The icon disappears, the screen goes black, and then the video comes back on. The image isn't of her on the bed—it's of me standing in my room.

I'm now leaning on the desk with both hands, but the me on my screen is still stroking himself.

I think of Number Eight watching himself vomit on TV.

I start writing that something's wrong, when a message appears.

i hacked ur facebook account if you dont give me ur credit card info ill post this video on ur page so everyone sees what a sick pervert u r

I sit. The dog in my lap backs into its house. The air that tingled with excitement feels cold again.

I write, *What is this?*

give me ur credit card or i will ruin u

I don't know whether "Vanessa" can make good on her threat, and it's unclear how much time I have before she will. But I think I've kept some agency by not reaching for my wallet. I write, *Why are you doing this?*

dont fuck around!!! / do u want everyone u know to see u jerk off??

My pubic hairs feel like they're retracting into my skin. I wonder if she's hacked other accounts too, like my bank or PayPal. But if she had, she wouldn't be pulling this weird stunt.

Unless she gets off on catching her victims literally with their pants down.

My parents. My aunts and uncles and cousins. Coworkers. Friends. I might be able to laugh about this with Gavin and Eli, but what about everyone else? My naked body touching itself on screens everywhere. I'd feel turned inside-out. It's one thing for a stranger to glimpse a private moment through the blinds; it's another for hundreds—thousands—to see it in their feed. With boxes to comment and buttons to share.

Another cold tremor and waft of sweat smell. I poke at the keys: *please don't*

She says, *fuck u pervert / posting now*

I quit Skype and open my Facebook account. Nothing new on my page. I change my password. I check the account's email address and phone number. Still mine. I wonder who else might be looking at this information right now.

I log out and log back in with the new password.

Check everything again. Everything's the same.

I sit naked and chilly in the dim room, hearing the foil on the window crackle, and I refresh the page again and again and again, waiting to see myself appear.

***

The grain of sand in my shell takes on another layer of nacre. It's smooth and round now, doesn't scrape anymore. But it's bigger. I've shifted myself to accommodate it.

I don't realize how much space it takes.

I CHECK MY FACEBOOK account every few hours and change my password every day. I assume "Vanessa" has moved on, but another part of me thinks as soon as I stop changing my password she'll be able to crack it.

I don't log back in to the sex site, but I do check my dummy email account for message notifications in case she sends more threats.

After a few days I'm notified of a new message. Red text at the top of the email explains that the message was sent anonymously—a feature available for premium accounts. It says, *Forgive me if I'm crossing a line here. I know your profile says you prefer women, but I wondered if you were open to the idea of receiving a blowjob from a man. If you close your eyes, it doesn't matter who's doing it. ;) Again, I don't mean to offend.*

I read the message again, then reread it.

This can't be "Vanessa" trying a bizarre new tactic. It's likely a real proposition. From a man.

I'm flattered to think he saw my profile and went out on a limb.

Is it difficult for him to find gay partners? Has he been through a similar wringer as me, and now we've got the option as two timid sex site rejects to settle for each other's company?

Or is this a kink that exists, homosexual sex with a heterosexual partner?

Has he seen the profiles of gay men claiming to be "clean," and does he not believe them? If so, why would a heterosexual man be any different?

Maybe I remind him of someone he longs to have back or could never have. An unrequited schoolyard crush, or someone with whom he used to exchange secret pleasures.

If he's still in the closet, maybe he feels I won't lecture him on the merits of coming out. Maybe he assumes I'd be embarrassed to receive oral sex from another man, and finds solace in our equal footing as two people with a secret to keep.

Something in my profile might imply that I'm in the closet myself and in need of a nudge in the right direction, permission from a stranger to live my truth.

Maybe he intends to get as far as the act itself, then slit my throat and bite off my penis to keep in a jar on a shelf with others he's collected over the years. Or he's a serial killer on the verge of self-realization, and mine would be the inaugural genitals of his collection.

Or maybe he isn't even gay—maybe he just quit smoking and ran out of gum.

He could've written the message in his sleep and he'll be horrified to realize it tomorrow.

Or it was actually written by a six-year-old girl copying sentences from a novel she found on her parents' shelf. Or sent by a parrot someone taught to type.

I log in, and respond that I'm flattered by the offer but that I'm looking for something mutual. And I apologize, because his being a man makes reciprocation unappealing to me.

I remember "P. erectus" again and feel dizzy.

But I thank him for the kind message.

Ships in the night.

ANOTHER MESSAGE TODAY.

The sender's name is "PainterLi," and the message says, *Hey, you seem nice.*

It doesn't come on strong like "Vanessa's" first message. There's hesitation in the word *seem*, implying the sender might've been burned like I have, but the vagueness of the message feints from further scrutiny.

I look at the profile.

No picture, and it's labeled female.

The bio says: *25. Doing some soul searching and looking for clean fun. Emphasis on clean. Geek at heart, corporate grunt by day.*

Short and sweet. If it's honest, we already have things in common.

I write back, *You seem nice too. From what little I see here.*

And I wait.

In the afternoon I'm smoking a bowl in my living room when I get a response: *That's it. / That's all there is to know about me.*

Green dot, ONLINE NOW.

I say, *That can't be everything.*

They say, *Well, I guess you've gotta dig a little deeper...*
Okay, what's your name?
Lili / Your turn.
Alex.

I wait, wondering where to go from names and half-expecting her to start spitting blackmail at me. I write, *You say you're a "corporate grunt." What do you do?*

Claims analyst / I always feel like that sounds like a compression of "anal cyst," which is apt because it's a pain in the ass. / What's your job?

I do closed-captioning.

Like subtitles for TV? / The news and stuff?

Not live. It's mostly reality shows.

bwahahaha / Oh, you poor bastard. / You've gotta also love it though, don't you?

No, Lili. I do not love it.

Uh-oh, hit a nerve?

Let me put it this way. If I have to listen to one more Real Housewife equate shopping at De Beers with "stimulating the economy," I'll put a gun in my mouth. / I think I'd prefer your "claims anal cysts."

Honestly, I think I would too!

We should trade jobs.

Nah, that's cool. / No offense, haha / Plus I think our bosses would notice.

You don't think we look enough alike?

Um, no.

I haven't seen what you look like.

What do you mean? I've got a photo up.

I load the profile again. *There's no photo, just a gray silhouette.*

Common mistake, that's actually me.

Huh. If that's true, your photo is all over this site.

I know. Everyone stole it from my profile. / Fucked up, isn't it?

It is.

That makes it easy for me to blend in here. But the real problem is when I walk around outside. / Everyone stares...

An image forms in my mind, a piecemeal assemblage of girls with whom I've had similar flirty banter.

We say nothing for long enough that my image slips apart. The person on the other end could be anyone.

Then they say, *Email?*

I type the email address I created for signup on the site, which is a handful of letters and numbers.

Wow haha / Are you a part-time spammer or what?

No, that's actually my email address. All the spammers copied me. ;)

Another long pause. They could be searching for a photo that fits the personality they've cultivated with me. A cute girl, glasses, snarky smile but not too severe. Maybe they use different photos with different people, pulled from a series of nesting folders labeled according to personality type. Now they're navigating to profile_pics/humor/sardonic/mild.

I refresh my inbox. If it's anything but a photo, I'll know that this "Lili" isn't who they claim to be.

Eventually an email appears from libsg2003@saymail.com with the subject: *pic of Lili*. I click, the photo loads.

There's one person in the photo—a woman who looks about my age, with dark brown skin, tilting her head over a plate of nachos. She has a round face, dimples, and deep eyes that smile along with her mouth. Her hair sticks out in chunky springs long enough that one hangs just over her left eye.

A weird sense of pride moves through me. She's Black. And she contacted me. Something in me is flattered to have received any attention from this woman, as if she's crossed some imaginary aisle. To her I seem "approachable."

Then a second feeling blooms, a nauseous recognition that my pride has nothing to do with her, only the "type" of woman she is compared to the "type" of man I am.

I feel a stir in my lap and wonder—moments ago, when my mind shape-shifted possible women for her to be, why were none of them Black?

The dot next to my name could turn orange any second. I've paused too long on her photo, which will give the wrong impression.

I quickly write, *It's nice to put a face to a name. / You're very pretty, Lili.*

Thank you.

We should meet up sometime, if you're interested.

Good idea.

SHE REQUESTED WHITE WINE, so I bought some on my way home yesterday morning. Then I realized that even her name connotes lilies and lily-white—maybe she prefers *everything* white...

I find myself glaring at the bottle or averting my eyes when I open the fridge.

In my profile photo I'm wearing the Robert Johnson T-shirt. Robert Johnson was Black. Two of the three prostitutes who've messaged me their prices were Black. The woman seeking a husband was fairer-skinned but from Madagascar. Had these women read my shirt as a coded indication of preference?

It's racist to think so.

I should sleep.

I smoke a bowl and listen to the foil crackle and cars pass outside.

I feel strange looking at her picture. Her eyes stare back, daring me not to think of this as some kind of new experience. Of course, it's really *me* staring from her eyes, daring myself. I look at her picture long enough to remember it clearly, then I lie in bed and imagine a scene in which we have sex. It's a dress rehearsal, to prove I can go through the motions without saying or doing anything stupid.

It's ridiculous, like steeling myself against walking into a grocery store and shouting "cunt" or "faggot" at the top of my lungs—something I've never done. But in a grocery store

I don't *have to* say anything. Conversely, time with Lili will be one-on-one, and whenever she isn't speaking it'll be my turn to say something, and each of those moments will be a chance for me to slip.

My brain outdoes itself conjuring such scenarios. They start innocently, with her knocking.

Then I open the door and say, "Get your Black ass in here."

In another version, I greet her with, "Nigga please."

In the next, I say, "You can start with the dishes."

My eyes clench tighter with each of these purges.

I never get hard. The buzzing warmth I cultivated looking at her picture dissipates. I finally let go, because touching myself during this ugly montage feels like a desensitization exercise.

Still, I'm determined to see one go right, so I restart the scene.

But now I ignore her knocks and leave her waiting at the door while I listen from the other side. A neighbor asks what she's doing here. She mentions my name, but the neighbor doesn't recognize it because I don't know any of my neighbors by name. They assume she's lying and came to rob the place. I hear the scene escalate and do nothing to intervene, until the police are called and she's taken away in handcuffs. Or they shoot her, strangle her, or beat her to death.

These scenarios are coming from somewhere in my mind; it's my fault they're happening. When I try to end them they get worse. Am I about to spend the evening swallowing back insults and slurs like stomach acid burps rising from my subconscious?

Are these the thoughts of a good person?

***

Minutes before our date, she calls.

"Hello?" I wonder if the same terrible scenarios occurred to her, and she's calling with an excuse to cancel.

"Hi," she says, in the voice of a woman about the age she claimed to be. "Can I park anywhere on the street? No weird rules like 'ten minutes only' or whatever?"

"Just street sweeping." I smile. She probably hears it. "But it's done for the week."

"Okay. See you in a minute."

Was that a genuine question about "special rules," or did she call to make sure I wouldn't bail on our evening? to save herself the trouble of knocking and waiting at the door? and possibly other worse things? Maybe she imagined them too, after all. Or she's already lived them.

I'm drowsy from spending the day thinking about how I couldn't sleep. My eyes burn. I successfully masturbated, which was important to accomplish before her arrival. I found an animated GIF and focused on that—no "people," just moving parts like factory footage. Now, having showered and brushed my teeth, I'm as clearheaded and calm as my exhaustion will allow.

The taste of toothpaste is still fresh, like I've scraped ugly language from my tongue. It's also good for the possible kisses Lili and I might share but admittedly not great for drinking white wine.

I go outside and down the stairs, and see her walking down the sidewalk. I smile. She smiles. A first date at my place with someone I've never met before. I think, *a new experience*, and the phrase turns my stomach.

I wait so I don't have to shout. Then I say, "Hey, there!"

"Hey, there." She puts her arms out and we hug, relieved that we're both who we said we were. I get a whiff of her hair, soft on my cheek—tea tree. It burns like blue-green ice behind my eyes and dissipates my lingering fog.

"Nice to meet you!" I say.

"Nice to meet you too."

I lead her up. The living room window is cracked, and a breeze pushes through the apartment like a slow school of fish.

"Something to drink? Wine? Water?"

"Water, to start. It's warm out there. AC's busted in my car."

"I know how that goes." I fill two glasses at the sink. "My old car didn't even have AC, just fans that moved the hot air around." I give her a glass and join her on the couch, the width of the middle cushion between us. "Still, it was better than what I've got now."

"What do you have now?"

"Minivan. Bought it from my folks."

"Hot." She curls a sneer that feels familiar from our messages.

"Not hot at all, thank god, it's got AC."

Her eyes roll. "Well, your 'dad joke' game is on point."

"I guess that's from all the time I spend driving around picking up kids."

She tilts her head. "You've got kids?"

"Oh! Sorry, no, I was making a pedophile van joke."

She almost spits back into her glass. "Wow, dad jokes *and* pedophile jokes. You've got range."

We sit for a moment. Lili puts the glass against her cheek and closes her eyes.

The scoreboard in my mind dings a point, because people don't close their eyes around perceived threats. "Do you want ice in that?"

Her eyes open halfway. "No, thank you, it's perfect like this."

"Good, because I think the tray in the freezer has totally evaporated. But I can fill it now for ice later."

She laughs and holds up a calm-down hand. "I'll be okay. Thanks."

The hand signal works; I am calm.

***

The bottle of wine is a welcome third wheel. The water rinsed the toothpaste flavor from my mouth, so when I tap my glass with Lili's and sip, the wine tastes as it should—buttery and tart.

I think about how instead of Lili sitting here now it could be the man who propositioned me. We'd be making small talk and possibly finding things in common, as Lili and I are, but all the while I'd wonder what it'll be like when he brings up our agreement and puts me in his mouth.

Or if I'd gone to the older couple's place, their strappy sex swing staring me down from the corner of the room, the wife in a day dress that presses her stretch-marked breasts into a jiggling mass, the husband in a T-shirt tucked into khaki shorts, scratching his beard and asking me, "Alex, wouldja like somethin' to drink?"

Or if I'd taken a prostitute up on her offer I'd feel guilty making small talk, like chatting up a pizza delivery person while they're on the clock. And which prostitute would I have chosen, Black or white?

I realize that since Lili's arrival I haven't once thought of my earlier apprehension. Then I focus on the glass in her hand to keep that thought from seeding.

She puts the glass down, touches her fingertips together, and says, "So, I didn't tell you this before... because I didn't want you to judge too harshly..."

Roller coaster cars sink past the point at which gravity takes over. Is she married with kids? Does she have an STD? Was my weirdness about the wine correct, and she's using me as some sort of white fetish object?

She tilts her head back. Her brown eyes widen and cower behind the hills of her cheeks. This is hard for her.

"Go on..." My own confessions prepare to draw straws. Do I tell her about my encounter with the Skype scammer? my twinge of animosity about her choice of wine? the terrible things I imagined this afternoon?

"I'm a virgin," she says.

"What? You—" An AC unit shudders on outside and the corrugated sound tremors through my body.

"I'm just playing with you." She smiles, her dimples deepen.

"Jesus, you threw me for a second." The roller coaster cars inch further down the crest. "So what's the real thing?"

She lowers her head, then winces and bites her lip. "I... worked on a reality show."

Deadbolts shriek in the basement door of my mind—*Keep your straws, all of you! Back under the stairs! False alarm!*

Aloud I say, "What show?"

"*All by Myself.* Heard of it?"

"I've captioned it." I try not to react. This coincidence would be welcome if I hadn't spent the last week thinking about the world watching Number Eight in his box, and if I didn't just now remember being seen through my window, and if I hadn't been recorded by a blackmailer, and if Lili mentioning this show didn't make me feel like these things are somehow connected. But now I feel small.

"I'm sorry." She winces. "Do you think less of me?"

"Of course not." I pour us more wine.

"It was just one day, to fill in for my friend who's a PA."

"Did you meet the contestants?" If she mentions Number Eight, this isn't a coincidence. My palms are cold.

"Only Jeremy. Number Four."

I take a hard swallow of wine and a bubble grates in my throat.

"I had to go pick him up and bring him to set, 'cause the whole thing was like this big, secret operation. They gave me a fat envelope with paperwork for him to sign and—get this—blindfolds."

"Blindfold-*s*?"

She nods. "Two of them. Kinky, right?"

"What? One for him and one for... you?"

"No, they were both for him!" Her hands curl into claws under her face. "Alex, I need you to understand how sketch this was."

I like hearing my name on her voice.

"My specific instructions were to put the small blindfold on him, which was like a sleep mask, and then tie the other bigger blindfold on over that to make absolutely *positively* sure he couldn't see where we were going. And he had to sit in the backseat of my car so I could watch him in the mirror and make sure he didn't peek."

"Did you know any of this when you agreed to replace your friend?"

"No! I signed an NDA and they were like, 'Pick up this dude, blindfold him in the backseat, and bring him to the drop-off point.'"

"Drop-off point?"

"The warehouse. I had to unload his stuff and hold his hand and guide him in because he couldn't take his blindfold off until he was in his pod. So I'm cruising up the five with this dude double-blindfolded in my backseat, praying I don't get stopped by the cops."

"At least you had the paperwork to back up your crazy story."

"If they would've even looked at it! Brothers and sisters get shot down for less."

My sip of wine goes sour. "They do."

She leans back and rests a hand on her forehead. Then she shrugs. "And for what?"

"What do you mean?"

"I mean *why*? How is *that* part of the plan?"

"The police's plan?"

"God's Plan."

I watch her eyes for the hint of another joke. "Dunno. You think God's racist?"

Her face hardens. "Whoa. Okay."

"No, wait, I'm sorry. I thought you were kidding, so I made a joke."

"Cold fuckin' joke, Alex."

This time hearing my name doesn't feel good. "I'm sorry, I didn't mean it like that." The shockwave of my mistake ripples across my skin. Of all scenarios, I hadn't anticipated this one. How could I have? We just met. I know nothing about this woman, including whether she's religious. She could be a total lunatic.

I ask, "You believe in God?"

"You don't?"

"I never really thought about it," I lie.

"Maybe you should."

I'm still not sure if she's kidding.

"Well," I say, "if my tiny life is serving a bigger purpose, I'd love to know what it is."

"That's between you and Him." She's serious.

Now it feels like there's a third person in the room—her omnipotent Imaginary Friend pulling both of our strings in some grand, unknowable scheme.

I shrug. "I've just never felt like my decisions were guided by anything but myself."

"You don't have to feel that for it to be true."

I resist the urge to roll my eyes. "Do you know *your* purpose?"

"I've got a pretty good idea, yeah."

"What is it?" I finish my glass.

She takes the bottle from the table and refills her glass, then reaches over and refills mine. "At the moment, it's making you help me finish this bottle so we're both nice and warm."

My cheeks heat up. She's about to laugh and admit she was kidding about the God stuff.

She drinks.

Any second now...

Eventually I break the silence. "I'm already pretty warm."

"Then I've got you right where I want you." She gives a flirtatious smirk, but now it feels naive. There's a glaze in her eyes—it could be the wine, but I read it as surrender to her Imaginary Friend and His Plan. I project forward to a version of things wherein we become an item, with more talk of divine supervision and manipulation. The idea makes my lungs tight.

Admittedly, our shared purpose *was* prewritten, by *us*, in both of our profiles: *clean fun*. She can't expect any more from this than I do.

I realize time is passing and it's my line. "I like you, Lili."

"I like you too, Alex."

We smile as the timer ticks. "I'd like to kiss you."

"I think you should."

I put my glass on the table to avoid spilling it.

***

I took the foil down earlier, which revealed my sooty safety glass window. The foil is folded under my shirts in the closet; I'm not sure why I hid it. I also changed the sheets so they're crisp and clean.

This is not my bedroom, it's a guest-friendly version.

I stop by the bed and remove my shirt, drop it to the floor. She removes hers, which I drape on the back of my desk chair. I'm struck by her dark skin, now seen against her light purple bra, and I get the impression that I'm somehow more naked, that even when she removes her bra she'll have the cover of her skin, like a wetsuit or a unitard she'll unzip and step out of, revealing a true base layer that's pink and raw and finally "nude."

My body tenses against the thought in a way I hope isn't obvious.

I motion to the bed and she lies down. I lie next to her. We kiss with our eyes closed.

Eventually our pants come off. I remove my glasses, kneel over her, pull her purple underwear from her legs. I lie between her legs, kiss her breasts, dark nipples, then her stomach, inner thighs, and finally I nuzzle against her pubic hair. I lick her.

I have only done this with two other women. I'm aware that the flora and fauna of each person's body is different, which creates an individual flavor. Lili tastes of rich leather, or the first pungent waft from a freshly-opened pack of rolling tobacco. I close my eyes and focus everything on my tongue, challenging myself to make associations unrelated to color. But this is how she tastes to me.

She holds my head and moans, says my name. Then shouts my name, draws it out, chops it to pieces with her breath.

I would enjoy this, but instead I wonder if she senses my distraction and is using my name as a mantra to ground me. My neighbors can probably hear her, which wouldn't bother me except for the fact that when I greeted her outside I had said, "Nice to meet you." Anyone who heard me say that, and who now hears her shouting my name, will likely make disparaging assumptions about her.

But I say nothing for fear of embarrassing her. I close my eyes tight and lick harder, which makes her shout louder, and eventually she quakes and clamps my head in her thighs and it sounds like we're underwater.

I take my shirt from the floor, wipe my face, and lie next to her.

She turns to me. Her fingers trace through my chest hair. "Now what do you want?"

"A bit of the same?" I know I'll be quiet. I usually am. And she'll be less likely to continue shouting my name.

She kisses me, then kisses my chin and my neck, my chest, my stomach, and eventually puts me into her mouth.

Does she think I taste like a white person?

I clench my eyes to swallow the thought, but it doesn't work. I want to stop her, to apologize and ask her to leave, but the "it's not you, it's me" excuse would be offensive if left unexplained or far worse if I'm honest.

She holds my testicles and gently kneads them. No one has done it this way before. It's new and thrilling and—don't say "exotic," you piece of shit. I wasn't going to, but my brain is like a car backfiring in a closed garage.

Lili is miles away across the blurry dunes of my torso, and I'm marooned in my head.

With my last girlfriend I used to make contact by stroking behind her ears and gently holding the back of her head.

My hand drifts over and meets Lili's tight, springy curls, and I realize my mistake. Jerking my hand away would indicate surprise or reinforce the idea that my goal was to touch her hair, so I commit to the movement and try to maneuver my fingers to stroke behind her ear. But I have to push her hair aside. I stroke behind her ear for a moment, and she doesn't seem to react either way.

When I decide I've done all I can to cover my tracks—because the damage is already done—I slide my hand down her neck and stroke her back. A neutral zone.

Though historically, it hasn't always been a neutral zone...

Beyond all logic, I'm still hard.

I withdraw from her and say, "I want you."

"I've got a condom in my purse."

"I have one here." I take a condom from my desk drawer and put it on.

She lies back, and I lie on top of her. With her face in sharp focus so close to mine, my eyes in hers, there is finally only us. For a brief moment it doesn't matter who we might be, or who anyone else has ever been.

NIGHT.

We keep the lights off even when she gathers her purse from the couch. We say bye and kiss in my open front door. Say bye and kiss again. Finally she pushes my lips harder, then steps away.

"Bye," I say.

She disappears down the stairs.

I don't close the door until I hear her shoes on the sidewalk. I go to the window and peer through the vertical blinds. She walks down the sidewalk like any stranger, like the stranger she was only a few hours ago, but now an invisible thread connects us. She passes behind the neighbors' house and is gone.

There's a near-silent residual ring of her voice in the room, a warmth in the air, a lingering charge from my first visitor here in a long time.

It's almost 11:30. Most other nights it would be time to go to work, but it's the weekend and a special occasion. I can't just sit here and let her energy dissipate, so I pack a few hits of weed in my pipe, pocket it with my lighter and keys, and leave.

Empty sidewalks. The night air is cool, but our sex feels like a covering on my skin, the layer I was missing when I stood naked in front of Lili.

She had joked that she was a virgin. She's sarcastic. The God thing could've been another joke. I can imagine her laughing and saying, "I totally got you!"

A car passes, muffled music through dark windows. The pitch of the music sags as the car goes down the road. When it's gone I take a well-rubbed notch through bushes and trees to the other side, a dusty path along the river.

The river is a wide concrete ditch with a narrow trickle of water down a gutter in the middle. A six-foot chain-link fence on either side keeps people from falling or jumping in. People jog and walk their dogs here during the day. At night I'm alone.

That would be a weird long-term joke to make, waiting until a second date to deliver the punchline. She must actually be religious.

When bad things happen she might say, "The Lord works in mysterious ways." All responsibility lies with her Imaginary Friend and none with her. But does this displacement of blame make her a bad person, or does her aspiration to serve a Purpose make her a functional member of society, unlike me in my quagmire of strongheaded, self-imposed insignificance?

The trees and bushes by the path are eventually replaced by a high concrete wall like a courtesy screen between the neighborhood and me.

Maybe all that Purpose stuff is just a superiority trip.

Superiority? In a country where every game is rigged against her? How dare I have sex with this woman and then assume the worst about her?

I light the pipe and take a long pull. My mouth and the back of my nose fill with salty, pine-flavored smoke.

Religious or not, I'm lucky if she doesn't hate me.

There's muttering across the river.

That side is commercial. Parking lot lights stand tall and blue-white above the trees. Grocery store, pharmacy, Goodwill, and restaurants are all blocked from view by trees and bushes full of tents and sleeping bags, crumpled beer cans, broken bottles, and sometimes clothes hung to dry on branches like silkscreened spiderwebs. The foliage over there is too dark to see any of that now.

Between patches of streetlight I hit the pipe again.

Quiet but distinct, a voice says, "There, you saw it?"

My thumb covers the ember.

Silence.

My mouth leaks thin smoke in my wake.

Further down I turn toward the wall and pull again.

"There it goes. I saw that one." It's a male voice. About my age, maybe older.

My thumb pushes into the bowl, crumples the ash.

"What do you think it is?" says another.

"Probably crack," says the first. "Or heroin."

"You can't smoke heroin, can you?"

"He's walking too much for heroin. That's crack."

They must be across the river. I pocket the lighter and keep the pipe concealed at my side.

"Yeah, crack for sure. Look how he's walking."

My walk does feel different, but I'm not sure how.

"We see you."

My chest tightens. I'm exposed in another patch of streetlight and my hand automatically lifts and brushes my nose. Casual.

"He just snorted a bump. That's a fucking crackhead, dude."

In the next shadow I turn toward the wall, lift the pipe to my lips and blow out the ash with a near-silent glassy hiss.

"We saw that, motherfucker."

The back of my neck hardens, blood rumbles in my ears.

"We'll get him at the bridge."

A car crosses the bridge ahead. Its headlights wipe the trees but don't reach low enough to reveal anyone.

If I turn around, the path back is flanked by chain-link and concrete for a mile and a half. No man's land. It's ideal for smoking weed in peace but dangerous for being chased. And halfway home there's another bridge where they could cross to my side. Maybe before I even got there. There's at least two of them, so if one crosses at this bridge and the other behind me, I'm trapped.

I pass a large storm drain with a shallow ditch of rocks spread from its dark mouth to the river. The opening is big enough for a person to crouch inside. Maybe someone's there. The side of my vision burns with attention as I step across the rocks.

Concrete stairs rise to the bridge. As I climb I listen for scuffling on the other side's staircase. If they meet me on the bridge, I won't run. I've done nothing wrong. My weed prescription is at home. Smoking in public is a misdemeanor, worst-case scenario is probably a fine.

"If the crackhead comes this way, we wait until he's here, then we jump."

But something tells me they're not cops.

No one is on the sidewalk at the top, I turn and walk away from them.

I won't look back. Not yet. I'll lull them into a false sense of security, then whip around and catch them on the sidewalk.

No sound behind me—no footsteps, no voices.

The street feels emptier than I've ever known. Even the car turning at the light in the distance looks empty. Orange light slithers on its black windshield.

"You think he heard us? Where's he going?"

"He's probably going home."

Do they sound closer than before? No, but also not further away.

"We're gonna find out where you live, crackhead piece of shit."

The dark car approaches like a ghost ship. Streaks dance along its edges like St. Elmo's fire. Not even dash lights are visible inside.

I turn and try to look everywhere at once, wishing I could catch them in a laser vision glare and watch their bodies fall to steaming pieces.

"Oooh, almost saw us! Gotta stay on your toes with this one!"

I kneel to look under parked cars. No feet.

"Ha! Peek-a-boo!"

"If he sees us, we'll just pound him."

I sprint across the street and toward Ventura Boulevard, where more traffic means more potential witnesses.

"What the fuck is he doing?"

"What do you mean? He's on crack."

I walk fast—not too fast—up Ventura, past car lots. Balloons tied to antennae bounce in the breeze like sentinel heads nodding at my presence. Slumbering strip malls, red window neon cast back into rows of empty salon chairs. Tobacco shops with curvaceous silhouettes of water pipes among rope lights flashing for no one.

In the '80s before I was born, Mom and Dad lived in this area, on a street called Arch Drive. It's a small street off Ventura that connects to nothing else, just a quarter-mile-long bend—an arch—away from the boulevard, then back to it. My confidence surges. I feel like Philip Marlowe, using L.A. minutiae to outsmart my pursuers.

I pass one end of Arch Drive without looking at it. Everything in me points forward down Ventura, as if I live at the end of the boulevard, or somewhere far beyond, among the hills of ragweed and creosote.

"What the fuck, man, he's still going!"

"He's gotta be home soon. He didn't walk all that way just to smoke crack."

The far end of Arch Drive approaches. I speed up, then bolt into the small street and slip between two parked SUVs.

"Where did he go?"

The back of my neck tingles at the thought of having tricked them.

I plant my feet in line with the tires and wait. Wedged bow-legged between strangers' cars, I'm glad everyone in this city keeps their curtains closed.

"Seriously? He was right there!"

"God damn it!"

Then it's quiet.

I walk, and glance back as casually as I can. Only a short length of sidewalk is visible before the curve slurps it away like spaghetti.

The apartment buildings stand quiet. A car ticks as it cools.

Darkness watches from dark windows.

A large man with a sagging face walks a small dog toward me. The dog stops at the base of a palm tree and pees.

I smile at the man. His eyes meet mine and drop quickly to the dog. He shakes the leash and says, "C'mon, let's go." The dog scrapes its claws on the pavement and skitters past me.

Past another palm tree a voice behind me tells the man, "Watch out for that guy. He's got a problem."

The man says, "I wondered. What's the problem?"

"Crackhead. We're gonna report him."

"Good. This goddamn city's full of 'em."

My scalp tightens.

I want to turn around. I want to tell them they don't know me, that I was just smoking some weed before bed, and that even if it *were* crack nobody deserves this treatment. But I'm too alone to do that. The man walking the dog was the last other person on earth, and he's not on my side.

Dialogue rolls across a giant marquee in my mind: *Aw shit, I forgot my wallet*, or, *I'm already late and I left the oven on*, or, *I got snacks for the party, but I left them on the counter!* I want these mantras of normalcy to bleed into my expression and demeanor. If strangers suspect I'm evading something, they all might side against me.

Arch Drive rejoins Ventura, and I'm finally pointed homeward.

I speed-walk, but slow enough not to arouse suspicion from passing cars, remembering how my gait somehow "proved" I was smoking crack. At this point desperation has probably made it worse.

I try to get a read on my appearance by watching my reflection traverse the car dealership's dark showroom windows. The glass pinches and warps my face, pulls it up to one side, then squishes it down onto my shoulders.

The lot balloons shake like heads, unconvinced.

The bars on Ventura are closing. That means I've somehow been out walking for over an hour. Time flies when you're being followed. The late crowds swarm by the doorways, buzzing at each other. As with bees, if I don't bother them, they won't bother me.

I pass through them staring straight ahead.

I hear one say, "What's his problem?"

"He's a creep, just let him go by."

"See how he looked at my tits? He's a sicko for sure!"

"Who, that guy?" Familiar voice. "Total sicko. We've been following him a while."

My neck is cold.

"Definitely saw him smoking crack."

Smile. I want to smile at someone and receive a smile back.

A group of girls walks toward me. A couple are laughing. I smile, and their eyes dart sideways and then away.

From somewhere else I hear, "Oh, you like that *brown sugar*, huh?"

Did they think I singled out the Black woman in the group? Had I smiled only at her? It's only seconds later and I can't remember. But the accuser is at my back—how had they seen where I was looking? I'm walking fast, so anyone standing in front of me is quickly passed. Behind me they merge into an advancing mass of snarls and dead eyes.

"Keep walkin', white boy! Ain't nothin' here for you!"

Don't turn around. The longer I hold my smile the heavier it grows, like an anvil dangling from a chain between my teeth.

My feet throb. My calves ache. I want to wave down a taxi and tell the driver, "Please, there are guys following me. They've been threatening me. I'm a good person. Please, I just have to shake them and go home. My wallet is at home, but I promise I live very close and I can pay you when we get there. I'll pay extra," but there aren't any green-lit taxis. The few that pass are red—protective bubbles of metal and tempered glass, other people on their way to other places faster than I can get on foot.

"Fucking crackhead pervert! Where the fuck does he live?"

Eventually I reach my personal stretch of Ventura Boulevard. My grocery store, my drugstore, restaurants, my bank... I worry arriving home will feel like a dream wherein I enter my front door but can't close it fast enough to shut out the person at my back. My body will twist like Silly Putty, only my legs will turn while my arms and head stay put. I'll try to reach behind me to push the door shut without touching whoever is there. My fingers might graze them. So I'll decide to run. But my feet are turned the wrong way and the floor will give like sand in an hourglass and I'll realize I'm not worried about the person killing or catching me; my worst fear is just having them *there* behind me. And I'll know they're already past the threshold, they're in my home, and they will always be behind me, everywhere I can't see, and I'll spend the rest of eternity trying to turn around.

Three blocks away small bones shift in my feet, my knees bounce under my weight, and I do slight finger and arm exercises to keep my limbs from turning to rubber. I pivot my torso one way and then the other, practicing to whirl around and shut my door. This is not a dream.

I leave the blue-white light of Ventura for the orange light of my neighborhood.

"You better be almost home."

"Yeah, we're gettin' too tired to beat you."

I wonder how long I'd have to walk for them to give up. I could reach Bakersfield in a day or so, with them behind me, drooling, hungry. My body would give up. I'd find someplace to lie down and sleep, and then they'd do whatever they want to me.

I have to focus on getting into my apartment and locking the door. Anything they do beyond that is breaking and entering.

"This one? Nope. How 'bout that one?"

They're following closer than before, speaking softer, but I hear them just as well.

"Maybe this next street. No..."

I grip the lighter in my pocket. Isn't that a self-defense move, grip onto something to avoid breaking your hand? Or jut your keys between your fingers to add spikes to your fist? Go for the eyes.

An old gumshoe trick comes to mind as I turn onto my street. First apartment building, then the second, and just before mine I flip the lighter into a hedge. It rustles and rattles. Throw the dog a bone.

Now turn on my driveway, get to the stairs and use the wrought-iron railing to swing myself around 180 degrees and I almost scream when I see nobody in the driveway or next to me because it means they're either still on the sidewalk or *right behind me*. My tailbone bursts in a tingling wave that thrusts me up the stairs. Too fast to focus on going two by two I whirl my legs like wheels. Use the railing again to whip around the switchback, almost scream again when I see nobody on the stairs below—they may *still* be right behind me. Keys—I forgot to get them ready! Plunge hand in pocket and bring keys up like a net of chrome tuna, find the right one in the narrow search-beams of streetlight through the branches and stab at the lock as I reach the door, turn to face the door expecting somebody next to me—no, behind me—and jut my butt back at the railing to pin them before they can get an arm around my neck. The key enters the lock, I twist key and knob simultaneously, push and hear the thick paint on the door crackle as it unsticks, the breathy whoosh pulls me through the airlock, gripping the edge of the door and throwing it back, hear it slam as I whirl around, palm pressed against it as my other hand turns the deadbolt—*thock*—and the knob lock—*click*—and I've done it.

I keep the lights off and squat with my back against the door, listening.

"I saw him throw it." Quieter now, through layers of wood and metal and glass. "It's gotta be the pipe."

My legs release and stretch out, thighs hot, calves tight, shins aching like they've been under metal rollers.

"Aw, it's the fucking lighter!"

"The pipe's not here?"

"He's still got it on him."

"Hey man, you're busted! We're gonna call the cops!"

"You can try to run again, but we know where you live, fuckin' creep!"

True. That is now true.

Orange blades of streetlight fan through the blinds, almost touch my feet. I cross my legs away from them.

"Hello? We saw someone smoking crack by the river here... Yeah, and he ran, but we followed him home." They say my address, followed by another pause. "Sure, thank you, officer."

I close my eyes and it all disappears. I'm where I can't see and no one can see me. The air outside isn't thick with faces. There is no outside.

"They're on their way! You're busted, crackhead!"

I stand, go to the kitchen and fill a glass of water, then sit back against the door.

I drink the water slowly. I keep the lights off.

When I leave the doorway it's 2:46 a.m.

The past two hours feel like endless fists unclenching in my legs.

I dig a spare lighter from my desk drawer and smoke a cigarette in my dim bedroom. My ashtray is an unrinsed jam jar. Clinging hunks of jam crackle when I push the ember into them. The air smells of smoke and burnt sugar.

On my rumpled bedsheet I find one of Lili's pubic hairs curled like a watch spring.

What would she say about those guys? That they were sent to teach me a lesson? That I should have stood my ground? Or were they meant to learn a lesson *from me* by beating me up and going to jail? By running, had I somehow interfered with The Plan?

Ridiculous. Wrong place, wrong time, that's all.

I brush my teeth, get into bed, and look at the nighttime light that's usually blocked by the foil. They're out there somewhere, sleeping soundly or still talking about the crazy person they followed home.

What did they smell on me, what scent of predator or prey?

MORNING.

I get out of bed and refill my water glass, sit on the couch and drink. Smoke a couple of cigarettes.

I could still be walking. Shuffling up mountain road switchbacks warming in first light. Or watching suburban sprinklers sprout from the ground and fan drizzling beams.

They might've been close to giving up. If I'd continued to the end of my street, turned back onto Ventura and kept walking, they might've tired of the chase.

Instead I led them to my home.

My blinds are still closed.

I spend a while looking at the corners of the room, seeing how the light is different on each plane—spackle scars under the paint where there used to hang picture frames or a shelf, wood floor so old the planks roll like a sea frozen in time, popcorn ceiling that looks like a painful planet to traverse with bare feet.

These walls represent the limits of hospitable space.

It's a fantasy I often entertain in public restrooms, that the rest of the world—the universe—is gone. The vacuum of empty space is too strong for me to pull open the door, so I'm trapped in that grimy, fluorescent-lit box.

The fantasy allows for running water and electricity despite the disappearance of everything beyond the restroom. With a working sink and flush toilet there wouldn't be the obligatory pileup of waste and filth, and I'd have water to drink.

The toilet paper's outermost layers would be soiled by exposure to the bathroom air, so I'd peel those away and flush them, then ration the rest, eating a square at a time. Two if I'm really hungry.

I'd only sit or stand because the floor would have layers of pee, under-shoe grime, and pubic hairs of all colors, shapes, and lengths. Eventually I'd give in and use soap, water, and paper towels to clean off a patch of floor to lie down. What a strange perspective, a public restroom from floor-level. The stall doors and toilets would look gigantic.

Sleep would be difficult in that small room, with buzzing fluorescent light cast into every corner, spread across the vinyl tile. With any luck there'd be a light switch, and I could sleep in windowless darkness save for the single blinking red star of a smoke detector. I'd settle into sleep by timing my blinks with the light to make it look like the light was either always on or always off.

I'd doze and wake later on that same greasy floor, reach and fumble for the light switch that would seem to have changed places, but when I flicked it on I'd see that everything was the same.

I saw a real ficus once, in a restroom decorated with Portuguese tile. I imagined eating the ficus leaves layered with toilet paper like sushi rolls. There was a small glass bottle on the toilet tank with bamboo sticks wicking lavender essential oil into the air. I could have endured for longer there. The tile was the same on every surface—hypnotic, infinite webs of blue-and-white tessellations; if I ignored the sink, toilet, and ficus, I'd forget which way was up.

If a bathroom has plastic plants, I could pull the plastic apart in strips and weave a mat to lay my head on. Better than touching the floor, but like any surface the plastic leaves would have a film of waste particles and deodorizing spray.

I might eventually go crazy and lick the floor just to sense the presence of other people. I'd remember people as being bitter and sour. I wonder how long it would take for the snap to happen, and after that, how long before I expired.

**

Lili sends me a text around noon: *Feel like a quickie at my place before work tonight? ;)*

My chest flutters.

Last night my whole neighborhood rejected me. Today yawns before me—hiding in the dark, hoping those guys don't show up, smoking cigarettes on the couch until I go to work under cover of night.

Her message on my phone screen almost radiates warmth, like her hand in mine.

I type, *I'm free!*

The exclamation point feels desperate, but changing it to a period—*I'm free.*—seems nonplussed or aloof. I wish something existed between the two.

So instead I write, *I'm totally up for that.* The "totally" might balance out the blank-faced period at the end.

Then I decide it doesn't.

Meanwhile, as I type, she might be watching a placeholder ellipsis bounce on her screen and wondering what the fuck is taking me so long.

That sounds great. Shall I bring wine? I can't say "shall," what a douchebag.

I tweak it. *Sounds great. I'll bring wine?*

I send.

I wait.

She might've stepped away.

Near the end of another cigarette my phone buzzes.

Bring wine if you want. You're the one working tonight.

I'll definitely bring wine—the grocery store is a good place to do some reconnaissance.

EACH PERSON I SEE in the grocery store could've been involved. Especially the young men. The guy in the beanie with a basket of beer and Doritos. Early twenties. Round face and a tiny nose. Does he look capable of following a stranger through nighttime streets for two hours? Or the guy carrying an eggplant and a three-pack of toothpaste. Mid-thirties. Neatly parted hair, crooked goatee.

I only get these impressions out the sides of my eyes when I know they aren't looking, blurry past the edges of my glasses.

I want to write on a card and stop each man on his way out the door and ask them to read it aloud. "You're busted, crackhead pervert!" If I wasn't convinced, I'd have them whisper, "Peek-a-boo..."

Instead, each time I see someone who might fit the profile I follow them long enough to hear them speak. This is only possible for the guys who are with someone, which is unfortunately rare.

The loners are the most suspicious.

I spot one guy, late twenties in a Lakers cap, bomber jacket, and basketball sneakers. He's pale and wiry like a baby bird without feathers. Long face, vague brown mustache under a nose that droops a little between the nostrils—the kind of nose that always looks like it's running. He pushes a cart with a family-size box of Frosted Flakes, a gallon jar of dill pickles, and a box of Cheez-Its. I follow him from the aisle where he adds a jug of whey protein powder and some chewable vitamins—for him, or does he have kids?—to dairy where he takes two cartons of whole milk, and then to produce where he collects five oranges, a watermelon, and four peaches. As he approaches the scale to weigh the peaches I cut around the pineapples and brush too close, look him almost in the eyes and say, "'Scuse me."

My heart pounds.

He stops short, says nothing, but I feel him frown at me.

I keep walking slowly. *Come on, call me a crackhead. Just say "crackhead" and maybe I'll go away.*

By the time I reach the dried fruits he's gone.

The next question is whether anyone here is someone my pursuers had spoken to. And if so, do they recognize me? Am I seen as "the crackhead from last night," now wringing the neck of a bottle of white wine and visiting every aisle but picking up nothing else? Staring at people?

A wave of nausea hits me in the checkout line. I sway, and the slight breeze it creates on my face helps. An old storm gathers in my mind, one I felt in elementary school every time we moved our chairs to sit in a circle—what if I threw up right now in the middle of the circle?

Standing in line we're too close. If I curled over, I'd let fly into someone's basket, softening the cardboard shell of that frozen pizza or dribbling into the wrinkled plastic on that loaf of bread. Soaking through that paper bag of mushrooms.

I fear the vomit might come so fast I won't be able to direct it or stop it. The fragile bubble of the store would burst—the bubble wherein we agree that purchases belong in the baskets and the baskets aren't helmets or slippers, we don't climb the shelves, we don't shout, we handle everything with care to avoid spills, we keep our clothes on, and we don't vomit on the merchandise or other customers.

I look at an old woman in the next line.

...and definitely not into someone's purse. Or the large pockets of their dress.

An acid burp rises on the back of my tongue and I swallow it back and grimace.

"He's gonna throw up."

"Please, oh god, that would be the fucking best."

Are they in frozen food behind me? Cereal, two rows down? Is it that guy in the polo shirt? I scan the lines out the corner of my eye searching for eyes looking back at me. I look for the droopy-nosed guy but don't see him.

"Peek-a-boo..."

My tired leg tremors on the brake at red lights.

In the stairwell of Lili's apartment building I meet a guy coming down, looking at his phone. He stops in the middle of the flight above me and stares, sees the bottle of wine.

"You're the guy, huh?" he asks. "Her new whiteboy?" He's white too, of course. Very pale, with freckles and a short nose with front-facing nostrils. Light blue eyes.

"I'm not sure what you're talking about."

He sneers and comes down the stairs, grazing me with his elbow as he passes. "Flavor-of-the-week motherfucker."

Lili opens the door smiling, even gives me a peck on the lips as if she hasn't just ushered that pasty specter out of her apartment.

"Got the place to yourself?" I ask.

"Yup."

"Nice." It's a spacious one-bedroom. Everything's new and modern. Large frameless paintings on the wall. A counter divides the kitchen from the living room. "No roommates?"

"No. Why?" She takes two wine glasses and a corkscrew from the kitchen.

I point my thumb at the front door. "There was a guy..."

She stops just past the counter. "Oh my god, you saw Eric? That's really embarrassing, I'm sorry. He was supposed to be gone."

"Yeah, he seemed to know who I was."

We sit on the couch.

"What did he say to you?"

"Nothing. He just glared at me on the stairs." She might know I'm lying. She might've sensed my awkwardness in our first meeting and arranged Eric as a test to see how I'd react. She *knows* he spoke to me, because she told him what to say.

"He's my ex. But we broke up a long time ago."

I want to ask if they met on the site. Instead I focus on opening the bottle.

"He dropped by as a surprise to give back my running shoes he was holding hostage. Super bad timing, I'm really sorry."

"No problem. Guess I'm just jumpy today."

"How come?"

I can't believe I said it. There's no taking it back. If I try to shrug it off as something stupid like "too much coffee," it'll be my second lie in a row, and she might be onto me already.

"Crazy night after you left."

"*After* I left?" She waits, eyebrows raised.

I pop the cork to appear casual. "I went on a walk and two guys followed me."

"Like muggers?"

I pour for her, then me. "No, they saw me smoking weed."

"Shit, were they cops?" She takes her glass.

"No. They thought it was a crackpipe."

"You had a pipe on the street? That's ballsy!"

I drink to the compliment. The wine tastes good.

She drinks too. "I used to smoke, but weed always made me way too paranoid to be outside. And then to get *followed*? Nuh-uh." She turns toward me and props her head on her hand. "So why would they follow you if they weren't cops?"

"They said they wanted to beat me up."

"Oh fuck, did they jump you?"

"No, I never saw them."

She jerks her head and frowns.

"They were across the river, in shadow. And they stayed behind me out of sight the whole time."

"You never saw them."

"Never."

"But you heard them."

"Yes. Talking to each other and threatening me."

She stares and sips her wine. "That's pretty freaky, Alex. You sure you weren't just high?"

"Not at all, it was just a couple hits." Now I regret bringing this up.

"Okay, but..." She looks at the ceiling. "How did they mistake your weed for crack?"

"They said I was walking strange."

She laughs and covers her mouth. "I'm sorry. Do you walk strange when you're high?"

"I didn't think so. Strange enough to look like a *crackhead*?"

Little smile. "Can I see?"

Irritation buzzes at the base of my skull. "See what?"

"Show me your stoned walk."

"But I'm not stoned." I sip, my mouth tense.

"Pretend. Walk like you normally do."

I take another drink.

She stares at me. Points. "Come on. Let's get to the bottom of this."

I stand and feel too tall. My shin hits the coffee table on my way around it. The buzz grows.

I stop in a corner of the room and pause, imagining the eggshell-colored carpet is the dusty path by the river, and Lili sits watching from the concrete ditch.

Which foot do I usually start with? It's unconscious, doesn't matter. I step and my foot skids on the carpet. My pace picks up and I move across the room feeling like a tin plate in a shooting gallery.

I look at Lili.

She's got her hand over her mouth.

"What?"

"Nothing, that was good."

"What? That's my normal walk."

Her eyes hold a smirking apology.

"Do I look like a crackhead?"

A laugh bursts from her. "No, I don't think so. To be fair, I don't know any crackheads, but I don't think they'd walk like *that*."

"Like what?"

"You're a little stiff. Maybe the shoulders. And you moved pretty fast, but I think this room is too small to judge. We should try it in the hallway."

I bristle. "Are you serious?"

"You wanted my opinion."

"I didn't, you made me do this."

"True. So don't listen to me. Your walk's fine."

I feel stupid standing here. Like I'm an extra person and the wine glass on the table belongs to a different, more relaxed guy who'll walk in any second and tell me to leave. I should leave. But the idea feels childish, and then I'd be alone again.

"I'm sorry I laughed at you. Come here." She finishes her glass.

"I speed-walked for two fucking hours to get home. My legs are sore."

"See? That explains the stiffness. Come here."

I walk to the couch, careful around the coffee table, and sit.

She hands me my glass. "Finish that."

I do.

She pours more for me, then more for her. "You had a crazy night and you're stressed out. But you're here, we've got wine, it's cool now."

We drink.

"Kiss me."

I do.

***

Later, crossing the room with pressure in my pants and the taste of her mouth on my tongue, I look at the paintings. I notice her name in the corners. This explains her username on the site: *PainterLi*.

"These are yours?"

"Yes," she says from the bedroom door, "but don't look too close. They're embarrassing."

False modesty. She's a skilled painter. "No, they're good. I like this one." I point to a large, gobby acrylic piece showing layers upon layers of sunflowers, heads bowed on their stalks like angels receding into infinity. A universe of only sunflowers in all directions.

She disappears into the bedroom.

I move my face close to the painting, my vision fills with yellow wheels. The effect is both suffocating and freeing.

***

On her bed I linger, kissing her inner thighs, covertly smelling for signs of Eric. I'm embarrassed by the impulse—the animal jealousy and human disgust with the idea of "sloppy seconds." Her leather and tobacco flavor is familiar now. It's warm and comforting, so individually and recognizably hers.

She says my name and I urge her with my tongue and hands to get louder because now I don't care. This is her place, her neighbors. Maybe Eric is still lurking in the hallway and can hear us. He wasn't warning me about Lili, he was asserting dominance.

He probably doesn't even like her paintings. I imagine him sneering like he did at me and saying, *That's it? Just sunflowers?* He's probably one of those white guys for whom it's a point of pride to have crossed that imaginary aisle, some badge of immunity or respect, a special notch in the proverbial belt or bedpost, some historical power trip. When he drinks coffee he probably can't resist making a "like my women" joke. *He's* the one preoccupied with race, not me. Seeing me as the "new whiteboy" means he sees himself as the "old whiteboy."

She comes, screaming my name.

If he's not in the hallway, I hope he's still on the street. It's probably inaudible through her third-floor windows, but I like imagining he hears it wherever he is.

She gets on all fours at the edge of the bed. I stand behind her, and she rocks against me.

"Al-lex..." Her voice is doing that breaking thing I like. "Talk... talk to me."

"You feel amazing," I say.

I watch her hair bounce, and assume Eric probably never hesitated to grab it or plunge his fingers into it.

"Fuck me, Alex—talk to me, Alex..."

In the stairs he'd had his phone out.

"I'm... fucking you."

"Yes... Keep talking, baby..."

Could he have taken a picture of me?

"You're..."

"Yes..."

I almost say "fucking me," since it's the natural continuation, and the rest would be something like, "We're fucking each other." If A = B and B = C, then I scream, you scream, we all scream for ice cream.

I bet Eric was a fount of dirty talk.

"You're..." I start again, as if derailed by pleasure. My mind fishes out a grimy flash card that says: *a nigger*. I hear it in Eric's voice.

Shut the fuck up, you racist piece of shit.

"What am I?" she says. There's no horror in her voice, so I know I didn't say it out loud. "What—am I, baby?"

"You're beautiful," I bend and kiss her back again.

"Oh..." she says.

He could be out there, waiting for me.

"THAT GUY'S GOT A problem."

I'm just home from Lili's when I hear it.

"Which guy?"

Yes, I wonder, which guy?

The living room window's cracked open, but the voice is too faint to identify. Did Eric follow me home? Is it the people in the house next door? Maybe the stranger who saw me. My blinds are almost fully closed, but I'm still glad to be wearing pants this time.

"The guy. Remember? The crackhead."

The clear water of my mind receives a drop of red ink that bursts in tendrils. I tilt to see past the edge of the blinds. No one down in the alley.

"Oh yeah. He's creepy, dude."

I fill a glass at the sink and stand in the kitchen, drink and listen.

"What's he doing?"

"Just standing there."

It's darkening out and my lights are on. There has to be an angle, some sliver they can see.

"What are you guys up to?" I ask loudly.

They're quiet.

I finish the water and pack a bowl on the couch.

"What's he smoking?"

"I think it's just weed. I can smell it through the window."

rt of me feels vindicated that they can tell it's not crack, so eave the window open.

I take the pipe into the bedroom.

"If he's just smoking weed in there, why the fucking foil on the window?"

"Probably so no one can see him jerking off to kiddie porn."

"You think he's a pedophile?"

"Oh, for sure. When we followed him last night..."

My stomach rises as if the floor has dropped out. I'm hovering over my desk chair, almost fully seated, but I don't dare move. The slightest creak of sinew might mean missing something.

"...of all the people he passed on the street, he only looked at the *young ones*."

Did I? Was it poor luck that my glances were toward the younger people on the sidewalk? They all had to be of legal drinking age to be at the bars, or at least old enough to fake it. In my memory all the faces are dark, illegible contortions. Anyone under the streetlight has a face of trembling leaves.

"Dude, next time he goes out we gotta follow him."

I look at the clock. Less than an hour until I have to leave for work. Not nearly long enough for them to forget their new mission.

I sit at the computer and search each term that comes to mind in a separate tab: *stalking*, *voyeurism*, and *harassment*.

One laughs. "Dude, holy shit, he's onto us!"

"What?"

"He just fucking Googled 'voyeurism' and 'stalking.'"

How do they know? The foil is back on my bedroom window, as they noted, which means they aren't seeing me from outside but somehow from *inside*.

The room is dark except for the screen.

The answer stares at me. Mere inches above the article on the legal definition and ramifications of voyeurism is the small, cyclopean pupil of my webcam.

I CAN'T TELL IF they followed me to work. I've gone out to the parking lot for a couple of cigarettes and heard a dog, a train, and the constant exhalation of the freeway. The rustling of leaves imitated their snickering. Two people spoke down the street, their voices muddied as they walked away.

Tonight's task is to caption *Rate Your Date*. In this episode contestants use night-vision cameras to watch and instruct their fumbling partners through the dark rooms of a mansion, searching for hidden "golden condoms."

The audio is raw, fuzzy, wildly uneven. When I turn it up to make out a phrase I'm punished with a shout or a clap that sounds like a blow to my skull.

The worst of the three teams is Justin and Kami.

Justin sits in the control room watching the monitors and vomiting words: "Over there, over there, over there, to the right, more right, more to the right, right, right, right, yeah, you got it, no up, yeah, there, got it, go, go—watch out, there's a—yeah, go, go, that's the door, you got the door, get the knob, it's right by your han—no, down, down, yeah, right there, you got it, go, go, you got it, go!"

In splitscreen Kami gropes through the dark over coffee tables and couches, dodging pedestals topped with breakaway Ming vases to increase the tension and hilarity, all the time matching Justin's blather with her own: "Here? Right? Going right, I'm going right, this way? Here? I'm trying, hang on, oh, this is here, wait, what is this? Doesn't matter, okay, never mind, that's not it, I'm going, more to the right? Up? Is this the door? Where's the door? I can't find the door—oh, this is the door, the knob is here, I got the knob, okay, I'm going, I'm going!"

I type it all verbatim, as it is my job to do so, and time it as best I can to the rapid-fire editing. I don't think any shot in the entire episode lasts longer than a second.

The intros and outros are the easiest parts to caption because the host is the only one speaking and his dialogue is rote: "Who's gonna go all the way, and who's going home empty-handed? Tweet your predictions with #DateRate!"

**

After a cup of coffee I sit in the restroom, hidden in the most central, private, bright space in the office. The lights hum. The toilet paper dispenser only fits one roll and the others are wrapped and stacked in a small pyramid on the toilet tank. The single toilet stall in the men's room is large. The room itself is spacious enough to lie down and still be clear of the toilet, urinal, and sink's respective splash zones. There's a floor drain too, which would facilitate cleaning a spot to lie down. I could take relatively thorough sink showers without concern for making a mess.

But at this point my apartment is still my desert isle of preference, despite knowing that they're watching through my computer.

The problem is I don't know how they got in, and I don't have the technical skills to kick them out. My laptop is a closed, dark room. Like Kami fumbling for golden condoms, I'll need a Justin to guide me through.

Soon after the end of my shift I'm at the back of a computer store watching the specialist drum his fingers on the counter while we wait for my laptop to boot up. He looks like he's still in high school, which means he's either inexperienced or tech-savvy. I tell him I believe I'm being hacked, that out my window I can hear my neighbors discussing things they see me do, which they're probably watching through the webcam.

He says such hacking is unlikely and runs a quick scan that reports nothing malicious installed. When he checks my security settings he notices the firewall is disabled. I had assumed it was on, but he explains that the firewall is disabled as a factory default and that I "just have to turn it on..."—*click*—"Go ahead and enter your password for me, and..."—*click*. The firewall status bubble goes from gray to orange. "Okay, you're all set. Can I help you with anything else?"

I've had this computer for almost a year with the firewall disabled. I stare at the orange bubble and feel suddenly naked. I wiggle my toes to confirm I'm wearing socks and shoes.

"But since the firewall was off... you're sure there isn't anything on here? Maybe something inactive for now that the scan couldn't see?"

"That's unlikely. They would've already gone after your passwords and money if that was the case. But keep an eye on your accounts, and keep that firewall turned on, and you'll be good."

A veil drapes over me. It's like the store lights have dimmed. Beyond my field of vision people's faces are dark and contorted as if under black pantyhose. Everyone looks everywhere except at me.

But as I pass them on my way out, I feel each head lift and turn to watch me go.

***

At home I use a small neon-green patch torn from a Post-It note to close the eye of my computer.

I search for the highest-rated virus and malware scanners, and pay for and install the top three. Each scan takes one to two hours. I busy myself folding strips from the Post-It pad into origami stars.

Every few minutes I glance up at the progress bar. The torn and folded strips of paper represent my brain's progress bar while it roots through a year's worth of emails received, messages opened, links clicked. The obvious first suspect is the sex site with all its popups and ghost windows opened and closed by my ad blocker.

"Vanessa," who caught me with my pants down.

Lili only ever sent a photo, which the scan doesn't flag as malicious.

The scan results are files with strange abbreviations and numbers, file types I don't recognize. But I read that they're important files deep in the operating system software. An article says, *If these filenames are listed in a virus scan, it is normal. DO NOT delete them!*

Unless the article is lying. That would be a big con to pull off, publishing fake articles framing malware as operating system components and then boosting the articles in the search results.

I tweak some settings and run each scan again.

The expanding scatter of neon green stars on my desk reveals no constellation.

RED ROPES ON GOLD posts draw the marble floor into an easy maze of switchbacks. A short line of people wait, and I join them in the maze.

A teller with a *closed* placard in her window peers at me over her glasses. I look at the ground, then hope I haven't done so too quickly. There's a hole in the left knee of my jeans, and the right knee is about to open its mouth. Does she think I'm here to cause trouble? Rob the place? I make a deal with myself to glance again—sweep my eyes across the windows to avoid looking directly at her—and if she isn't still watching, it means I'm not suspicious.

I start at the right side and move my eyes across customers at the windows, the others in line, and... she isn't looking. Nor is the security guard further to the left.

The back of my neck tingles like circle time in school again, but now I have to pee. I can already see how the bank's marble bubble of quiet murmurs would burst at the sound of my urine stream hitting the floor.

Would the security guard charge at me? Would he tackle me to the ground?

He might approach slowly with his hands out to show how much he doesn't want to have to touch me. The line of people would flush out against the teller windows. The tellers' heads would pop up over clients' shoulders to see. Would they push that secret alarm button under the counter I've seen in movies?

What would it feel like to stand in the middle of a bank with my penis in hand, exposed to the cool marble air, emptying onto the floor? There'd be a magical several seconds before anyone noticed what was happening. Would it be freeing, if only for a moment? A perfectly normal tableau of afternoon in a bank, but there I'd be in the middle of it like a mischievous fountain cherub.

Repercussions would follow—charges, fines, jail time, psychological counseling, a mark on a record—but my body knows nothing stands in the way of me doing it in the first place.

I've seen something like that once, waiting at a light downtown. A man at a bus stop wearing threadbare sweatpants and T-shirt posed in a subtle lunge, a hand down the back of his sweats. He waited. My light turned green, and he was already small in my mirror when he pulled his hand from his pants and dropped something on the ground. I was alone in my van, others were in their cars, none of us could share or come to a consensus on what we'd seen. I wasn't even sure the other cars had seen it. The man's appearance may have rendered him invisible by default.

Which is why this isn't the same. The hole in my jeans is from wear but not hardship. And I'm not at a bus stop, I'm in a closed space with other people.

More line up behind me. Everyone watching the back of my head is, by association, waiting and counting on *me* to do something.

Which is worse to do on the floor of a bank: piss or shit? The physical act of shitting stimulates the prostate, which induces pissing. So shitting is worse because it means both will inevitably occur. I'm in good health; my shit would stay well-contained. It'd be like picking up after a big dog. Bleach wouldn't stain the marble, but psychological stains would persist in the witnesses who might forever make a point of stepping over that particular spot. They might adjust the red rope maze around the "no-go zone." Eventually the detour would become normal, and maybe someone would ask why the red ropes seem to steer around this small patch of floor, and the person asked wouldn't know because they were hired after "the incident." Or maybe "the incident" would gain layers of infamy and insanity with each retelling, and twist into me shitting *onto* someone or pinning them down and trying to feed it to them.

I'm next. This is the moment to do it in full view, pivoting to hit the calves and shoes of everyone in front of me.

A teller to my right says, "Next customer, please," looking at me. She isn't smiling. Can she tell what I'm thinking? Is there an expression someone makes when they think about peeing in public? I try to relax all the muscles in my face, then fear it's become a worse "pee face."

I slide her the twenty I got from the ATM and ask for quarters.

What do people look like when they think about normal things?

She slides me two rolls of quarters. "Can I help you with anything else?"

I consciously think the sentence, *I am preoccupied by normal things happening in my life and everything is fine,* and I smile with that energy. I say, "Thank you," put the rolls in my pocket and walk around the maze, past the guard, and out the door, leaving their civilized bubble intact and the marble floor dry.

THE METAL FRAME OF the pay phone's wall box is bent, as if it had softened in the sun and a giant hand lowered from the sky and pinched a corner of it. I imagine two punks with metal bats alternating blows like blacksmiths pounding folded steel bars.

Below the phone hangs the segmented metal cord that used to hold the phone book in a plastic shell, but someone cut the book and shell from the cord and now it hangs umbilical, vestigial. The phone's earpiece is caked with something that was once thick and wet but is now dry and dusty after days—weeks? months?—of direct sunlight. The number pad buttons are cracked and pushed in.

I get back in my minivan and drive, seeing all kinds of places where a pay phone would be, but where there isn't one now.

Flash of pay-phone blue in a liquor store parking lot. A booth! I park and walk to it before realizing the phone is gone. Now it's just a small bubble in the middle of the neighborhood. Clear out any condoms or needles, scrub away the scum. There's a shelf—limited counter/desk space. Sleep standing up, or sit with my legs crossed or hugged against my chest. My universe would shrink to the size of the booth; the world out the smeared glass would be illusory.

Regardless, it would need curtains.

Getting back into the minivan, I hear a laugh. I wait with the door open. Maybe from the next lot, behind the hedges.

"What is he doing?" one says.

"Two busted. Third time's a charm!" says another.

Two pay phones, and I'll be seeking a third. Could be another overheard coincidence, like the stranger.

But when I'd heard the stranger I was on my computer, and its eye saw me switch hands. That was no coincidence.

They saw the virus scans, my searches, they may have followed me to the computer store or watched through the webcam and laughed as the specialist turned my laptop, swinging their view from his skeptical face to my own sinking bafflement—*go ahead and enter your password for me.* They could've prepared for the quest I'm on now. I thought I was clever, avoiding my cell phone for this call. I even turned it off and left it in my desk drawer. Nice try. But they're not following my phone, they're following *me.*

I'm grateful to have my cigarettes. I hadn't expected this to take so long. I smoke a couple driving down Moorpark, up Coldwater, and back on Riverside. Liquor stores, laundromats, payday loans, psychics, nail salons, more liquor stores, and only the ghosts of pay phones. A rusted pedestal against a brick wall, an empty shell with the word *PHONE* above it like a joke.

What happened to them? Were people trying to get at the money inside? Or did the decay of obsolescence produce a pheromone that attracted violent riffraff?

Then there's a park, and on the wall of the concrete block of restrooms is a pay phone—with the phone part intact.

I park and open my door in time to hear them say, "—fucking creep-o." Maybe it's not them, maybe it's a parent. Maybe they mean someone else.

The restrooms are near the playground, where parents sit nudging strollers back and forth and chatting with their phones in hand. Kids run, climb, scream, laugh.

"He picked this one 'cause there's kids."

I feign interest in a tree to my left, away from the playground.

"Don't look at 'em, perv."

"We should warn all these parents."

"They've already clocked him. Lone dude with a minivan."

I drag on my cigarette.

"Hey... *Hey*!" It's louder and clearer than the other voices. Female. "Hey, excuse me, uh, you can't *smoke* here!"

To my right is a woman on a bench with an incredulous face and her arms up in a shrug.

"This is a park!" she says. "With *kids*! There's a sign!" She points at the bathrooms. Near the pay phone is a red circle-slash over a cigarette. I know it's illegal to smoke in parks, anyway. I'm just distracted.

I stoop and smush the cigarette on the ground. "I'm sorry," I tell her, "it totally slipped my mind. Sorry. I was thinking about something else."

She looks at the black smear on the pavement. "Great. Now that's filthy."

I scrape the spot with my shoe, which does nothing, and look for a trash can to toss the butt. There isn't one. So I put the butt in my pocket, which the woman appears to expect from someone like me.

"He got fucking *told*!" says the familiar voice. They're somewhere nearby. "Just so you all know, we're keeping an eye on that guy. He's a perv. If he so much as looks at your kids, we'll take care of him."

I dare to scan the playground again—blurry, speeding past the children to the parents—to see if I can catch my pursuers evangelizing. I don't know what I expect them to look like. Maybe they're dressed like these people. Maybe they know the locations of all the pay phones within a certain radius, and could anticipate where I'd stop, so they arrived ahead of me and planted themselves.

That woman is still looking at me and saying something to a woman next to her, who is now also looking at me. I turn away.

I want to find another phone. But that could take hours, and leaving would make me more suspicious.

The phone's receiver is cracked and a couple of buttons are missing from the number pad.

I take the receiver and hear a dial tone—a distant, familiar sound. A hum like the universe thinking aloud. A long, flat plane with no obstructions. I tear open a roll of quarters, feed the phone and dial, pushing my finger into holes where the buttons are absent and hoping not to receive an electric jolt. The line rings.

"Probably scheduling a drug deal."

Ring...

"Around a bunch of kids and parents? That's way fucked up!"

Ring...

"He's a desperate crackhead. What do you expect?"

Ring...

"Hello?" I almost don't recognize the difference in this voice compared to the others. This one is less muffled by distance, more thin and electric. My ear clings to it like a buoy.

"Matt? It's Alex," I say. "Porter."

"Hey, what's going on?"

"Something's happening, and I need your help."

Matt is a friend of Dad's. The most knowledgable computer guy I personally know. I tell him about the neighbors' comments, the firewall, and my suspicion about the webcam.

A kid on the playground starts screaming.

Matt asks, "Where are you?"

"I had to find the last working pay phone in Los Angeles. Happens to be next to a playground."

"You mean your cell phone's messed up too?"

"Might be, yeah. I don't want to take any chances, so it's at home turned off. But I think they followed me anyway."

"You saw them?"

"No, I heard them. Shouting stuff at me."

"But you haven't seen them?"

"No, they always stay just out of sight."

"What were they shouting?"

"You have reached the prepaid limit for this call. To continue, please insert fifty cents."

I dig in my pocket for more quarters and Plinko them into the phone. "Matt, you still there?"

"Yeah, I'm here. What are they—"

"Is it too late for my computer and phone? Virus scans got nothing. I feel like the disabled firewall left the door wide open and they've just been squatting in my basement this whole time, y'know? I have no idea how long this has been going on."

"Did they go after your money?"

"No, I checked everything. No weird charges on my cards. Changed my passwords. I think they're doing this to fuck with me."

"Right." He pauses. "That's a lot of work just to mess with someone."

"I know." Truth tickles in my spine. Matt understands the extent of their obsession—this is an unreasonable amount of effort for nothing. My hope is that if they're clever enough to infiltrate my privacy, logic will prevail. They'll reach a point of diminishing returns and realize how much time they've wasted following me around. I might already be close to the end.

Then I feel another tickle, imagining a day when they'll disappear from my life and I'll be left perplexed but at peace.

"I wonder if I got hip to them sooner than they expected, and now that *they* know that *I* know what they're up to, they can't take my money or anything. 'Cause that would give me concrete evidence, you know? And maybe they're just using me as a guinea pig, trying out tactics to use in other scam jobs."

"Have you told your folks about this?"

"No, I don't think they'd know how to help. I figured you'd know best."

"Hmm..."

The line between us crackles like the foil over my window.

"Do you know of anything I could do in the meantime, while I wait for them to wise up and go away?"

"You said your firewall's on now?"

"Yeah."

"Good. We could tweak some settings on your router, too."

I cup my hand over the receiver and my mouth for the rest of the call. I glance over my shoulder—only once, avoiding looking directly at that woman—to make sure no one snuck up behind me to listen.

I strain to hear grit underfoot, or breathing, or the swish of fabric. But I can't hear those things under everything else. I wish the children would shut up and sit still for a goddamn second, and the air would calm and the leaves would settle, and the cars would park and the planes would land. The world beyond my field of view is in an unknowable quantum state, constantly shifting and trading places, peopled with things popping in and out of existence. But when I turn to look, everything jumps back into perfect position, twiddling its thumbs.

The world grins and says, "Nobody here but us chickens!"

I BET THEY THOUGHT I'd go straight home. As I pass my street I imagine them saying, *Where the fuck is he going? This guy's crazy!* And I rise and meander in the hills for the length of a couple cigarettes, along humps and ridges, appreciating how these ribbony roads allow me to swoop in and out of sight, with steep slopes of brush and rock on either side. Eventually I point myself back down with a hasty right turn, and I hope I've lost them there.

Gavin's street is a small loop where parking is rare even on a weekday. I find the closest possible spot and walk fast to his building, through the unlocked front door, and up the stairs to his apartment.

I knock. No answer. I haven't seen the time, but I guess it's still too early. So I sit on the doormat and imitate someone waiting for a friend.

People enter the building through the whining front door, and if I hear them enter the courtyard below, I lean forward, listen to their footsteps, peek over the railing where sometimes I see a shoulder, and I make sure each passerby finishes by unlocking and entering an apartment.

All strangers are accounted for.

Regardless, my pursuers might've anticipated this trip to Gavin's—though I can't imagine how—and found a silent way in, and now they could be standing right below me, heads upturned to sniff the air and listen.

A window in the building next door has its curtains open just wide enough to peer through. All they had to do was act confident, flash some fake identification, a 3D-printed badge, and they could say some bullshit like, *Ma'am, we're sorry to bother you, but we're tracking a potentially dangerous suspect and he's in the building next door. May we look through your window?*

Who would refuse?

The door whines again. Shoes mount the stairs. The top of a head bobs into view, then a face. Not Gavin's. A Black man's. He sees me and I look at a spot on the floor, conjuring a facial expression that says: *I am just waiting for my friend. We have been friends for a long time, and neither of us is a threat to anyone.*

I squeeze myself against Gavin's door to make room for the man to pass, smiling upward but not quite at his face. "Hi," I say.

It works—the man goes by, then unlocks and enters an apartment a few doors down.

"That nigger was onto him."

"Totally. He saw right through it."

I watch the man's door. He might've heard what they said, and he might think I was the one who said it.

A thought forms too quickly to swat away—the man might know Lili. They might see each other soon, and she'll happen to describe the strange white guy she met online, and the man will recognize her description and tell her about this encounter. I'd been so careful to dodge my personal landmines, and in the end she'll think I'm a racist because of something *someone else* said.

But this scenario in itself is racist—where does the knee-jerk assumption come from that this man and Lili know each other, just because they're both Black? Does the fact that I have eyes make it more likely that I know any random person on the street who also happens to have eyes?

My pursuers have eyes, but they're still little more than strangers to me.

And where the fuck are they? The window looking at me is closed. It could be another window next door, or further down—

"I thought that was your van." Directly to my right. I turn expecting a gun, or suits, or disguises like the parents in the park, or bunches of rustling fake leaves with green-painted faces and white eyes staring.

It's Gavin.

I stand. "Hey, I locked myself out of my apartment."

"Oh, shit." He thinks a moment. "How did you drive here without your keys?"

Good question. "I keep 'em on separate rings, like an idiot."

"Well, that was a dumb move. At least you've still got your car keys." He thinks again. "Do... I have a copy of your apartment key?"

"No, but my phone's at home too. Can I use yours to call a locksmith?"

"Yeah, dude." He thumbs the code and hands me his phone.

We're still standing at his door, so clearly my urgency hasn't translated through my voice or body language. Or Gavin isn't paying close enough attention. "Also, could I get a glass of water?"

"Yeah, sure, sorry." We enter his apartment. "Help yourself." The day-old air inside is hot and thick. He leaves the door open and lowers onto the couch groaning, "Uh, boy..."

Standing by the far end of the couch I can still see the bright world outside. The window with the slit in the curtains stares like a giant reptile eye sunken into rough plaster skin. And there's Gavin on the couch, head back, eyes closed, with the door open right next to him, oblivious that he's exposed, visible, vulnerable.

He gets up and moves to open the window. "It's fucking hot as balls."

"Wait, can you keep the window closed?" I point at the door. "And close that? Just for a sec."

He pauses by the door, then pushes it shut. "What's up?"

"Can you lock it?"

His face is confused, but he turns the deadbolt. "Did something happen?"

"Do you—" I motion around the corner from the living room. "Come here."

He follows me into his kitchen, which is long and narrow. I go all the way to the back wall and stop short of a small huddle of empty beer bottles. I hand his phone back. "I didn't lock myself out."

"Oh. Okay... You still want that water, or was that a lie too?"

"No, yeah, I'll get it. Thanks. Do you still have that PCM recorder?"

"Yeah."

"How sensitive is it?"

"Pretty sensitive. I kept picking up the neighbor's AC unit in the background, which was a nightmare to mix out."

I lean. "Can I borrow it?"

"Yeah." He raises his eyebrows. "Uh, why are we whispering about this in my kitchen?"

Calling Matt was a risk. I have to assume that no amount of mouth covering or whispering kept them from hearing what I told him. But Matt is far away in Milwaukee. Gavin is only a few blocks from my apartment—ground zero. I've already fucked up by coming here in the first place; the last thing I want is to drag him further into this. "I can't say now, but I'll tell you when I know more."

"Is something going on?"

"Nothing big. I just need to borrow the recorder."

"I don't know if the battery's charged. You've got a... project?"

"Sort of, but I can't say much for now."

"You gonna record a murder or something?"

"Nothing like that." I sort of chuckle.

"I'll go get it."

I grab his arm. "Can you—do you have a bag or something to put it in? Preferably not see-through."

Gavin stares at me, blinking, and says, "Yeah, I think I got a bag," and goes into his bedroom.

I follow.

The apartment is well-sorted except the dishes in the sink. But Gavin's bedroom has only a bed, a desk, an armchair, and then things strewn and stacked as if he emptied his moving boxes onto the floor and left it that way. I'm grateful for the disorder, because while he digs through it I have time to scan what I can see from across the room, out the window over his bed to the roof of the next building and the leafy branches of trees.

Shadows move, but there's nothing substantial, and I regret the few minutes it took for me to get into the apartment and talk to Gavin—enough time for them to climb a tree? or relocate to another neighbor's apartment? maybe somewhere with a view through this window? Gavin is close enough to the window, it's possible they have line of sight.

I wish he wasn't a separate person. Or I wish I could disguise myself as him and get the recorder myself, because as Gavin I could look through the window to confirm whether they were there, and they wouldn't duck from view because they'd think I was him.

Or if it were possible for me to be both Gavin and myself, I could coordinate an elaborate shell game between our two bodies so they'd never notice the handoff of the recorder. I could even use Gavin to tail *them* while they tailed *me*.

But he and I are two separate people, which means anything I want to communicate to him has to be either written and made visible to the world, or spoken and made audible. Communication is exposure.

Gavin holds a medium-sized gift bag out for me to take. It has party hats and colorful metallic spots printed on it. "This'll do?"

It's conspicuous. But it's also thick and opaque, specifically made to obscure its contents. "Yeah, it's—it'll work."

"I can't wait to know what this is about."

"Soon, I hope. Thank you. I'm sorry."

"Smoke a bowl?"

I sit on the couch drinking water from a big plastic cup that's comfortably unfamiliar. A friend's cup. The tap water is the same as at my place, but it tastes different in this cup.

The gift bag stares me down like a bomb on the coffee table. I let Gavin open the door and window, because opening to the world and adopting a "casual hangout" atmosphere might take some attention off of him. It may even relax their focus on me, too.

He packs salty-smelling weed into the small water pipe he calls Kobayashi. The pipe is clear glass that's turned purple and grainy with use. A long, sky-blue dragon wraps around it, aiming its crooked hand-blown sneer at the weed in the bowl. I remember the day Gavin bought it. I was the second person ever to smoke from it in our shared bedroom sophomore year.

He hands me the pipe and a lighter. I draw bubbles, remove the bowl and feel the smoke rush into my mouth and throat. I hold.

Gavin rubs his folded hands on his head, stares at the wall.

I exhale and taste blue cheese smoke on my tongue.

"So," he says, "where should we go next?"

I hand him the pipe and lighter. "I'd like to hang here a little bit, if that's cool. Then I should head home."

Gavin draws on the pipe, staring at me, and then his laugh draws out in stoned-motion like the quiet call of a large bird. "No, I mean where should the next trip be? Did I show you the map of Los Padres?"

"I don't think so."

"Hang on." He goes back to his room, and I watch the apartment door.

Someone walks past it. No, that was the sound of Gavin moving something in his room; I hadn't actually seen anyone walk past.

"He's fucked up. What a fuckin' lightweight!" That wasn't Gavin, it came from outside. Nearby, but still far away.

Laughter. "Are you stoned, Alex? Are you ffuuucking *sssstoned*?"

"He's scared."

"Yeah, look, he's terrified. He hasn't even blinked yet."

Test movements of my eyelids prove they're dried stuck on my eyeballs. I blink. Blink again. Did something move out there when I blinked? Where are they watching from?

A map lowers onto the coffee table like a manta ray settling on the sea floor. Concentric amoebas drawn over shades of green and brown. Red dotted lines twist through illusory crevices and across blue line creeks. Gavin sits on the couch. "This is Los Padres." He circles a large portion of the map with his finger. "Up by Santa Barbara."

"Did you just hear someone talking?"

"Who?"

"Someone outside. About me being stoned?"

He laughs, "Well, you're clearly stoned." He waves his fingers, "Focus." Then he moves them in a magician's flourish, "This..." points back down at the map, "...is Los Padres."

I want to stay in this moment where there is only me, Gavin, and the map. It's a small, safe constellation—a triangle—with simple vertices: he points at the map, and I concentrate on his pointing. There's no way to fuck it up. Why can't everything be like this?

I watch his finger but channel all my attention through my ears. I give quick sideways glances out the door. Gavin's on that side of me, so each time I look I can pretend I'm looking at him. This is the kind of trick I'd pull if I could control both of us. I'd orchestrate entire outings wherein he and I would talk to each other about whatever bullshit, always staring just past each other to keep a 360 watch for my—our—pursuers.

"There's a campsite here, with picnic tables and stuff. I found some pictures online. Nice shady spot. No shitter, but we don't need it." He traces with his finger. "There's a creek here that might be dry when we go, so we should pack in extra water."

"Sounds fine."

He removes the bowl from Kobayashi and goes to the door. I half expect a shape to pass the doorway and swallow him. Then the walls and furniture of the apartment would crumple like paper, exposing bright light behind everything. Some of that light is already piercing through in extruded beams of smoke over the coffee table, centering on the gift bag and glaring off its metallic spots. I move the bag to the floor by my feet, in shadow.

Gavin doesn't disappear out the door. He fingers the crusty remains, blows out the bowl, returns and pushes more weed into it.

"And this is a canyon, kind of like when we went to the springs. The fires a couple years ago cleared out a lot of this area. Want the green?" He offers the pipe and I shake my head. He draws flame into the pipe. The smoke held in his lungs changes his voice like a mouthful of whipped cream. "But now it should be growing back. Lots of wildflowers and stuff. Probably beautiful." Long exhale.

"I'll bet."

***

When I leave, I step out the door looking both ways. Splotchy yellow sunlight through the trees spreads like alien lichen across the wall. Brightening, darkening, breathing.

I turn back to Gavin. "Thanks for the help." I hold up the gift bag. "He's gonna love this."

"Right on." Gavin nods, chuckles. "Tell him I said... happy birthday?"

Gavin is a good friend, and this breaks my heart.

MOM PUT AN ORNAMENT on the mantle every Easter. A hollow sugar egg the size of a softball, its two half-shells glued together with a wavy crust of purple icing, crowned with a red rosette and blue ribbon. It had a window through which you could see sprouts of green grass, clusters of tiny plastic eggs, a pastel-rainbow wicker basket, and a fuzzy toy bunny sitting on its haunches and staring at you with bulbous pink eyes.

Now the bunny sits on a couch. Rather than plastic eggs there's a glass of water, a pack of cigarettes, and a jam jar ashtray within his reach. As he stares out the window of his egg, he knows something that you don't—there's a recording device hidden from view. You didn't see him turn the recorder on at a red light on his way home. Nor did you see him place it on the windowsill, which is just deep enough to hide it from view. He seems harmless sitting there. Big pink eyes.

He stubs out a butt and stares at the walls of his egg with a soft smile on his face. You may be surprised to hear him speak, and feel at the base of your skull that he's addressing you.

"Can you hear me?" I ask the giants peering in. "Can you see me?"

Silence.

I light another cigarette and take patient drags, seeming harmless in my sugar egg.

Then I prop the cigarette in the jam jar and stand. I do tai chi. My hands curl and stretch, pass an imaginary orb from palm to palm, push it away and pull it back in controlled waves, a slow step here, another slow step there. The orb swirls with color like a soap bubble.

A window AC unit somewhere outside clicks on and hums.

"What the fuck is he doing?" a voice says.

Got 'em. I try not to smile. The AC hum becomes the sound of the orb in my hands.

"Look at this fucking idiot."

"There you are," I say. I sneak a look at the neighbors' window where their Venetian blinds are closed. But I don't linger, I turn my back to them while cradling the orb in my arms and then push it away with a long exhale. I look again. Did the blinds flick shut? They might be peering through the holes where the blinds are threaded together. Clever.

I move to the coffee table, raise the orb over my head, curl my hands around it, then swoop it down to the table and scoop my phone up, thinking of how it might look to them through the phone's camera, seeing my hand descend from the popcorn ceiling, grow to gargantuan size and smother to black.

"Now," I say, "let's talk."

"What do you wanna talk about, you fucking creep?"

Holding my phone, the voice is no louder. The phone is not the source.

Turn and push toward the kitchen, then a careful step on sideways foot to my bedroom where I toss the phone onto my bed. My laptop sits wearing its Post-it eyepatch on the desk in a nebula of green paper stars. A graceful pull of the doorknob shuts my traitorous electronics in the dark.

The orb dips low, I lean to catch it like a falling balloon. "How am I a creep? What have I done that's so creepy?"

"*Look* at you!" one says. "Dancing around like a fuckin' faggot!"

There it is. The familiar frequency of the schoolyard in their voices. This is about getting a rise out of me, maybe nothing more.

"Clearly all of this isn't for money, or you would've taken it by now," I say, calm, eyes on the orb.

"Oh, but it *is* for money, Alex."

"We've got viewers."

A tingle sinks from the back of my neck to my stomach.

"Lots."

"They say this shit's better than TV."

"They're placing bets now."

I dip to take the cigarette and pinch it in my lips, then lift the orb again. After leaning in the jar for so long, the cigarette has gone gray up one side and tastes stale.

"Alex, we're livestreaming you to viewers all over the world. You have no idea how much money we're making. You're a star!"

It's hard to keep my movements deliberate. I tell myself I don't hear them anymore.

"Most of 'em tune in when you're jerking off."

"Yeah, how 'bout it, Alex, feel like jerking off now?"

"I'll make a poll in the chat." Then speaking slow, as if while typing, "Place your bets! Shit... piss... or jerk off?"

I shift my weight from one foot to the other and feel a sting at the tip of my penis. I have to pee, but doing so would look like giving in to their suggestion. They're kidding about the livestream. How is it happening anyway, if my computer and phone are turned off in the next room?

The air is evening blue. The last claws of pale yellow scratch the neighbors' wall. Eventually it'll be too dark to see me. I sit on the couch, cross my legs, and light a fresh cigarette.

I can probably hold it for another half-hour. Be the rabbit, as still as the plastic grass and the colored eggs. Wait for everyone to get bored and go away.

"Alex, you got a message from a girl on that perv site. She's super hot. You want me to respond for you?"

"Why're you spoiling the surprise? We didn't tell him we got into his email."

"Come on, he knows. He's not a total idiot, right, Alex? He knows we have his bank stuff. But do you think he realizes that access to his email means access to basically everything else?"

"*Everything* else."

"Oh, someone just placed a bet that you'd jerk off in the bedroom instead. Now it's getting interesting! Will he go to the bathroom or the bedroom?"

I can't do either now.

"Actually, stay on the couch for a minute while these side bets come in."

"Oh my god, the chat is going fucking crazy! Who's gonna win, Alex?"

"The beauty is, *we* win no matter what. You're sitting on the fucking couch doing nothing, and no one can stop watching!"

Where's the camera? It hurts now; I won't make it thirty minutes.

"Alex, you wouldn't believe the money riding on these bets. Whatever you do, you'll make someone very happy."

How did they get in to install the equipment?

My apartment building is owned by an agency with other properties. To go out on a hypothetical limb, is it possible that my observers live next door, in a house coincidentally also owned by that agency, which they work for—or have connections to—and they used those connections to copy my key and sneak in while I wasn't home?

Is this a new reality show? A slapdash webstream proof of concept? Will a guy with a head mic and a clipboard knock on the door and ask me to sign a release?

I'll take the pen and sign his goddamn eyes.

"Alex, if you go to the bathroom right now, someone'll win more money than you make in a month!"

It hurts to sit still, and hurts even more to move. I could wait for my bladder to split and seep urine into my abdomen, and refusing to satisfy these motherfuckers will cost me my life.

If there's a viewer out there with half a conscience, they could leak this to the press, and my neighbors would be arrested on counts of voyeurism, harassment, and manslaughter. Or proof of malicious intent could make it homicide. Mine would be the first case of its kind. Someone would play me in a movie, reenacting *this exact scene*, and the realization would wash over the country that all our possessions have sprouted eyes and ears, that this could've happened to anyone. But I wouldn't get to see my observers' twisted empire burn to the ground because mine would be a martyr's death, the kindling of that revolutionary blaze.

"Come on, faggot, let's go! Everybody's waiting!"

"What's it gonna be, Alex?"

"If the people who bet you'd stay on the couch win, everyone's gonna be pissed."

"Yeah, boring is bad for business."

"Dead air is only suspenseful for so long, Alex. Come on, Alex, let's go, Alex!"

I slide to the edge of the cushion and a pang radiates. If I stand, I'll lose my careful muscle configuration, it'll all go into my pants and onto the floor.

Everyone will have a good laugh. Money will change hands, if some were smart enough to bet on this outcome.

The recorder still listens at the window.

But what if this doesn't work? What if nothing works, and they elude capture indefinitely? Would it be possible to continue living like this? Could I cultivate apathy and ignore the warped faces looming in the terrarium glass?

I rise on weak legs and the ache shifts, but I keep my urethra clamped tight and shuffle to the bathroom.

"Oh, motherfucker's going for it!"

My zipper takes a moment to pry up and pull down. Some on my pants, some on the rim of the toilet bowl. Better than on the couch and the floor, or elsewhere inside my body.

They laugh.

It hurts to let go—everything stretched to maximum capacity, muscles strained now releasing, relaxing, shrinking. My frayed bladder folding back together is excruciating. I go up on my toes to accommodate the pain.

"Holy shit," one says. "That's a ton of money!"

***

There's nothing on the recording.

Well, not *nothing*, but nothing helpful. I hear a faint AC unit buzz, I hear myself move around the room asking questions.

"Now, let's talk," I say.

But their responses aren't there.

The microphone was sensitive enough to pick up the pop in my ankle when I shifted my weight. I turn the audio up high in my headphones and fumble through the EQ menus on the recorder's LCD screen.

Scrubbing, adjusting, and listening on the recorder itself is like conducting a delicate archaeological dig with a shovel and a broom. A bug scratches at the back of my mind—if I put the SD card into my computer and open the waveform in a program with more range, more tools, I might find the evidence.

But copying the file onto my computer would give them access to it. Not to mention the risk of letting my computer's voyeuristic tapeworm infect Gavin's SD card, and later his computer.

In the headphones a door closes, when I shut my phone in with my computer. *"How am I a creep?"* I hear myself ask. Electric air whooshes. *"What have I done that's so creepy?"*

The buzz of the AC unit, the cars on the nearby arterial and distant freeway, the air of the room and the alleyway beyond the window all combine in an eternally-cresting wave that spittles foam into my desperate ears.

"Clearly all of this isn't for money, or you would've taken it by now."

The wave rushes in. For the rest of the recording, my movements are underwater. I hear the suffocated *shick* of the lighter. I hear the couch creak under my weight. I feel the sense memory of attempting outward normalcy while I ached and contorted like a tangled marionette. And I hear the moment when I slid from the couch and fell to my knees, then rose, my ankle popping again, and shuffled into the bathroom. Then from the next room the stream growls on denim, breaks on the edge of the porcelain bowl and into the water, sounding my simultaneous relief and defeat.

Breath held to listen, turning the whoosh louder in my ears...

Is that laughter?

AFTER THE FIRST KNOCK it's too late to turn back. Maybe this demonstration of bravery will prove that I know who they are and I'm serious about getting them to stop. They could take the hint, and we could save ourselves a confrontation.

But since it's 10 p.m. on a Monday, and I'm standing in front of their quiet house lined up with all the other quiet houses, lights on and curtains closed, their other option is to pull me in and make me disappear. If they have the means to torture me at a distance, they have the means to torture me in person.

Matt expects me to call when I get to work tonight. If he hears that I went missing after our conversation—for which I sought the last working pay phone in Los Angeles—he knows enough to give the authorities some rocks to turn over.

I've got the recorder's SD card in my pocket on the off chance they'd use this moment to sneak into my apartment and mess with the evidence.

I knock harder. If they answer or peek through the curtains, I'll have a face to remember.

The deadbolt springs back, the knob clicks and opens.

A young guy stands there with blond hair buzzed short. He's got eyes like holes cut in cardboard, somehow both flat and sunken-in. They make him look defiantly illiterate. But that doesn't mean he isn't good with computers. Maybe his eyes got that way from scanning pages of hacker tips, reading all that broken, impersonal coding language computer people trade online. It's probably been a long time since he's read a whole, unadulterated sentence.

His eyes narrow, or maybe they're always like that. I search them for signs of recognition. He says, "Yeah?"

Without it sounding tinny and distant, I can't compare the voice. I say, "Hi, I'm your neighbor. Alex Porter." I wait.

"OK."

"Look, I know what you guys are up to. I don't know if it's you or your housemates, but I'd like to call a truce. What do you think?"

His tongue flicks over his lip. His eyebrows go up in the middle like a golden retriever's when it can't find a stick you only pretended to throw. "What do you mean?"

"I'm *the guy*. From over there." I point at my window.

He looks but can't see my window past his hedge. Then he looks back at me. "And?"

"And I want my privacy back." I don't even feel the urge to make my language more severe. This clearly isn't the response he expected.

"Dude, I don't know what the fuck you're talking about." He frowns and runs his tongue over his lip again.

That's one of the tells, isn't it? Proof someone's lying? The tongue thing, and looking up to the left? One side means lying, the other side means trying to remember something. Lying is to the left, I think.

"I'll bet your buddies know what I'm talking about."

"Well, they're not home."

"So you admit you've got housemates."

"Yeah. What does that mean?"

"Are they just cowards, or what?"

He shakes his head like an Etch A Sketch to erase me from his doorstep. "Look, dude, I don't know what your problem is, but whatever it is, it's not us."

"You sure they aren't home?" I look past his shoulder. It's dark in there. I see a couch with clothes draped on the back. There's a heavy wood coffee table and burgundy recliner—ugly, found, frat-house furniture. Video game console and controllers on the floor with jumbled cords like a disemboweled alien.

"They're at work. Do you work?"

"Nights." I smile. "But you already knew that."

He just squints at me.

I return his squint. "Do *you* work?"

"Not right now. But I've got other shit to do." He closes the door, satisfied it'll wipe me from view. But just before the bolt catches he adds, "See ya, creep."

He said *creep*.

THE CONFERENCE ROOM COMPUTER is old, shows me those generic, green nowhere hills. I disable its internet connection and plug my router into it.

I blow dust off the desk phone and wipe the handset on my shirt, leaving a thick gray stripe.

Matt answers. Right away he says he's got good news and bad news.

The good news is that he found a PDF of my router's user manual. He learned that there's a "superuser" login that allows advanced configuration. This is how we'll boost my security.

The bad news is that by default the superuser password is "password."

Of course, it would've been a good idea to change this password when I got the router. I'm lucky the hackers haven't already changed it themselves to lock me out.

"We'll fix that when we're done here so they can't get back in," Matt says. "But first, you know when you turn on your computer's wifi and it shows a list of available networks? We're gonna make it so yours doesn't show up in that list."

"Yes! Invisibility! Please, how do I do that?"

"See the checkbox that says 'display SSID'?"

"Yes."

"Uncheck it."

"It won't let me. It's grayed out, permanently checked."

"Gray?" A pause. The sound of dead air is too familiar. "You're in the superuser preferences, right?"

"Yup."

"Ah... Shit. Sounds like someone did get in and fuck with things."

My hands go cold. The worst of the good news is that I'm not crazy. I hadn't just spent the evening talking to myself in my apartment. I hadn't listened to two hours of the neighbor's humming AC unit for nothing. I was on a quest for proof, and now with Matt's help I've found it.

He says I need a clean device, and to avoid this happening again he'll configure a router he has handy and send it for me to use. I give him the office address, which is more secure than my apartment.

Walking back to my desk, my compromised router sags like roadkill in a grocery bag tied shut. Old CRT monitors lurk in dark rooms along the corridor, slivers of hall light reflected on their glass faces. The tower in the manager's office is silent and hidden in shadow except for its tiny green light. Asleep or awake? Our big room has twenty desks, each with a PC tower. Screens hunch like flat-faced gargoyles.

I imagine if I peel away the face of my screen, I'll find eyes staring back from a howling void.

They might be the navel orange eyes of my neighbor. Behind him I'd see his room. Unmade bed, clothes everywhere, a backpack hung on the doorknob, posters on the walls for stupid movies or shitty bands.

He and his housemates might be surveillance or tradecraft hobbyists.

They could have suitcase-sized electronics stacked against the wall. A battery bay plugged in and charging, blinking red and green lights. Headphones. A filing cabinet labeled with my name full of documents concerning me, my behavior, and the behavior of others around me. Records of things I bought, maps of places I went and the paths took to get there.

Matt said as long as my phone isn't jailbroken, only people with NSA-level clearance could get into it the way I fear they have.

What if they do work for the NSA? What if they're young interns or new hires training for a job in surveillance? After a series of tests in controlled, closed-circuit conditions, wouldn't they eventually have to prove themselves in the field with a live, unpredictable subject?

Maybe theirs is a special assignment: does mocking a rat's attempt to navigate a maze impair its ability to solve the maze?

EVERYONE ELSE AT THE grocery store is preparing for something.

I would say I can see it in their eyes, but I'm making a conscious effort not to look at anyone's eyes. I move around and past people like they're wheeled furniture on a rocking ship. No one rushes, but in my hair follicles I can feel they're biding their time. I'm their countdown clock. Carts and baskets packed with family-sized bags of chips and jars of dip, boxes of beer, ribbed bricks of hot dogs, pink mounds of chuck, buns for meat of all shapes, pretzels, popcorn... Spectator snacks.

My own cart is full too. Among the staples are beer and ice cream to celebrate my imminent freedom. *You don't want to miss the series finale, folks.*

A mother pushes a cart with a baby in it, and a little boy of about four dances beside her, pulling cans off the shelves and then putting them back per her request. He wobbles near and looks up at me. I don't look at him, but I can feel his sticky gaze on my cheek. Then he turns his back to me, puts a few cans on the floor and squats down to stack them. In the blurry part of my view I see his shirt rise to reveal a band of flesh dimpled by shadow in the middle. Obedient as a wind-up toy. Disgusting, to wrap children up in this twisted experiment.

"Is he looking at the ass?"

"I can't tell. Can't see his eyes."

Tightness at the back of my head, blood rumbles in my eardrums. Don't run. They'll see what they want to see: a sweaty, white-knuckled pedophile fleeing the scene of a near-crime. Well, I'll show them I can stay planted in place, happy to focus on my task. That kid may as well be a pack of canned beets.

"He'll look, if he didn't already."

Olives on the top shelf. I don't need olives, but there are gratefully enough brands and varieties for me to play-act a discerning shopper.

"He's resisting for now. Give him a minute... Oh, reading the label on those olives, huh? What's in there? Hmm, vinegar... oh, right, and olives... Seem pretty good to me. Are they good for you, Alex? Lotsa vitamins? How the fuck can he look at that label for so long? Should you buy those olives?... Ah, didn't think so. Yeah, put it back. Maybe no olives today, you fucking pervert faker bullshit artist."

As soon as I put the jar back on the shelf, I defiantly take a jar of the next brand and put it in my basket.

"Oh, need olives after all? Hope those are good ones, Alex, you didn't even take the time to read the label!"

"What if they're bad for you, Alex? What if they're *poison*?"

"One of the jars on that shelf is poisoned. Did you pick the right one?"

Laughter.

"You think he'll put the jar back now?"

"Probably not now. Maybe later."

"How long before he puts it back, you think?"

"Probably when that lady with the butt-kid is gone."

Doesn't the mother hear them? Shouldn't she react? I arc my stare over her son. She peruses the mustards. Don't you usually just grab a mustard and go? Most people have a brand, right? There aren't many options—bright yellow, goldenrod, or goldenrod with the little seeds in it. She's avoiding my stare and ignoring what they say, playing her part in their sting operation.

"Disgusting," I say to her.

Her son looks at me, but she doesn't.

"Hell-o." I wave.

She turns. "I'm sorry?"

"Disgusting." I point at her son.

Her son looks back at her. They clearly didn't cover this scenario when they coached him.

"Jeremy, come."

The boy stands and walks to his mother's outstretched hand, turns to look at me.

"Let's go," she says.

"You all know I'm onto you, and you can stop right now." My voice never rises above speaking volume, but my delivery is firm enough that the mother turns her cart around and leaves the aisle, watching over her shoulder, visibly shaken.

Maybe they collect volunteers on Craigslist. Desperate amateur actors who don't know what to do when the mark goes off script. Are the posts labeled "scientific study," or do they list them among the acting gigs?

I can't tell who is and isn't a plant, but everyone else in the store avoids my stare. Maybe the mother and son were the only plants and the rest are viewers, eager for me to check out and leave so they can race home to their TV sets. Then, seated on couches and in armchairs, kids on cushions on the floor with bowls of popcorn, chips, and pretzels, the sliding glass door open to the patio where meat sizzles, they'll see me walk onto their TV screens, entering my apartment with my own groceries.

"There he is, Dad," a kid on a cushion will shout without turning from the screen, "he's home."

And the reply from outside under the sound of sizzling meat, "I'm coming. Tell me if something happens."

All the world abuzz over how long before I crack. Money sealed in separate envelopes marked with prognoses like a demented game of *Clue*...

In his bedroom with a rope.

Or, *in the public library with underwear on his head.*

Or the signature option of this brave new century, *any public place with an automatic weapon.*

I could climb the shelves and scream and tear off my clothes before they finalize their bets. Take me away. Put me where you want. Leave me the fuck alone.

The only people who meet my gaze are printed on cereal boxes. The cereal box people are at ease with being watched; they smile back at me, wink at me, laugh with me. My laughter is internal, of course, to avoid drawing attention.

If they haven't died since taking these photos, these people are somewhere out there right now, worrying like everyone else. Self-conscious when they reach for something sugary in full view of a wall of themselves scooping into a bowl of muesli.

But the most sympathetic cereal box people are the cartoon characters—birds, rabbits, leprechauns, et cetera—because they don't have real-life counterparts weighed down by obligation and judgment. Their smiles are always the right kind. And they've already gone crazy—cuckoo, silly, whatever the individual case. Society encourages their weaknesses, insanity burns bravely in their wild eyes.

They never blink. They gaze back, grinning, while dust collects on their painted eyeballs. Stab forks into them and they'd still be last to blink. Their stares would endure through creeping flames.

But TV proves that they too are prodded and tested. After hacking through miles of jungle, dodging poisonous snakes and spiders, surviving deadly booby traps of darts and pits in some long-lost temple, and finally standing before a holy grail of neon corn balls and slow-motion milk cascading from the mouth of a monolith, what do they do when a bunch of giggling kids show up and snatch it away?

On the boxes they smile through their anger, goggle-eyed, oblivious that their treasure sits just behind them, through a thin layer of cardboard and plastic.

I SAVE EVERYTHING IMPORTANT from my phone and laptop onto a couple of thumb drives, then set them to wiping their memory. Full cleanse.

I lie on my bed, close my eyes, and watch a phantom progress bar.

When my phone finishes, it lights up and stares at me with the blank face of a post-op lobotomy patient, wearing its factory-generic color gradient background like a hospital gown.

It asks a list of questions it used to know about me.

My computer does the same, emerging from its wipe empty-headed and woozy, its face showing stars and a bright smear of aurora. Post-coma haze.

At first it isn't even sure what language to speak.

I tell it English, and enable the fucking goddamn firewall.

Then I turn both devices off and shut them in the bedroom.

Step one complete.

I slip the SD card bullet in the chamber, put the loaded recorder on my coffee table in plain sight with the LCD screen cocked, lit orange, and press record. With the jam jar ashtray it looks like an impromptu interrogation.

I light a cigarette and sit on the couch.

"Hey, you," I say. "Both of you fucks." I drag smoke. "However many of you there are."

"Us? We're two, for now."

"No, there's just one of us."

"Right, what he said. Just one of us."

"Yeah, haven't you been listening, fuckin' moron?"

I say, "Well, I've *heard* you. There's a subtle difference between the two, but *listening* implies a receptiveness to what's being heard. You haven't gotten that deep into me yet."

"I bet you'd like us to get deep into you, wouldn't you, faggot?"

I stop the recorder and plug my headphones in. Hit play. Turn the volume as high as I can without hurting my ears. My voice booms and reverberates, the rest of the air in the room is loud like waterfalls, and I strain to hear their replies through the whoosh. Nothing distinct. Sensitivity at 100% must be too high; the sound of their voices is drowned out by dust motes colliding closer to the microphone. I unplug the headphones, tune the sensitivity down to 80%, and hit record again.

"Sounds like you've got a recorder, Alex."

"Sounds like? You can't see me?"

"Nah, you wiped out our cameras."

A tingle slides through me. "And now I've recorded you saying you have cameras."

"Yeah? Play it back. Are we coming through nice and clear?"

"You are, actually."

"Bullshit."

"I don't understand why we can't resolve this face-to-face," I say, knowing I blew that chance when I heard them that night by the river, and instead of confronting them I zig-zagged for two hours like I had something to hide. Big mistake. Of course they followed me.

"If we did, it'd ruin the experiment, you fuckin' idiot! That's not how science works!"

"You're right," I say, "let's keep things 'fucking scientific.' I'd like to play a little game."

"We love games. What's the game?"

I lift the recorder from the table. "You're gonna tell me where it is."

"Where what is?"

My smile spreads. "I want to know... where's the bug?"

"We're not gonna tell—"

"Where's the bug?"

Silence.

"Where's the bug, motherfuckers, where's the bug?"

"Dude, you must think we're—"

"Where's the bug?"

"There's no way—"

"Where's the bug? Where's the bug? Where's the bug?"

Incredulous laughter. "Holy shit, he's lost it!"

"We broke him."

I stub the cigarette and take a deep breath.

"Wheresthebugwheresthebugwheresthebugwheresthebug-wheresthebugwheresthebugwheresthebugwheresthebug-wheresthebugwheresthebugwheresthebugwheresthebug-wheresthebugwheresthebugwheresthebugwheresthebug..." over and over, "wheresthebug," quietly, "wheresthebug," under my breath, knowing they can still hear me, "wheresthebug," listening for changes in their reactions.

At first they're quiet. Nothing but one-word questions like "what..." and "why..." Then they laugh and call me names, but the volume bars don't rise perceptibly on the LCD screen.

I continue without missing a beat, like a television announcer doing a vocal warmup in a time loop.

"...wheresthebugwheresthebugwheresthebug..."

It becomes a mantra, a rhythm as easy as breath itself.

"...wersabugwersabugwersabug..."

The sound is part of the air, slicked across surfaces like colored light, hanging like garlic smell. As I flex my mouth and throat muscles I imagine my voice echoes in a vast space of tile or metal or concrete, swims with choruses of itself in a round, an aural moiré: "Where's bug the, bug where's the, the where's, where's bug the bug, the where's bug the bug, the bug..."

I'm a sonar device. The first sound "where's…" casts an expanding sphere through the air, and "thebug" is the surface of that sphere bumping up against the objects in the room. "Where's… the-bug, where's… the-bug, where's…"

"You're never gonna find it, Alex!"

They don't have to answer my question; it's not even a question anymore—if I keep this up I'll find the device through echolocation. I pace the walls until I reach an object—the couch, the bookshelf, the TV—and search the object. Near the front door there's a plaster scab under the paint where the knob would hit. Likely benign. I spot other little backfilled dots like whiteheads in the living room wall where previous tenants probably hung pictures.

"We just drained your bank account, fuckhead, you've got nothing left!"

The caulking in the bathroom looks newish…

"…wersabugwersabugwersabug…"

…but if there's a wire hidden there I can't feel it under my finger, running the length of the tub.

"Be sure to check everywhere, Alex!"

"What if he finds it?"

"He won't, he's a moron."

I pull books from the shelves and stack them on the coffee table and floor like pillars of wind-eaten desert rock.

Silverware crashes onto the counter, my fingers scratch deep into the drawers and curl up against rough wood substructure, feel along the edges, into the corners, anticipating a slick patch of tape or the thin line of a wire.

"Getting warmer… closer… Oh, nope, now you're freezing."

"Wait, yeah, warmer… warmer… oh, hot, you're red-hot!"

"Burning up!"

"Scalding! Holy shit, he's gonna do it!"

"Aaand… go fuck yourself, shitbag, there's nothing there."

I move the contents of my cupboards to the living room. A box of rice spills between the couch cushions. Stacked books topple and sugar gushes across the coffee table and onto the floor in a gritty haze.

"...wersabugwersabugwersabug..."

In the cupboard behind my pots and pans I notice a wood panel. It wiggles when I push. I hook my finger in and dislodge it. A secret space. The scratched and stained floral-print shelf liner stretches into this unexplored void.

"Oh, shit, is he gonna find it?"

"Well, later, faggot. It was fun while it lasted."

Flashlight on, I climb in headfirst and slide until my head touches the wall. There is no tape, no glint of wire. The observers are quiet.

The space is large enough to pull my legs inside.

"...wersabugwersabugwersabug..."

My toe pulls the cupboard door shut. I turn off the flashlight. I'm cramped and whispering in perfect dark.

"...wersabugwersabugwersabug..."

I've seen photos of ancient catacombs, rows upon rows of skeletons folded into this position. Death shrinks us.

The whisper seeps from the wood around me.

...wersabugwersabugwersabug...

I stop to listen to it—but then it stops. I'm falling. Shut in a wooden box, spinning into space, with only as much air as is closed in with me. It's beautiful to be so alone. I touch the wood, feel the lines of its grain against my fingerprints. It's so close, protecting me, and beyond it is the vacuum of space for billions of miles—light years, even. My breath is the only sound, close and deep.

I blink my eyes. The dark doesn't change.

But something is here. Dim, shifting blobs of deep purple and green expand in a stygian tunnel. I touch the wall again, admire the conundrum of the tunnel's depth despite feeling wood inches from my face. My breath is warm on the back of my hand.

The box should get colder the further I travel, but it's still warm. Getting warmer? I could be approaching a sun.

The heat will increase to a cozy level, become stifling, until the wood itself is too hot to touch and the corners ooze blue-hot plasma and my darkness explodes into yellow flame. Maybe I'll survive long enough to watch the box burn away around me, and my consciousness will blink out just as my last breath ignites in my lungs and the firelight overwhelms my eyes.

***

There's no bug in the kitchen, that I've found. There are parts of the oven I can't take apart. I pull the fridge from the wall, feel along its coils, careful to avoid the hot parts. I run my fingers up around the underside of the sink basin.

"...wersabugwersabugwersabug..."

Either they work on batteries or they're wired into a constant power source.

When did they install them? Busy shadows in the night, while I was at work. They could've left the lights on, no need to tiptoe; the only place with a clear view into my window is their house. Footsteps on the floorboards heard by my downstairs neighbors who don't know me anyway. Some of the observers' exhaled breath could've been in the air when I returned home. I might've breathed it myself. Or touched hair or skin cells they left behind. Might've swept that evidence right up and thrown it out long ago.

I could be one in a long line of people come and gone in this apartment, so many seeds flung onto this hostile patch of soil. Each attempt to sprout and grow scrutinized with a magnifying glass of such focused intensity that each of us shrivels and burns. This stain on the wood floor—could it be old blood? Are there convenient places to hang oneself? There's the coat closet by the front door—would I find that the bar is strong enough? How many tortured ghosts lay with me in that coffin in the kitchen, seeking the source of their madness or at least a place to exist out of sight?

The bugs are like blisters in the walls. If I drill in the right places, they'll burst and bleed out all they've seen and heard.

Power sources—outlets, one on each wall. And light switches. Tappable veins of energy. Clamp little metal teeth on the wire and the parasite will drink.

I can feel them under my own skin like botflies ready to hatch, larvae like eyes all over my body. Their queen watches through them from her hive.

If I drill the right holes...

I unscrew all the plates, make my way around the room, scatter rice on the floor when I slide the couch from the wall to make sure I haven't missed one.

When a plate is removed, the two outlet faces stare at me with innocent surprise in their cockeyed slit eyes and small O mouths. Their home is just a metal shell with copper veins passing through it. The light switches are similar. Pull the plate away to expose the switch in its cave like a thin, white bat.

"...wersabugwersabugwersabug..."

Nothing is anywhere. Everywhere is nothing.

"Shut the fuck up, Alex."

"...wersabugwersabugwersabug..."

"Shut the fuck up, Alex!"

"...wersabugwersabugwersabug..."

The ceiling light is a simple glass dome over a bulb, easily removed. Dust floats down and I sneeze, and there's nothing there. Standing on the coffee table makes the tacky soles of my bare feet grainy with sugar.

But several feet away is the smoke detector.

It's a big one. Not one of those little white plastic things you buy in the checkout line and double-stick tape to the ceiling like a cheap clown nose. This one's the size of a saucepan, with ridges and grilles to snort the air. Beige plastic with sloppy smudges of ceiling paint at its base. This thing isn't a gadget, it's a fixture. The round, red-eyed head of a gargoyle peering into my world.

"…wersabugwersabugwersabug…"

"Shit, I think he's got it."

"At this point I don't care, if it means he'll shut the fuck up."

I slide the coffee table beneath it, brush the sugar onto the floor, make two stacks of books—one for each foot—and I still have to go up on my toes to reach.

But all it takes is grasping its face, holding tight and jiggling to break the crust of paint, a turn, another jiggle, the books under my feet slide a little, and the thing pops from its hole. Plaster snows into my eyes.

I break my mantra to shout, "Fuck!"

"Serves you right, faggot."

I drop my head and brush at my face, grit pinched in my eyelids.

"Well, do we call it? Kinda relieved to be done."

Are they louder? I'm so close to the source now; it's in my hand. Does it contain the speaker *and* the microphone? That would explain how they sound both omnipresent and distant, and how they can hear everything no matter where I am in the apartment.

I let it hang by its wires, and I step down. My eyes sting and dribble chunks. I remove my glasses, wash my hands, and search in the bathroom mirror to remove the rest.

My throat is dry. I drink from the faucet and stare. I only have to cut their source—squash the bug, and silence will fill these rooms thick and sweet like molasses. Maybe I'll turn out the lights, too. No photons, no vibrations. Just stillness, silence, darkness. The occasional *shick* of my lighter, the *psitch* as I open a can of beer. The softest, deepest gulps. Silent drunk buzz in my brain so quiet it ends at the tips of my hairs and disappears on the air vague, undetectable.

I stack more books and cradle the thing in my hand.

"You got us, Alex. Congratulations. We're gonna order pizza. You wanna come over and have some with us? Bring the beers."

"Yeah, you've earned it."

Tilting it, I can see the wires stripped of insulation where they attach to the smoke detector. They aren't long, so I have to lift as I turn it to get enough slack.

"I can't believe how well you did. Others have cracked, but you held your own throughout. That's admirable."

"Come on over, and we'll explain everything."

Tilting it as much as I can with my fingertips, I see the screws. Then the wires touch with a loud pop and a white burst edged in blue.

FOOTSTEPS IN THE DARK? Circling me. Marching. How many are there?

The cream-colored grid of my kitchen floor stretches from my cheek to a vanishing point under the oven.

Not footsteps.

Ringing, like a choir of air conditioners. The growl of the fridge? No, the fridge is silent.

My jeans sting against my scraped shin. Extending my leg simultaneously feels good and hurts more.

I look up at my looming fridge. A hole in the sky. The smoke detector hangs from it like a peeled scab ripe for the final pluck. I hit a nerve when I pulled. The scab screamed and gave a jolt, a pop of blue-white heat. What a fucking idiot. Jabbing a screwdriver into power outlets, light switches, then pulling on this live-wired smoke detector!

The footsteps fade as my heart calms. No one is here.

The blown fuse took everything out. I imagine any other hidden bugs have burst and are dripping in my walls. Sweet relief.

The indicator light on the smoke detector stares down at me, dark and unblinking like a dead eye. I'd spit at it, if the spit wouldn't fall back in my face.

I laugh.

For a short while this cocoon, this cave, will be cast back to a time before electricity. My TV sits blank-faced and useless.

My fridge—shit, my fridge. All my groceries. The ice cream. For now, everything is sealed in cool compartments. But as soon as I open the door, that trapped cold will spill out. Slow rot will set in.

I need to go to the fuse box and power everything off. Never too late for safety. It'd be just my luck to short out the apartment, then reach up to pluck the golden fruit at the end of my quest and touch the one remaining live wire.

They'd love for that to happen. I wonder if they were watching my window moments ago, maybe they saw the flash and the lights go out through the blinds. Maybe they think I'm dead, and are having their own celebration.

Or maybe they're gathering their tools to come and remove the evidence before anyone finds my body—sprawled on the kitchen floor, cupboards empty, rice and sugar and stacks of books spilled around the coffee table, the table itself askew in the middle of the room below a hole in the ceiling where the smoke detector hangs by its wires.

They might clean up some of the mess. Put things back in the cupboard. Sweep up the rice and sugar. Make it look like my smoke detector went off, maybe malfunctioned, and I climbed up to turn it off.

I open the blinds to let in orange light from the street, but not enough for them to see me.

The fuse box is in the coat closet, and I check the front door locks again before I open the closet, push my coats aside, and flip the main switch off.

I take pliers from the shoebox of tools in my bedroom. Then I climb, reach, and feel the jaws slip around one wire. I'm staring at the window, the soft streetlight squeezing through the hanging blinds, knowing they're on the other side cursing their fate or toasting my death. The wire clips like a finger bone. The smoke detector settles heavier in my hand.

The pliers open and seek the other wire. Find it and close. Clip. I catch the thing on my fingertips like a platter. Deliverance is served.

Now to relish the removal of that most damning of evidence: the microphone and the speaker. That terrible tinny speaker like the voice box in a child's toy. Pull the string, and it calls you a faggot.

I'll crack this nut and eat its heart.

My face hurts; I realize I'm grinning. Like Tom every time he thinks he's caught Jerry.

I leave the smoke detector on the coffee table while I go back to the toolbox for the hammer. I saunter, spitefully slow, like I've just pummeled the bad guy and he's a pulpy mess gasping for breath behind my car, and I'm about to put the thing in neutral and blast exhaust in his face before I finally drive off. I can already taste the beer. Intoxicating, bitter victory. The ice cream is still cold; I'll eat the whole carton.

The clipped wires stick out from under the screw heads like lopped-off antennae. The parasite sits frozen with fear in my lap. I can see the seam where its carapace fits together. I pull, and it opens just a hair's width.

I note that the device itself must stay in working order so I can reinstall it, in case those fucks try to set me on fire. If they could still hear me, I'd dare them to come over and set me on fire right now. I'd use the hammer and pliers on *them*.

I grip the halves and turn, but nothing budges. Of course it's tamper-proof. But then how did they get the bug in there? Is this a custom device made to *look like* an old smoke detector? Or maybe it's real, but after installing the mic and speaker they superglued it shut.

At the very least it's disconnected, powerless; they have no ears, no mouth. God, the fucking *mouth* on that thing. It's one thing to know you're being watched, and another to have the watcher shouting, "Here I am, I'm here, I hate you and I'm here, motherfucker, I'm here, I'm *always fucking here!*"

My other option is to pound the whole thing to pieces and examine the rubble.

"Should we tell him?"

"Not yet. See what else he does first."

The voice sends a cold buzz across my skin like white noise.

This is when Tom peels his hands apart to find them empty, and looks up to see Jerry wave at him from across the room.

My grip is so tight it's rattling.

"What's that weird sound?"

"I think he's—hey, Alex, are you trying to shake the mic outta that thing?"

They laugh.

"You know that's not gonna work, right?"

Batteries. In case of a blown fuse or power outage. "Clever motherfuckers," I say.

"We've thought of everything, I guess."

"You didn't think it was gonna be that easy to get rid of us, did you?"

I drop the smoke detector onto the kitchen counter.

"Hey! Fuck, that was loud!"

I lean close, lips almost touching the grille, and shout, "I hope you made this shit waterproof!" then push the stopper into the drain and open the faucet.

"I wouldn't do that, Alex."

"I'm sure you wouldn't! Ruin all your careful electrical work, huh? How much did this thing cost you? Or did you not pay for it yourself? Maybe you'll be in deep shit with your supervisors. Sloppy spy work."

"Alex, there's shit in there that's dangerous in water."

I settle my chin in my hand, smiling, and shout over the rushing water, "Dangerous, huh? For whom?"

"For you. As soon as that thing gets wet, it'll release toxic gas into the air and you'll be dead in seconds."

"And why, pray tell, would you give me this information, dearest pals o' mine? Don't tell me you care about my well-being."

"Fuck no. But we don't need a murder charge on top of everything else."

"I gotta tell ya, I'm this close"—my fingers pinch together—"to denying you the satisfaction of helping me. This thing is dangling over the sink, fellas. I'm calling your bluff." The sink is full enough that it's draining off. I shut the faucet.

"Alex, you crazy fuck, this is the truth! If you get that thing wet, you will *die!*"

I've talked myself into a position wherein my demise is the ultimate rebellion. But what do I stand to gain? I don't believe in an afterlife, so I can't look forward to seeing them punished. Worst-case scenario, my death is an inconvenience. They'll show up in plastic suits, use some kind of government-grade chemical vacuum to clear the air, drain the sink, drop the smoke detector in a protective bag, and leave me here for someone else to find. The corpse of a lunatic after what was clearly an eventful afternoon.

No, it's much later now.

The one thing in my apartment that isn't dead—besides the smoke detector parasite and me—is the wall clock. It says 10:47. Forty-three minutes until my shift.

I take my phone from the bedroom, turn it on, and call work, feigning food poisoning. It's a lie I can ride for a couple of days, if necessary.

When I hang up, the quiet in the apartment is overwhelming. No sound from outside. None of the usual hum of fridge, lights, or wires. I can almost hear my muscles move.

"What's your plan, Alex?"

***

When I was six, I had a hamster named Cocoa. At one point I was playing with her on my bed, and she burrowed under the pillow, and I pushed down on it to keep her from getting out the other side. I remember seeing her head peek out, and her eyes bulged. I thought if I pushed harder her eyes would pop out. I could imagine them hanging on the optic nerves, wetting her fur with slime. I could see her scramble to find safety.

Even at six years old, the idea that something would have to seek safety *from me* gave me vertigo. I could've done it. A hamster is easy enough—just tell my parents I rolled over on her, an accident.

But it wouldn't have been an accident. And the thought of *just wanted to see what would happen* made me imagine all the nights I'd spend staring at the ceiling and remembering the way her eyes bulged, the way I pressed down harder, her tiny muscles and bones unable to move between the pillow and the bed. The worst part would be when her eyes came out, like tiny black corks from pop guns. The point of no return.

Maybe because I didn't do it, I'm exactly the kind of subject they were looking for. They want to see if I can be moved to do otherwise. Their goal is to pummel me into pressing down until the eyes come out. Any eyes. Even my own.

I stare at my reflection in the TV screen. The streetlight and blinds paint a barred trapezoid over me. One bright strip falls across my left eye. It haloes, and I see the floaters inside my eye, little watery amoeba shapes drifting through the glare. When I blink, they swirl like patches of sea foam in a rocky inlet. I keep my eyes as still as I can and the floaters calm, pushed by the subtle throb of my heartbeat. Then, when this is the only movement, I blink again.

I take the smoke detector from the counter. Into the grille I say, "I want to try something with you guys."

"Oh, yeah? Audience participation?"

I lean over the recorder, there's a thin bar left in the battery. "You could call it that. But I want to see..." I sit on the couch. "...how long it takes... for this to become so incredibly annoying... annoying... annoying... annoying... annoying..." and I don't finish the sentence; I stick on the word, "...annoying... annoying... annoying..." Rhythmic. Three syllables and a pause, each the same length, said in 4/4 time, the most monotonous time signature there is. The word itself has a bend in the middle like whiplash on an old wooden roller coaster. *An*—then it levels and rounds a turn—*noy*—then dips back down and speeds up—*ying*.

I say it faster, and it morphs into "anoing anoing anoing anoing anoing..." When I have to inhale, I do so quickly to keep pace.

If I change the sound in any way, it'll become too interesting. They'll wonder how it will change next. For my idea to work, I have to make it clear they'll get nothing else from me. I'll line this word up like bricks in the mud as far as I can, then work my way back, stacking another layer, back and forth, until I've built a wall.

I want to cultivate an allergy or phobic response to my voice. I want to make their ears bleed with one word.

"...annoying, annoying..."

I lie on the couch with the smoke detector on my chest. I fold my hands behind my head and stare at the ceiling. I feel myself smile occasionally, and hear the smile creep into my voice—a change I consciously allow, a torturer's glee—while imagining the crystalline silence that will envelop me when this is over.

Teleportation would be a dream. I could disintegrate before their eyes, then materialize somewhere far away and go on living my life.

But the viewers of this "show," whether it's just the idiots next door or a vast audience, would be fascinated by the "teleporting guy."

It'd be an adventure for them—every episode they'd tune in to see me disappear, and then try to track me down. The observers might offer a reward for the person who finds me.

The winner would get to mess with me as punishment. The punishment would be shot on whatever camera, webcam, or phone the winner had at their disposal, and broadcast for the others to watch and froth at the mouth, eager for their turn.

The one rule would be that I'm kept alive and physically mobile, in the spirit of the hunt.

The only way I could rid myself of them would be to zap somewhere they'd never guess to look. Once there, I'd either have to dig a hole and stay put or continue moving from unthinkable place to unthinkable place for the rest of my life. My teleportation ability would have to be at the ready to get me out of split-second scrapes.

When powering up, it might sound like an old flashbulb charging in my head, that high-frequency rise. Maybe it'd be audible to others around me, so I'd have to be careful where I did it. It might sap my energy to reach that level of charge, so I couldn't maintain it all the time, and they'd catch on and coordinate to ambush me in moments of weakness. Maybe while I slept. I'd grow to distrust even those who seemed to want to help me. I'd only trust people who didn't look at me, who ignored my voice, and who seemed not to care. But I'd wonder about everyone.

Of course, as news broke about some guy zapping himself here and there all over the world, eventually everyone would care.

***

I should've looked at the clock when I started. I didn't think of it until now, long into saying the word. I say it once per second. That's 3,600 times per hour.

"...annoying, annoying, annoying, annoying, annoying..."

This is Chinese water torture—I have to hit the same spot on their forehead with the same size drop every single time.

I lift the smoke detector in front of my face to approximate where it was on my chest while I walk to the bedroom. The foil on the window makes the bedroom very dark, so I use the flashlight to find a pen and Post-It pad in the desk drawer.

"What's he doing?"

"I don't know, but if he doesn't stop fucking repeating over and over, I'm gonna flip out."

I return to the living room, put the detector on the coffee table, hunch to keep it the same distance from my mouth, and in the streetlight I write on the pad: *3,600 x 24*.

If I keep this up for a whole day, I'll have said the word 86,400 times.

If I say it for a year, it'll be... 31,536,000 times.

I'd have to sleep. Lack of sleep makes a person go crazy. But I imagine showering and saying it. Driving to and from work, muttering it under my breath. It'd be hard to keep it up while trying to listen and type at work. Part of my brain might partition off and become solely responsible for speaking the word from the moment I wake to the second I fall asleep. Maybe even while I sleep. It would become a thing about me that I'd have to explain to other people. How would I have conversations? I couldn't go to the movies—people in the theater would beat the shit out of me.

But none of this will happen. There's a magic number long before 31,536,000 that marks their breaking point, especially if one of them is already talking about "flipping out." I can't imagine them even making it to 86,400, but that's only because I can't imagine going that long myself.

Their part is easy. And because they're at least two people, they could crack at different times. Take turns. Or they could stop listening for a day and check back in later. If they ever noticed that I'd stopped, they'd be back, and probably eager for another "crackup" like that.

Why can't I just dunk the thing and short it out? There's no toxic gas waiting to burst in my face. Let's be honest, the mic is probably waterproof anyway. I can see myself finally dousing the thing and hearing the speaker laugh underwater, "What an idiot!"

Well, they aren't going to find my next move hilarious.

"...annoying, annoying, annoying, annoying, annoying..." I pick up my phone and turn it on.

"Hey, he's got his phone again."

"He does? But is he still saying that shit?"

"Yeah, but now his phone is starting up. Put your headphones back on."

"It's two in the morning, dude! Who are you gonna call?"

"Are you gonna tell 'em you've had a nervous breakdown?"

"Ha ha, yeah, he'll call his mom, and his mom's all waking up, like, 'Hello?' and he's all, 'Annoying, annoying—Hi, Mom—annoying, annoying, annoying...'"

"They'll put you away in a heartbeat, you crazy fuck."

"And we'll be rid of you."

Two missed calls. The phone doesn't remember who they're from, but I recognize the number as Dad's. They're right; it's too late to call him back now, and the phone battery is at 7%. It's probably draining faster than normal with their hacker bullshit running in the background.

"He's on Google."

"What's he looking for?"

I can't believe I didn't think of this earlier.

"Hello, yes, I'd like to report my neighbors for stalking."

"Do you feel you're in danger now?"

"To be honest, no. But this has gone on for a while already, and they know that I know."

"What is the nature of their stalking?"

"They hacked into my computer and phone, and—"

"The phone we're speaking on right now?"

"Yes. They're listening to this call, which could provoke a dangerous situation, but so far they haven't made good on any threats of violence. They did follow and harass me, though. And I believe they bugged my apartment."

"You located a bug in your apartment?"

"Yes."

"Okay. All of my units are busy at the moment, but I'm going to send a couple of officers over. Again, do you feel you are in immediate danger?"

"No, I don't for now. Door's locked."

"Okay, I'll put this request out, and the officers will be there when they can. I'd estimate sometime within the next two hours. Is that all right?"

"Sure, okay. Thank you."

She takes my name and address, and we hang up. Now my phone shows 5% battery. Fucking parasites. I turn it off.

"God fucking *dammit*! We're gonna *murder* you!"

"I'd like to see you try." I push the hammer headfirst into my back pocket and check the door locks. I lean my forehead on the door and let out a breath. It stinks against the glossy paint, the sour acid of a long-empty stomach.

Looking sideways at the window, I see a sliver of glass at the edge of the blinds. Just enough to shine a red dot onto my temple? Take the shot quick. Maybe lead on me a little, knowing I'll jerk back from the door, so I still get it behind the eyes.

I flatten and slide against the wall into the living room and close the blinds.

Perimeter secured, I put a pot of water on the stove and use my lighter to ignite the gas and light a cigarette.

Even without electricity, I'll have ramen noodles in no time.

And the hot water will serve in case they surprise me before then. In fact, I hope they arrive before the police so I can let them have it with the hammer—face and claw—and the pot of boiling water. I'll stub out my cigarettes in their nostrils.

I imagine the cops arriving at my dark apartment, and me showing them the two culprits, weapons in their limp hands, blood in their hair, ashy filters in their noses, bloated burnt faces obscured by soft stringy noodles.

Please do come. I'm waiting.

Salty broth vapor rises from the bowl as my fork squishes in the mush.

The sound is repulsive.

When I stayed at my grandma's as a kid, she always ate an English muffin for breakfast with the crossword puzzle. The only other sound was the ticking clock in the living room, so quiet that my brain amplified it, which amplified all other sounds—including the crackle and squish of grandma biting into her English muffin, the cavernous mush and churn of saliva. Muffled teeth clopping. Her tongue dislodging glop from her bridge. It sounded like hunks of raw meat in a hot water bottle. I could practically see the X-ray view of her oral cavity expanding and contracting, thick tongue writhing and contorting the pap until it was soft enough to swallow.

I had to actively remind myself that I loved my grandma, holding my cereal spoon tight enough to hurt my hand, struggling to eclipse her with the sound of my own chewing.

I tried excusing myself early, but I only made it a few steps before she asked why I didn't finish my cereal. Then she took another bite of English muffin and chewed while awaiting my response.

"I'm just not hungry, I guess."

She packed the lump into her cheek and pointed. "That's a whole bowl of cereal you're leaving there."

"I'll finish it later."

"It'll be mush later."

That was only true because she insisted on putting milk in it. She said it was for my bones. I preferred dry cereal because it crunched until it was ready to be swallowed. As far as I was concerned, the best thing "for my bones" was to send hard vibrations through them, not the spine-melting, fist-clenching sounds of milky salivary pulp.

"I just don't want it anymore."

She relented.

Later, when she'd finished her own breakfast and I jumped at the chance to eat mine, she trapped me in another conversation about how I'd wasted a perfectly good bowl of cereal just an hour before.

Then she poured another bowl for me—with milk—and sat at the table to watch me eat it. To pass the time, she took an overripe pear from the fruit bowl.

So I ate in a race, but she was always too fast with her knife, as if she *knew* what she was doing. My only recourse was to gulp the cereal whole, rough pieces grating all the way down, and I concentrated on the whoosh of my breath. I choked on the milk and coughed.

"Slow down!" she said.

I wasn't listening, I stared at the floor wishing I could burrow through the floral-pattern tile, the foundation, deep into the earth, and finish my bowl of cereal in peace.

I ate apples all the time as a kid but avoided most other fruits when I could. I ate peaches before they were ripe. Mom would say, "Who the heck likes a crunchy peach?"

"I do," I'd say.

They gave me stomachaches.

Eventually I did learn the pleasure of an appropriately ripe peach. With the right music at the right volume, it's a heavenly experience.

Now, leaning against the kitchen sink in the dark, I wince at the squish of ramen noodles in my skull. But that anger funnels into the hammer in my pocket. I hold my fork as tight as I'd hold the hammer.

When the ramen is gone I light a cigarette. "So? Where are you guys? Too scared to come over?"

"No, the cops came."

A breeze passes through me as if the walls disappeared. "When?"

"Just a few minutes ago. We said it was a false alarm."

"Yeah, he pretended to be you, and I said I was your roommate and you hadn't taken your pills."

"The cops think you're crazy now, Alex."

"They won't take you seriously anymore."

I consider that. "But if I talk to those same cops, they'll see that you and I are different people. And I have ID to prove who I am."

"Actually, funny story—when we put the bugs in your place, we found your expired driver's license. That's what I showed 'em. And are you ready for the best part? You and me kind of *look alike*, Alex!"

I wonder where that old driver's license was. In the desk drawer? And they took it?

"Yeah, Alex, he and you don't look exactly the same, but close enough. It's uncanny. I'll admit, sometimes I see him standing there, and I think he's you, Alex, coming to get us! Freaks me the fuck out!"

"Isn't that fucking crazy? What are the fucking chances?!"

THE SMOKE DETECTOR LAUGHS at me from the living room while I empty my desk drawers onto the bed with the flashlight in my mouth.

"You're not gonna find it, Alex, we took it!"

There's a knock at the door.

I enter the living room. "Hello?"

A voice comes through the door. "LAPD." It doesn't sound like the neighbor, but it's not clear enough to compare. "You called about an issue in your apartment?"

Ah, he's carefully stepped around any mention of "stalking." The true stalkers might've come out and said it, believing specificity would earn my trust. But this person—whoever he is—understands the risk of blabbing such things out loud.

I pull the hammer from my pocket and open the door to two silhouettes. Crisp-shaped uniforms, the bumps of radio handsets on their shoulders, arms bent with hands at their hips, weapons ranging from pepper spray to pistol within easy reach. In the light slipping around their faces I can see they're both white men in their mid-twenties.

The one on the left isn't fat, but his cheeks round out so his face looks like a cherub mask. In other contexts he's probably the easier of the two to make laugh.

The one on the right has cheeks that come straight down to a pointed jaw. He looks like a strategist of some kind for sports or the military. On the plane of his cheek is a patch of dark stubble he missed shaving, like a smear of sand.

Neither resembles the guy I saw next door, but they could be participants. If that's the case, I'm about to allow the enemy into my apartment. Two of them. With handcuffs and guns.

But I also consider how I look to them if they're real cops. I've opened the door at 3:30 a.m. in a dark apartment, holding a hammer.

I say, "Sorry, I hadn't mentioned this to the dispatcher, but I blew a fuse. I was prepared to defend myself, since the stalkers heard me make the call. That's why the hammer. It's not for you. I'll put it down, okay?"

The Cherub guy nods.

The Strategist's eyes remain on the hammer. He says, "You're safe."

It's strange to hear those words from someone who's about my age. It occurs to me that as you get older, those who respond to your calls for help are by comparison younger and younger. Children come to save a full-grown adult. A peer saying I'm "safe" feels like lip service from a student put in charge while the teacher takes a bathroom break.

"Go ahead," he says. "We'll follow you."

I go to the living room and drop the hammer on the couch.

The Cherub looks into the kitchen as he enters the living room. The Strategist follows. They leave the door open, and the shimmer of a moth enters and disappears.

The Cherub says, "Pretty dark in here. Could you open those blinds?" pulling his flashlight from his belt.

The Strategist does the same.

I partially rotate the blinds. "I'd prefer not to open them all the way. It's actually *those* neighbors who are the problem, and I'd rather they not see us."

They look at the books and cans of food stacked around the bookshelf and TV, the glinting pile of silverware on the counter, the clipped-off smoke detector on the coffee table, the hole in the ceiling... The air is smoky, and their flashlight beams on the spilled rice and sugar make the apartment feel like a sunken ship.

"So," says the Strategist, hand on hip, "what's the problem?"

"Well, about a week ago I was walking by the river, as I often do, and I heard a couple of guys say that they were gonna 'get me.' And they followed me all through the neighborhood, threatening and insulting me."

"Those neighbors," he nods to the window without moving his eyes from mine.

"I believe so, yes. I actually never saw them because it was night and they stayed well-hidden. But I heard them."

He slowly nods.

"They never 'got me,' clearly, or I wouldn't be here now." I chuckle.

They don't chuckle. Not even the Cherub, who might be more inclined to.

"After that happened, I heard them—from over there—commenting on stuff I was doing in here."

"What'd they see you do?" the Cherub asks.

"Everything. They claim they've got a livestream going, with people betting on what I'll do next. I don't believe that, of course. They're just trying to push my buttons."

The Cherub says, "Sure," like he gets it.

"The other day I got out of the shower and had to poop." I feel strange saying "poop" in the presence of their uniforms. "And they were like, 'Oh, my god, who takes a shit *after* they take a shower?' It was the highlight of their day." I hope the observers are embarrassed to hear me say this.

"That is a little weird..." The Strategist tilts his head and raises an eyebrow. "Normally you try to do it the other way around."

"Yeah," I shrug, "but sometimes it just happens that way."

"Uh-huh," he says. "Huh."

I don't like his attitude, but at least all of this seems like new information to them.

The Cherub points. "That's the bathroom?"

"Yes." I look at the light spilling through the open front door. Someone could be hidden there; a sudden shot could blast apart the Strategist's head.

"It doesn't face their window. How'd they see you... do your business?"

If the attack came fast enough, when the Cherub turned to look they might get him in profile, through his cheeks, scattering syrupy shards of teeth on the floor.

I say, "Could you guys move into the kitchen? Or could we shut the front door? I'm concerned something... will happen."

The Cherub's hands rise to his belt.

The Strategist shares a look with him. "What do you think is gonna happen?"

"I don't know, but they threatened to come here before you guys arrived. Just to scare me, of course." I watch for changes in their expressions. "You know, they also claimed they already spoke with a couple of officers, and pretended to be me and my roommate. As you can see, I don't have a roommate. They said they showed my old driver's license to prove they were me, which they'd stolen when they broke in here to install the bugs."

"There was a break-in?"

"Not that I knew about. I think they might have a key."

"Have you given your key to anyone?"

"No. But I was looking for that old license before you got here, and I can't find it. I know it was in my desk drawer."

Both frown. The Cherub's is a rumpling of his forehead, the Strategist's is downward and sharp.

"If they showed your ID," the Strategist says, "wouldn't the officers see that it wasn't them in the photo?"

"Like I said, I haven't seen them, but they claim we look alike. Actually, that's not true, I've met one of them. I confronted him about watching me and the comments they made. He was standoffish and denied everything."

"But he wasn't the one who supposedly looks like you."

"No."

The Strategist works his jaw sideways. "You said they bugged the place. You found something?"

"Yes, that's why it's dark in here. I blew the fuse when I pulled out the smoke detector." I point at the hole in the ceiling.

"That's pretty dangerous," the Cherub says. "I got zapped doing something like that once."

"Yeah, I got lucky."

"That's the smoke detector?" The Strategist points.

"Yes."

"May I see it?"

"Absolutely."

He shines his flashlight through the grille, rotating it like a piece of alien technology. "Where's the bug?"

"Inside. I tried opening it, but they probably glued it shut."

He guides his light along the seam. "I think they make these so you can't open 'em. For safety."

"Yeah, I wondered about that."

The Cherub eyes the wires hanging from the hole in the ceiling. "How long have you been living in this apartment?"

"About a year."

"Have you had this problem anywhere else you've lived?"

"No."

He nods and frowns. "Any history of mental illness in your family?"

"I know how this looks. I appreciate you guys humoring me."

He raises a hand. "Oh, it's not like that. We're obligated to ask, no matter the call."

"Look, I've been having conversations with them through that thing. I've recorded the conversations on there." I point to the recorder.

The Strategist holds up the smoke detector. "You've picked *them* up on it too?"

"I haven't listened to the recent stuff, but it's possible." I turn on the recorder and play the last file from the beginning.

"—*ying, annoying, annoying, annoy—*"

I stop it and scroll through the files. "I was trying to frustrate them so they'd shout at me. The mic in the smoke detector is so small they're impossible to pick up otherwise." I select another, advance to several minutes in and press play.

"—*sabugwersabugwersabugwersabugwersabugwe*—" Under my voice are clattering pots and pans, spilling fistfuls of silverware.

"That was the same thing, to annoy them. But before I cut the smoke detector from the— Look, I won't waste more of your time. I've heard them. I know that's not enough proof, so I've got to listen to these recordings, possibly make more, and if I pick them up on here I'll let you know."

The Cherub's eyes search the air. "Could you... get them to say something now?"

"No, they won't say anything now. They know you're here." I tug at my hair. "It's like that frog in the cartoons. He sings and dances, but only when nobody else is around, so everyone thinks the guy's crazy. You know what I'm talking about?"

"I can't say I've seen that one," the Strategist says. He puts the smoke detector on a stack of books.

I mutter a bit of the frog's song, "'Hello, my baby. Hello, my honey. Hello, my ragtime gal...' And he kicks his legs. Know it?"

The Cherub smiles the way one smiles at a stranger monologuing under their breath when they pause to ask for change. The difference is, the monologuer in the street is strapped into a personal rollercoaster.

Can't they see I'm being proactive about this? My rollercoaster ride is long over. Now I'm clinging to beams somewhere inside the mountainous framework of the thing, navigating its skeleton while the car continues its eternal circuit, dipping and looping, empty.

It's just a matter of climbing down, but I can't see the next hand- or foothold. So I called these two for help, and there they stand safely on the ground, suggesting I climb back up and get back into the goddamn coaster car!

Sometimes people have to shit after they've taken a shower. And sometimes people's apartments are bugged without them being crazy. I don't know the reason. Whatever it is, it's bigger than me.

At least it's clear the cops are too dumb to be in on it. There's no way a secret government program would collaborate with these meatheads; it actually works in the observers' favor to keep LAPD stooges in the dark. Their captain might know something about it, but he'd never tell.

Get a load of the mugs on these two. The Cherub's rumpled brow, not understanding and unable to extend himself enough to understand. I'm not surprised he got burned while doing electrical work. I'm operating under duress and self-preservation. What's his excuse?

And the Strategist—clearly not much of a strategist. He held the key to the puzzle in his fucking *hand*. He shined his flashlight through it. The appropriate response to being presented with that kind of evidence is: *Let's crack this motherfucker open and take a look together*. But he's not looking at it anymore, now he's just looking at me.

They'll probably lock me up somewhere for "treatment" and unwittingly employ my voyeurs as janitors or orderlies. Then I'd see them every day, peering in through my tiny window.

The Strategist puts his hands on his hips. "So, how long ago did you blow your fuse?"

Fuck you, I want to say. *I don't need your "help." Go filch a jelly doughnut, rookie pigs. We don't need shit heels like you or my neighbors twisting the mind of a good person into believing he's the monster. Yet here you are, two chimps in hand-me-down uniforms, come to tell me I'm crazy.*

Cherub, go store some more nuts in your goddamn cheeks. And you, "Strategist," should stretch yourself beyond your sudoku puzzles on speed trap duty. A little more attention to detail would do you some good. Oh, and when you see a mirror, check your cheek. You missed a spot.

But instead I say, "It was earlier this evening. When I isolated the sound of their voices to the smoke detector. I'm positive the answer is in there."

"Well, so," says Mr. Strategy, smiling, "with the power cut, the bug's not getting any juice, so they can't hear us now anyway. Problem solved."

"You could be right." *Sure, I'll just climb back into the coaster car. Lulled by the ratchet-ratchet-ratchet of my ascent into the clouds, I won't even notice when they pull the blade across my throat. But you'll have to clean up the mess. I hope I shit myself when it happens. When you come to collect your evidence, I hope you don't have a clean spot to stand.* I smile. "Well, I'm sorry I don't have more to show you in the way of proof. I know this isn't much." *It's everything.*

"Hey, no, we're sorry we can't be of more help," Cherub says. "Fact is, this is a fairly new type of crime, so we're still figuring out how to deal with it. But here's my card." He pulls a card from his shirt pocket.

I tilt it in the light through the blinds and read out loud, "Officer Brian McCormick."

"That's me." He smiles.

So you're telling me you haven't seen the old cartoon with the singing frog, but when you picked an alias for your cop disguise you went fucking Irish? *Go buy a box of doughnut holes and string 'em up your thin blue line, you cliché piece of shit.* "Thanks."

"Give us a call if anything else comes up, okay?"

"I will. Thank you."

They move toward the door.

"Now, try to get some sleep," Cherub says. "Maybe wait to clean this stuff up tomorrow, when it's light."

Good advice, numbnuts. "Sure, I'll do that. Thanks for coming out so late."

"Hey, we prefer this kind of call to the others."

Bravo. That's exactly what a real cop would say. What helpful, brave fucking gentlemen you've been. I wave as they start down the stairs. "Fu— uh, thanks to you."

Cherub waves back, smiling. But ah, god dammit, he heard that slip-up. I'd done so well, and that last bit lost me all credibility. Now I'm just some wack job spinning his wheels and breathing rubber fumes in the dark. If those cops are for real, I just joined their clueless caller hall of fame alongside parents who call 911 to get their kids to do their homework and old people who report stolen TV remotes.

A sad smile, a pat on the head, and those dutiful sentries of the city are gone.

It's 4:00 on Wednesday morning—nineteen hours until my next shift at work—and I'm still my only hope.

WHAT SHITTY SPIES, THOSE cops! True spies would pretend to take my claims very seriously; they'd nod empathetically and placate me with phrases like, "yessir, it's a big crazy world we live in," while feeling along every surface in the place, dabbing more sticky eyes and ears into corners, under ledges.

No, those were true-blue LAPD officers, fresh from the Elysian Park Academy, thumbs still wet from sucking.

Get some rest. What did they think I was gonna do next? I'm fucking exhausted.

I need to change the locks, because they clearly have copies of my keys.

The couch slides snugly into the entryway, so even if someone can get through the locks, the door will only open a couple of inches.

From the street comes a clipped honk. The same as when I lock my minivan with the key fob. But my van isn't visible from the window. I make a mental note—when possible, park within view. I don't see a police car, either. They might not have come in a car. Maybe they walked, or materialized from a sulfurous mist.

Was it them locking my van with their own copy of the remote?

The window is dark next door. Are the "officers" over there now, slipping out of their uniforms, hanging them in a closet or folding them into duffel bags? High-fiving their buddies?

I'll search the van in the morning.

For all I know, the honk is an attempt to lure me into the street where—enough is enough—I'd finally go missing. They want me to go check now, at 4:00 in the morning when no one will see.

With the couch blocking the door, window locked, blinds drawn, foil taped, and most importantly the power cut, my bubble of security has re-expanded to the size of my apartment. I breathe deep and feel a surge of fresh energy.

The question of help from an outside party was a weak point. But I know now that things are far too weird to explain to anyone else. It's only from my position that the stars align to reveal Orion's arrow pointing at me. Seen from any other angle, there is no Orion.

I brush my teeth in the dark. No light at all, save for the dark purple rectangle of safety glass above the shower, too dim to illuminate anything beyond itself. I turn away from the window and brush my teeth while staring into the black void. The wall is somewhere in front of me, I don't know how close. I reach, touch it and jump—only inches away.

It feels good to lie down. I'm naked, how I usually sleep. Behind the foil the window is still open just a slit to let air into my protective bubble, and to stoke the soothing crackle of the foil's quiet metal fire. It makes me sleepy. My eyes burn. My feet are still cold under the sheets. I brushed them off but can feel some grit followed me into bed. I run my hands up and down my torso, my arms, my legs, push my blood around. These are things over which I still have complete control.

My hand rests on my penis, and I feel it come to life a beat at a time. All that blood pumping logic in my head for so long, other parts of me have shriveled with neglect. But now I'm confident I've solved enough of the puzzle that there's blood to spare, to wake those parts from hibernation.

I wish Lili were here with me. We could fuck and both scream loud. Pour white wine on each other and drink it off. I'd probably be free of my toxic thoughts. We'd just be two people using each other's bodies.

My mind flashes with imagery of past crushes like a zoetrope—I watch a head move up and down on my cock, but each time it rises it's a different girl, and they go around and around, changing every second. All of them suck me in unison—in celebration. I'm so hard I can feel an aching line through its core from the base to the head. I wish they were all here. What a party we could have here in the dark. We could eat and drink the contents of my fridge and each other. One of them could put a big scoop of ice cream between her legs, then sit on my face and put me out of my fucking misery.

A sound catches my attention. Small and far away. Like howling.

I stop.

I get up, still hearing the sound, intermittent now, and I walk into the living room feeling my newly-sprouted limb bounce and swing with my steps. The sound gets louder, as I suspected it would, and is loudest when I reach the smoke detector. Oh, if only those cops could hear this now. That's what it took to wheedle them out of silence—a feeling of joy in me, and the fuckers piped right back up.

They say, "Alex, what the fuck? God dammit! Are you thinking about those cops or what, you faggot?"

I pick up the smoke detector, feeling myself at half-mast still heartbeat-bobbing against the pull of gravity.

"You can see me?" I ask.

"We can see everything, you sick fuck!" The voice is tinny and desperate in my hands. This would be the moment to dunk the thing in the sink.

But now I have new information. Probably infrared. I don't know if omnidirectional thermal cameras exist, or if they have multiple eyes planted in places where I somehow missed them. Placing cameras is a different art than placing microphones, since mics don't need line of sight.

The cameras roll wherever I am. They probably watched me brush my teeth facing the wall minutes ago. Maybe my behavior is starting to frighten them—I feel my erection returning at the thought. They might watch a bit longer out of morbid curiosity, knowing it's only a matter of time before I knock on their door again, hammer in hand.

They want a monster? Well...

I put the smoke detector next to the bed and lie on top of the sheets. "You see that?" I ask. "Get a good fuckin' look." My erection has fully returned and aches. I stroke it hard, slow, feeling like the skin could split and peel down to reveal a standing iron beam. My other hand cups and pulls on my balls. "Keep watching."

I see the girls again, and the zoetrope spins slower. I pause on some of my favorites.

A girl from high school lifts her head to curl her hair behind an ear and says, "I always wanted to do this to you, Alex."

Then she puts her mouth deep on me again and changes into the girl from the tobacco shop by work. "I think about this every time I see you." She smiles and licks along me.

You're beautiful. Let me see your chipped tooth.

She pulls me into her smile.

"You have desires too," she says. "Everyone does."

We're only human.

The smoke detector screams, "Fucking gross!"

A girl I saw once in traffic says, "Be gross with me, Alex. Let's be animals together."

Disgusting. I want to be disgusting with you.

She grips me tight, out of breath, her eyes stare into mine. "We're all disgusting, Alex! Be disgusting!"

Then I see Vanessa from the ill-fated webcam session. I force her head down. *Choke on it. Put that on Facebook.*

"God, what the fuck?!"

The smoke detector's disgust mounts with my pleasure. Eventually all my muscles tighten, the ache reaches an excruciating pinnacle, and a thick blast explodes through me. I feel it land up to my neck, and I keep working until it's over.

"Jesus fucking Christ! You sick fuck!"

I tremble, and the dark room sparkles like faint TV fuzz. My toes curl and uncurl. A warm hum sweeps slowly back and forth through my brain.

When the buzz calms, I take my T-shirt from the floor and wipe off, then slip under the sheets.

The smoke detector continues chattering to itself as my eyes close, and the warmth radiating through my body pulses me into a deep sleep.

"Maybe he's dead."

"He's not dead."

"The pleasure was too much for him, and his brain exploded."

"That was fucking disgusting, I can't believe we had to watch that. But he's not dead."

"Alex, are you dead?"

Seconds pass.

"See? Heart attack or something. Stroke, maybe."

"His heart's still beating."

"Ah, good. Then I guess we keep going."

"Sure, I'm in for the long haul. Hear that, Alex? We're here to stay."

Initially I think I'm dreaming. Hearing my name tugs at my attention.

"Come on, Alex, we're bored. Do something."

"He is doing something. Look. The beats are closer together. He's awake."

"Alex, we know you're alive. Yawn to confirm you can hear us."

My throat shifts in the back, pulls cool air through my teeth, expands, and exhales.

"Oh, my god, he did it!"

Laughter. "God dammit, I can't believe that worked!"

"Look, his heart's going faster."

"Are you scared, Alex?"

My heartbeat thumps in my ear against the pillow. I slow my breath to try to slow my heart.

"Yes, breathe. Is that working? Are you less afraid?"

"Holy shit, calm down, Alex, your heart is going crazy."

Breathing isn't working.

"Man, I thought this was gonna be boring, but this is already pretty fucking fascinating. Alex, now stretch your legs."

My legs do feel tight. I was too distracted to notice when I awoke. I still haven't even opened my eyes. Now I feel an overwhelming urge to roll on my back and extend my legs.

But I don't. They can't be right. Don't make them right. I don't have to do anything but breathe, just keep breathing, and listen to my heart. Gain control of that first, and the rest will come easier.

So I lie still, feel my dewy legs stuck together, hairs pressed itchy between them, and the longer I stay like that, the more I prove that their suggestions don't mean control.

How long must I wait to ensure that stretching my legs is *my* idea and not *theirs*? I don't have a way to time anything. I can count seconds—what number is high enough? Several minutes, I suppose.

How many heartbeats go into five minutes?

My heart is fast again, so a lot in five minutes.

"He wants to. You can tell he wants to."

"Alex, are your legs cramping up yet?"

"Just stretch 'em. You'll feel so much better."

"Oh, man, wouldn't it feel good to stretch your legs? Maybe roll over? You've been in that position for hours, Alex. Doesn't your body ache on that side? Roll over and get the blood moving."

"Come on, up and at 'em, tiger!" Laughter.

I am the plastic bunny in its sugar egg. My joints will fuse in this position like petrifying wood.

My grandparents had a *Ripley's Believe it or Not* book from the 1950s. It was full of amazing people—a guy with a hole in his skull that he used as a candleholder; a guy with two pupils in each eye; a boy born with his heart on the outside of his ribcage, pumping like an alien blister on his chest.

But the one I remember best was an Indian fakir who held his arm straight up in the air, wrist bent and hand cupped, and he held it there so long that his whole arm fused in that position. Supposedly a bird built a nest in his hand.

The book had a pen-and-ink drawing of this man, his nether regions wrapped like a diaper and his head wrapped in something like a turban. His arm was a thin vertical beam, the muscles atrophied, knobby balls of bone at the elbow and shoulder. The nest was held aloft in his hand. It even had a couple of eggs peeking over the edge. One egg was open, and a tiny beak strained skyward. The parent bird swooped toward it with a worm in its mouth.

I will be like the fakir.

My side aches where it presses into the mattress. I can only imagine the pain the fakir experienced in the weeks it took for his muscles to turn to jerky. But if I keep it up long enough, mine will give up too. My heart rate will find an equilibrium, there will be peaks and valleys, moments of pain and panic, but the observers will lose interest in watching those. I will be a still life.

"Well, he's gotta take a piss or eat sometime."

I do have to pee. I was so focused on my legs and heart that the ache in my bladder felt like just another pain. But if I don't move soon, I'll pee in the bed.

"Is that it? Did we nail it? That series of blips there means we're right? He's gotta pee."

"By all means, Alex, when nature calls. But you should stretch your legs first."

I toss the sheet and slide off the edge of the bed, staying curled. The side of my body beats and aches. The room is dark except subtle leaks of sunlight at the foil's edges. I walk to the bathroom, still hunched from the pain in my bladder. My legs zing like static and steel wool.

The wall clock says 7:00.

I slept for two and a half hours.

The bathroom window holds blue sky and creamy light in its net of chicken wire safety glass. I sit on the toilet and pee. I flex my legs and feet and shoulders. I've failed to resist. It's the beginning of another day and possibly the rest of my life with them.

The wall clock ticks.

From the toilet I see the dim mess in the living room, the place where the couch should be, grains of rice scattered like insect eggs. I'm disappointed things aren't somehow back to normal.

"Is he taking a shit, or is he *sitting down* to pee? Alex, we know you're our bitch, but we didn't expect you to become an actual bitch!"

I press my face in my hands, massage my temples, feel my feet turn the cool tile warm.

There's the ceiling hole with the wires hanging out, and I remember I have no power. As further proof, I notice a moth faintly outlined against the bathroom wall. Probably the one I saw fly in last night.

If I had resisted and stayed in bed, the moth might've come to rest on my shoulder or my face, nibbled at my hair, eaten away the sheet draped over me.

***

Rinsing the shampoo from my hair, I stare at the yellow calcium haze at the bottom of the cheap plastic shower curtain, and looking down at my fleshy, hairy body I *know* that I'm a mass of meat washing off its bodily excretions. I get the feeling I'm a pig at a slaughterhouse. I watch the water fall around my face, stare at the bumps and ridges of my feet, my fleshy pads pressed against the basin of the tub. And beyond the shower curtain, someone is waiting.

I stand there a long time, and nothing happens. I wonder if they'll turn the water off and call through the curtain. "Come on." A close and empty voice. I'll pull the curtain aside to see not what I long imagined was my bathroom, but a giant concrete building with conveyor belts and hooks on chains, swarming with flatbed electric carts driven by men in bloody overalls. One such man will be standing next to my shower stall. He'll have a hairnet on his head, another over his beard, and I'll see only his eyes looking through me. He'll lead me out of the shower basin, one in a row of identical basins. "C'mon, let's go," he'll say. And I'll go wherever he tells me to go. Because somehow everything will make sense.

I'm having a drawn-out dream of life as a human, but the illusion only lasted so long, is now breaking down, and the world of the dream and that of my reality are now superimposed in harsh clarity.

How else could they monitor things like my heart rate and breathing? I search my body. An internal chip. When was it put in? Did I eat it? Did they drug me and install it? Somewhere in my gut or far up my nose? In my ear? Ever-present and so close, just millimeters from my fingertips yet completely inaccessible unless I damage myself to reach it.

When I turn the shower off, it's quiet. I pull back the curtain and feel overwhelming relief and disappointment to see my bathroom. No answers. There's no one here to lead me to the next phase. It's not over, keep going. My legs weaken, and I crouch in the tub and stare at the mess in the next room. Everything is still here.

The observers stay quiet while I brush my teeth and get dressed. Return things to the cupboards and drawers. Sweep the floor.

I even open the blinds—just a bit—to let in some light.

Energy expended the day before hangs in the air, almost literally rings in my ears. I think of the words and phrases I repeated. I had filled the air with them, enough to warm the walls with sound. The recordings prove my stamina. I know it's impressive how long I went. It wasn't a day or a year, but impressive.

I keep the couch in the slot of the entryway and lie down on it, stare up at the walls boxed around me and the narrow strip of ceiling, and I think about how snugly I fit here.

"He's relaxed now."

"First time in a while, I think."

They speak softly, like young parents over a crib.

"Alex, the experiment is over."

"We can't share the results with you, because they still require quite a bit of analysis. But let's just say things got very interesting."

"Yes. A lot of things we didn't expect to happen."

"We're also very pleased to see how you maintained through it all. We haven't had many subjects, but you're the strongest we've seen so far."

I chuckle to myself, remembering how frightened I was in bed earlier. If only I'd known it was so close to being over. A couple hours more would've seemed like nothing, but I didn't know, so I prepared for forever.

Light comes golden through the blinds and stains the wall yellow. Slits of bright blue in the window. I might go for a walk later, if this all wraps up in time.

I chuckle and say, "You guys are fucking assholes, you know that?"

"Yes, and we're sorry."

"So, what finally did it? Why now? Was it me figuring out about the chip? Or having the will to clean this place up? Keeping my cool? Or was it actually when I found the smoke detector, but you decided to keep stringing me along?"

"We'll explain everything very soon."

"Are you coming now?" I ask.

"Yes, just let us get some things together here and then we'll head over to you. Thank you for your patience."

"No problem. I'll be here. Just knock or say something so I know when to move the couch."

"Yes, don't worry, we'll stay connected on the microphone so we can speak, if necessary. You don't mind that we leave it on for now?"

"Hey, you've already seen way more of me than most people ever have, or would ever want to see."

A chuckle. "You've got that right. You really put us through the wringer. But I think if I were in your position, I would have done the same."

I CLOSE MY EYES, feel the couch cradle my body, wonder where they'll pull the chip from and what the tool will look like. Will it be as simple as tweezers in my ear or nose, or will I have to be sedated? Will I need stitches to close the removal site? Will it hurt?

"Guys, I don't know what this was all about," I say, "but what you've done seems wildly unethical. I'll warn you, I only sound calm because I'm relieved it's over. And exhausted. But I'm actually furious with you."

"We understand. There is an explanation for everything. Sometimes research takes us places where, at first glance, it seems ill-advised to venture."

I say, "Like *The Three Christs of Ypsilanti*."

"I know I've heard of that. Remind me what it is?"

"Book, nonfiction. Three paranoid schizophrenic men each think they're Jesus Christ. And they're brought together to see what happens when their delusions are forced to confront each other."

"Ah, yes, I'm embarrassed to say I haven't read that one yet."

I smile. "It's fascinating. But spoiler alert: it doesn't go well."

"You've certainly done your research, Alex. That might explain how you fared in this particular study. I look forward to sitting down with you to record your side of all of this."

"Well, come and get it while it's fresh. And before I decide I want revenge."

A chuckle. "Yes, well, as I said, we need some time to get our things together. We'll be over to see you shortly."

"I'll be here." Such a big smile. Such a sunny day. If it wouldn't bother the other tenants, I'd move my couch out onto the terrace and drink a beer or two, smoke, while waiting at the top of the stairs. I'd eventually see them round the corner in their suits or lab coats, carrying their bags of equipment and notebooks. *Ah, you've come out to greet us, Alex. Let's hold our interview session out here. It is a beautiful day. We do apologize for everything, we really meant you no harm.* He'd point to a man with a tool belt. *Our technician here will enter your apartment—with your permission, of course—to remove our devices from your home. He can do this while I fill you in on what this was about. You may find it hard to believe at first, but by the time we're through you will see that all of this has served a great purpose.*

I get up and fry some eggs. I picture myself giving speeches to publicize the injustice and prevent it from happening to others. TV appearances. I'll look back on this and laugh. Despite their apparent change of heart, my observers might be imprisoned. I'll testify against them. I'll sit on the stand and stare at their faces, which they'd kept hidden for so long. They'll look like complete strangers.

Start small, Alex, don't get ahead of yourself. First, eat your eggs. From now on you will take better care of yourself. You will get more sleep at the appropriate hours. Eat better. You'll only keep smoking as long as it takes for the residual waves of this experience to wear off. Like a shellshocked veteran, you'll probably have moments among friends when you'll stop to stare through the smoke, remembering the night you were followed, or the night you tore your apartment to pieces looking for hidden microphones. You'll remember the blend of terror and relief you felt when they removed the chip that allowed them to read your heart rate and your thoughts.

I imagine recounting all of this to Lili over a glass of wine.

Unless they decide to wipe the experience from my memory. Would this be like cleaning a petri dish when the experiment is over? I am a container. They'll scrape me out and put me back on the shelf, crystalline and clueless.

Maybe they'll just make me sign a nondisclosure agreement, and I'll have to keep it a secret for the rest of my life. But if this is truly the end, I'll sign anything to make them go away.

Sure, vengeance and justice are preferable, but at the very least I've proven my strength. Despite their influence, I didn't emerge as a pedophile or a racist or one prone to violence. I didn't buckle.

That might have to be enough.

What a relief when they remove all the bugs, pluck all the blisters from my walls, and take the smoke detector away, take my computer and phone for a government-caliber spyware wipe, or simply replace them with brand-new, bug-free exemplars... I'll open the blinds and tear the foil from the bedroom window. I'll buy more ice cream just for the occasion. I'll go on long walks every day through busy parts of town and smile into the eyes of each stranger I pass, because I'll have emerged from this gauntlet with scientific proof that I am a good person.

PINS AND NEEDLES EXPAND through my mind. Crevices parched from disuse are flooded with fresh blood. The tight rumble of anxiety is gone. I feel an openness, an all-encompassing awareness. I have a band of eyes all around my head, and I can see there's nothing behind me, nothing hidden anywhere. I'm the only one, motionless. Everything moves around me. I am the center.

Because I'm still on the couch and my head is next to the door, the knock is loud.

The pins and needles descend into my chest. I want to skip the next few minutes. There are obligatory introductions to be made, because these people are strangers. But that unfamiliarity is only one-way—they know *me* intimately.

Though I'd argue they don't know me personally.

I'm relieved to have cleaned up and showered, so we can meet each other as close to equals as I can manage.

They've seen me at my worst, watched it all happen through their omnipresent eyes. The whole big mess. They understand that everything was their fault.

I drag the couch from the entryway into its normal position. Then I stand at the door.

What's the point of my hesitation? If they haven't turned off the cameras, they can see me waiting. But I have to savor opening the door to the beginning of my post-observation life, whatever that means. Will I need therapy? I don't feel like it, but maybe just because I'm buzzing with adrenaline. Mentally, I'm on top of my game. I had to be to keep in stride with their shenanigans. They pushed my logic to limits I didn't think possible. They said they were surprised by my resilience. How many other people have they put through this? Apparently those other poor souls broke. I didn't.

Another knock, harder. Afraid of blowing their cover? Maybe all their time spent hunched over a computer in a dark room engendered some agoraphobia in them, too.

Give me a second, god dammit. I need a moment. I don't say this out loud because I'm not ready to hear their voices yet, unadulterated by tinny microphones.

When the other subjects opened the door, were they just a blubbering mess? Did this sort of meeting even occur, or did the observers have to rush in for damage control? The others might've been permanently changed, involuntary patients, rendered forever incapable of coping with normal life.

But what's so special about me? Maybe that's something we'll talk about. I wonder what the first question will be. Something like, *How do you feel?*

I'd laugh. *Well, I feel like dancing and scooping your eyes out with a spoon.*

How could I ever answer that? How do you feel. I'd probably ask, *How am I supposed to feel?* And what would they say to that?

Another more urgent knock.

I wipe my hands on my shirt and unlock the door. But when I open it there's only one person, and his first question is: "Dude. Can I use your bathroom?" It's Gavin. He's in his running clothes, sweaty and out of breath. "I'm sorry, it's an emergency."

No one else is with him. Or behind him. Or anywhere; it's just the two of us. The look in his eyes pushes me back, and I step behind the door. He moves past me, around the corner, and into the bathroom.

A breeze enters after him.

"Can you still hear me?" I ask quietly.

"Yes, we're listening."

I close the door. "Did you see what just happened?"

"Yes."

"What do I do?"

"We wait for him to leave. Only a slight hiccup."

"He might notice the hole in the ceiling. I assume I shouldn't say anything."

"You assume correctly. This is to remain between us."

"Even though I told the police?"

No response.

"What, you're gonna tell me those weren't real cops? They were agents of yours?"

"We won't confirm anything until we can speak in person. We must be very careful, you understand."

"I didn't tell him anything, but he knows something's up."

"We know."

"And you know I told Matt."

"Yes."

I lock the front door. I want to close the blinds again. "He might notice the power's off."

"You mustn't tell him anything."

"What does that mean? If I say something, you'll have to kill him?"

"Don't try our patience."

The toilet flushes.

"You said this was over." I take the smoke detector from the coffee table and put it in a cupboard.

"This unforeseen interference arrived before we could end things to our satisfaction. Now we must wait, and you must avoid complicating things for yourself and your friend."

The sink gurgles and splashes.

"Your accelerated heart rate shows that you understand the gravity of the situation."

I sit on the couch and light a cigarette.

Gavin comes out of the bathroom. "I'm really sorry, man. Were you jerkin' it or something?"

I try to smile. "Funny. No."

He points at the hammer on the coffee table. "Doing some handiwork here in the dark?"

"No, that's from—I was gonna take a nap. The hammer's from another thing."

The splash pattern on his shirt shows that he rinsed his face. "Ah, sorry, I should let you sleep." He takes a step. "Oh, how'd the recorder work for you?"

"Good, yeah. It's cool."

He waits.

"What?"

"You can't tell me what it's for yet?"

A large hand grips the back of my brain. Between my blinds I see enough of their window to know it's open, just a crack. Their screen blocks any visibility beyond it, but they have a clean line of sight to Gavin.

"Not yet," I say. "But soon. And thank you, it was a big help."

"Sure." He waits.

He probably sees the way I'm sitting, unwilling to move at all, breathing slow but shallow breaths. I keep my eyes on his face, because as soon as I look away their red dot will appear on his temple.

We're in another triangle constellation, like when he showed me the map. But now the third point is an unseen intruder. My point is fear. Gavin's point is care, confusion, and fragile human meat that could spray across my kitchen at any second.

"Do you have to go?" I ask.

"Sure. I can. If you're good."

After this cagey performance of mine they might decide Gavin is too suspicious. I can't send him back out there.

"No, that's cool. Stick around." I stand. "Want a glass of water?"

"Oh, that'd actually be amazing." He sits on the couch.

I go to the window and give a serious glare in their direction as I pull the plastic chain, rotating the blades to block their view of Gavin on the couch.

"Dark in here."

"Yeah, I'll try to sleep in a bit."

"I can go, I don't wanna keep you up."

"No, I'm up now anyway. Stay." In the few steps to the kitchen, I realize that if they're using infrared, they could line up a clean shot through the blinds. At least putting the smoke detector in the cupboard might keep them from triggering its self-destruct or gassing mechanism.

"Smoke a bowl?" he asks.

"Nah, thanks." I need to stay clear-headed for my interview. "But you can." I hand him the water. "So, there's a story? You were running and suddenly had to pee?"

"No, man, I had to take a *shit*." He drinks and gives a sheepish smile. "Sorry."

I laugh. "No worries." I get my pipe and weed from the desk drawer and blow out the ash.

"So, okay, you remember that girl Tiff from the dorm? Remember when she was talking about running marathons and how she said sometimes she'd 'poop a little bit'?"

"Oh, no."

He laughs, and slips into Tiff's Jersey accent, "Yeah, sometimes when you're runnin', you know, you just kinda poop a li'l bit."

"I think she realized she sounded crazy." I join him on the couch with the weed.

"She *did* sound crazy... until today. But dude, she was right. Something about the movement, I don't know, of your legs or your guts or both, it just shakes loose. Never happened before. I almost lost it and had to duck into someone's yard. I was literally targeting every large bush to figure out if I could hide behind it or not. Problem is, in most peoples' front yard, if you're behind a bush it means you're *in front of* a window."

I pass him the loaded pipe and the lighter, and he takes a long pull that cuts short into coughing.

I revel in the fear and courage of that moment. Sure, I've had similar thoughts for years. But here he's telling me his body was about to force itself to evacuate in public. All the awkwardness of squatting in the woods, but with cars and windows and other people all around.

I think of the man I saw at the bus stop. I was one such onlooker, watching him go into his own hand. I don't think anything happened to him as a result. He probably left it there on the ground and moved on.

Maybe the trick is not to care.

I'd care. And Gavin cares, which is why he panicked.

"You were lucky it happened nearby, so you could just come here."

"It wasn't nearby! It started over on Moorpark! But I didn't have the balls to do it in a yard, so I went to the river thinking I could find a patch of trees. But everybody's walking their goddamn dog there. They probably knew what was up, too, I was probably walking funny."

What a story for the observers to overhear after piling such judgment onto me. None of us are immune. Everybody walks funny sometimes. Everybody poops.

They probably watched Gavin use the toilet here.

"So you walked all the way from Moorpark to my place on the verge of shitting yourself?"

"Yes. I waddled all the way here." In the dim light his eyes are comically serious. "That's like a quarter-mile."

"Well, I'm glad you made it."

"Me too. Jesus." He takes the pipe again.

Then I hear it. Quieter than normal, so maybe from the smoke detector or somewhere else further away. An observer says, "We couldn't stop him."

I look at Gavin to see his reaction. He holds a hit with his eyes closed.

What do they mean, "we couldn't stop him"? Do they mean me? They couldn't stop me from letting Gavin in? Or do they mean they couldn't stop Gavin from coming here? How controlled is the area around my apartment? After I borrowed the recorder, did they start watching him too?

"Yeah," the observer says, muffled, "he's still there."

"Do..." I begin.

Gavin looks.

"Do you hear that?"

He exhales and listens. "Hear what?"

"Like a small, tinny voice." I wait to hear it again myself.

"No. Like someone outside?" He listens. "What did they say?"

The fist tightens in my skull. "It said, 'We couldn't stop him,' and then it said, 'He's still there.'"

"Rate's up," the muffled voice says.

"No." Now a question on his face. "I didn't hear it."

"Okay."

His eyes burn my cheek. "Alex, what's up?"

"What do you mean?"

"I mean, what's going on? Are you in trouble? Does this have to do with the recorder?"

"No, I'm just tired, I think." I watch him chew on that.

"Work?"

"Yeah, I guess. Catches up with me sometimes." My throat tightens. "I'm fine."

"He's in the orange. Alex, keep breathing, and get your friend out of there for your own safety."

The chip must be in my ear. That explains the heart monitor and the fact that only I can hear them. And the eerie quality of hearing their voices at the same volume wherever I go—whichever room of the apartment, with the shower on, the neighbor's AC unit humming, out on the street...

Maybe it's somewhere under my skin, against a bone. In science class, I clamped my teeth onto a metal wire with sound played through it, and I could hear the sound faint but clear as it vibrated in my jaw. When other students tried it, I couldn't hear a thing.

The voices are only for me.

I start a breath pattern I learned in a yoga class. The instructor said inhaling through the nose and exhaling out the mouth is a way to ensure regular oxygen absorption without hyperventilating. I do this as subtly as I can to keep Gavin from noticing.

The world past the blinds rises and falls like the horizon on a ship.

In the nose and out the mouth, it's a bit like circular breathing. But then thinking the phrase "circular breathing" is a mistake, because it makes me feel like the ship isn't rocking but rotating, like a slow-motion bullet over the sea. The water rises to fill the window completely, all swells and chop, and eventually the sky reappears as the ship keeps turning, righting itself, only clouds for a weightless moment, and water rises again from the bottom. Spiraling between sea and sky.

"What's that?"

I look where Gavin is pointing, feel my gyroscopic inertia shift as I turn my head toward the hole in the ceiling.

"Ah, my smoke detector. Had to disconnect it."

"It was bugging out, or what?"

"We're at high orange, imminent panic attack."

"No, just beeping at me. I've gotta talk to the landlord about it."

"Huh. I've never seen a wired one before. I guess it makes sense, though."

I had never seen one before either. What if wired smoke detectors aren't a thing?

"I'll be right back." I rise from the couch, leading with the lower half of my body. My legs guide me around the coffee table into the bathroom, turn me so my hands can close the door, then take two steps and kneel me at the toilet.

The first pushes are empty, but the third brings a mouthful of sour, syrupy bile and gummy gobs of egg. I convulse two more times, tears squeeze from my eyes. The giant imaginary hand holds the scruff of my neck, and now its partner wrings my torso.

When the clenching subsides, I try to breathe out through my mouth and in through my nose. I inhale sour breath from the toilet bowl.

"He's breathing. Rhythms are leveling out."

"Are you okay?" comes muffled from the living room.

"Yeah." My voice is loud and close in the bowl. My breath ripples the sludge.

"Alex," they say in my ear, or bones, or wherever, "your uninvited guest has to leave."

I whisper, "Between you and him, *you're* the uninvited guests."

"This is not a game. We will use the necessary force."

"Empty threat, like everything else you've said." I listen to make sure I don't hear Gavin struggling and trying to scream through a gag in the living room.

"Have you ever had a panic attack before now, Alex?"

Never.

"Where do you think this one came from?" They wait, to let it sink in. "Our finger is on the button. Do not test us."

"Rate's rising," another says.

The cloud of bile slows its swirl in the water. I wipe my mouth with toilet paper, flush, wash my hands and brush my teeth, dab my eyes on my sleeve, and return to the living room.

"Are you okay?"

"I think I ate something bad. I'm good now, though." I fill my glass at the sink and drink. "I'm sorry, man, I think I do need to sleep."

Gavin puts the pipe on the coffee table and blows a cone of smoke. "Sure. You should do that. I'll see you later." He gets up and stretches, all meat and bone.

Their finger is on the button.

"Actually," I say, "I could use a walk first. Some sunlight. I'll walk you back, then sleep."

***

One person jogs on the opposite sidewalk, their head bobs above parked cars. An attack could come from anywhere. Maybe behind us. I pretend to stretch my neck to look back. I laugh, too—carefully timed with things Gavin or I say when it might make sense to laugh.

On Ventura I realize Gavin is the one walking street-side. I hang back, pretend to get a better look at a billboard, then run up around a palm tree to his other side, to ensure I'm near the street. He veers to make room, oblivious to my trick. I can breathe a little easier, confident that if they send a car to jump the curb, it'll probably hit me first.

No one on the sidewalks or in cars seems to look at us, which is concerning. I assume when I look away from each person, their glare snaps back onto us. But they hide their glares from Gavin so he doesn't catch on.

I turn and walk backwards for a moment, knowing that between his field of view and mine, we have 360 degrees covered.

"Fancy walking," he says.

"Don't wanna poop a little bit when you're going backwards," I joke, "you might step in it."

"That's true," he says.

I turn back around.

He says that he and Eli decided on Los Padres, if it's okay with me. Of course it's okay with me. He describes what he's seen in photos of the campsites and surrounding area.

And I think, *How is this of interest to anyone but us? Who the fuck cares what I'm doing right now? Nobody should. Not even them. They can't murder us in plain sight. Maybe kidnap us, but someone would see it happen. Unless the entire city is in on it, but that's a massive operation. And for what?*

The sun is high, the light is warm, our shadows are short. I resume my breathing pattern and feel the ground harden beneath me and stay beneath me. On the horizon buildings sit, cars come and go, lights change—all of it passes beneath me, around me, as I walk fixed in place. Gavin, too. We're two small gears turning the giant roller of the earth.

I imagine walking through Los Padres, over hills of scrub brush, my booted gear teeth digging into the ground to move the earth beneath me. With Gavin and Eli contributing, the three of us could get it turning pretty well. Roll on into forever.

***

We reach Gavin's apartment and hug good-bye. I reassure him that I'm fine, that the walk and visit have done me good, my stomach has settled, and now I'll go home to sleep.

When he opens his door, I sweep my eyes through his apartment and see no one there. He turns and smiles, "Later, dude," and shuts the door.

I wait, listening for sounds of a struggle.

After I pass back through his building's creaky front door, it feels much harder to turn the earth by myself. Going downhill from his cul-de-sac it's like a big hand cranks the earth beneath me, forcing my pace. And when the sidewalk flattens out I have to push off with each step, pull with my knees and lift my feet so I don't catch and fall.

"He's gone," I tell the air in my living room. "Are we doing this?"

No response.

"Hey. Guys. He's gone. Come on over."

I still spin scenarios of Gavin getting jumped in his apartment. They could've been hidden further inside. But they would've told me; they love to gloat.

Plus they heard us, so they know I said nothing incriminating. They have no reason to hurt Gavin. Killing him would be messy.

But in the worst-case scenario they wouldn't kill Gavin, they'd adopt him as a new subject in the experiment. They could knock him out and implant a chip, or put it in his food, or do whatever they did to me.

Unless he's already involved.

What if Gavin was the original subject? Maybe he's more stoic than I am, and he's trying to get me to admit what's happening because he's afraid to bring it up himself. Or maybe he hasn't connected the dots yet. Maybe his dots are different than mine. Maybe they don't use his chip to talk to him but to do other stuff, like make him have to shit while he's out running.

If he's cooperating with them, maybe the shit story was just to scare me or strengthen my trust.

"I'm prepared to learn the truth," I say.

Gavin is too old and close a friend to willingly double-cross me. Using him to get to me would've required years of grooming, starting the moment he and I met, or before.

He wouldn't do that to me now.

"Ready when you are," I say.

Maybe Gavin's visit was meant to do exactly this—make me believe he's involved and not to be trusted. Is this a final test? Have they planted that ugly seed and now sit silent, awaiting my reaction? Do they want me to shrink from everyone until I implode?

They could be standing outside with a cake and party hats; all I have to do is open my door for the cherry atop this grand, twisted experiment. *Congratulations, Alex, you chose the path of no fear! We had hoped for this outcome but didn't believe it possible until now!*

I don't expect them to present me with an oversized cardboard check or anything, but I do think I merit a handshake, maybe an approving nod of surprise. They said it themselves—others haven't fared as well as I have. I still don't know what that means. A couple hours ago I was close to stepping out of my shower and living out the rest of my life as a pig to slaughter. Is this success?

"Hey, guys."

The window across the alley has its blinds drawn. I crack my window open and listen for voices from their house or their fenced-in backyard.

Ah, but the question answers itself, really—if you could focus a beam onto a specific individual and drive them to such a depth of self-loathing, fear, and paranoia that they find it more plausible that their life is the desperate fever dream of a sick animal on its way to the blade, wars could be skipped.

Kill the head, and the body will die.

I imagine a future wherein a despot paces his private quarters, wringing his hands and repeating certain words and phrases under his breath, until something fragile cracks inside him and urges him to the door. He opens it to find two men dressed in bloody overalls and hairnets. He gives them a look of resigned recognition and climbs into the back of their electric cart. They drive him to a concrete room with a drain in the floor.

"Hey," I say. "He's gone. Coast is clear."

It's been quiet for so long, I have trouble placing the sound. Like a creaking. I look to my door, but it's still closed and locked. No, it's a giggle in my ear.

"There you are. Are you guys coming now?"

The giggle blooms into laughter.

"Alex, you are hands down the fucking stupidest person alive."

Tremors rack my body, my head empties, my volition rises from deep inside and thrusts out of me like a silent scream.

We imagine the moment of death as a separation. In movies, a glowing phantom version of the person rises from their inert body like double-vision. The phantom looks around, suspended in midair and surprised to find itself there. And they fly. They haunt others. Throw chairs. They have jealousy or sadness or anger—unfinished business. They are pure volition.

But when it happens to me, my awareness stays with the rest of me, limp on the couch, still staring out through my body's eyes, still feeling the weight of my bones, muscles, and organs. The difference is that I feel nothing else. No sadness, no anger, no fear. And I have a thought. I believe everyone must have this thought the moment before their energy scatters in that final pump of the heart, the final crackle of electricity through the mind, those several seconds of awareness they say occur in a head freshly chopped, when it's lifted by the hair to stare at a jeering crowd.

I think, *Of course.*

Death is freedom. It's like being alive, but you don't care. You're not too warm or too cold, you don't get hungry or thirsty or tired. Opinions don't matter; there's no wrong way to be dead.

It is boundless relief.

I wonder if dead people piss and shit themselves, not because their body has ceased to fire the electrical impulses to stimulate their muscles into holding waste material inside, but because they stop caring. They no longer worry about aiming it into a toilet, or what other people will think if they release it wherever they are. They don't feel or smell anything, so they don't mind the mess. For them it's not a mess.

Dead people are nihilists.

The dead even surrender the task of breathing to all the little creatures in their bodies. They bloat, because the breathing creatures are not just in the lungs but everywhere. Those tiny lives dismantle the dead and go every which way. From our perspective they are destructive, but among themselves they are builders. If it were up to everything else in the universe, they'd take us all apart and make something new.

"You are an absolute fucking goddamn idiot."

I barely recognize it as speech anymore. It's like wind howling or beams creaking in an old house by the sea. It's as ever-present as scratches dragged through the floorboards of that house. Ubiquitous and eternal. I know those scratches well. I was there when they were made, though I can't remember the shape of the furniture that made them or who moved it. Sometimes it was me.

"Alex, we're government scientists."

"Yeah, we're doing an important study. For the government."

The roof leaks in this house of the dead. If I were still alive, I'd hold up my hand to catch a drop of rainwater in my palm, cool and slipping down my wrist into my shirtsleeve. I'd think, *Should replace that shingle when the weather clears up*—the living call it "planning"—and I'd foresee how I'd collect a hammer and nails and a new shingle, and taking care not to slip, I'd climb a ladder and patch the roof.

But I'm dead and don't care. Shingles or not, it doesn't matter. Let rain seep through the roof and drip into my ear.

Let the drops tap a slow hole through my head to the floor. Let the wind push and weaken this house. Let it flex the walls and crack the windows. Let water puddle around the foundation and eat its way into the basement with soft teeth of black mold. Let the dark corners flourish with mushrooms. Let fauna find shelter here. Let them eat of my flesh and take me with them to be filtered through their own bodies, mingling with plants and fruit and pieces of other animals, and let them deposit me in dissolution far from this place to feed a patch of wildflowers, or a field of nettles, or the roots of a great tree.

"The government is paying us a fuck-ton of money to video you jerking off."

"They're paying us to make you go crazy, Alex. And it's working. We thought it'd take a lot longer, but you've progressed quickly."

"Yeah, we're proud of you, Alex."

"So proud, you stupid piece of shit."

Let the skeleton of this house weaken and collapse around my remains, and let its heavy mound squeeze the gases and fluids from me.

"Alex, how the fuck could you actually believe we were government spies?"

Let it press me into the rubble, hidden away. Let me seep into the broken wood and the soil.

"We were just bored, really. But we're so glad we found you! My god, what were the chances we'd meet such a freak? It's like watching a fuckin' movie."

Bed me beneath a thick carpet of moss. Let me feed tiny life that doesn't know my name and has no tongue to speak it.

"We never want this movie to end."

I'm tired. Let me sleep.

I WAKE IN BLUE twilight, a lump on the floor. My limbs are cold and stiff, like empty clothes dug from the rubble of that collapsed house by the sea.

Something slips into the clothes. Uncrumples and animates them.

Volition returns to my body, buzzes in my core, pushes outward, stings through my arms and legs. I find I can move. I can stand. I am the vengeful undead.

The light is on in their window. Bright points shine through the holes where their blinds are threaded together.

I put on a coat that's long enough to hide the hammer handle sticking out of my back pocket.

The air is cool and fresh on my skin. I witness the moment when the yellow orbs of the streetlights come on. Crickets chirp in the hedges. Let my ears bleed, and let it hurt if it must, as long as after healing I hear only crickets.

A car comes down the street. The driver looks at me. This is the end of the movie, is it not? This is the moment I take drastic action, and they intervene. They knock me out, throw me into the car, and drive me somewhere secluded where, when I awaken, one of them monologues an explanation, and at the climax of the speech another shoots me in the back of the head.

The car keeps going, stops at the sign, and doesn't even stay long enough to see me turn and start up the neighbors' walkway.

I remember this view of their house from when I first stepped through the invisible wall at the sidewalk. Now I reuse the hole I tore into their world, float up the walkway. I fantasize pounding through the door with the hammer. It would take many swings, but each dent would bring me closer to them. I'd pound until a hole formed, and then I'd pound around the edges of the hole. Eventually the hole would be big enough for me to reach through and unlock the door for myself.

I'd listen to their screams, focus as intensely on them as I have their tiny voices coming through the smoke detector. I'd record their screams in my mind. And after I'd destroyed them, I'd destroy my ears and replay their screams until I grew tired of them. And then I'd play the crickets and live out my days in that indifferent seesaw buzz.

I knock.

Crickets in a nearby bush quiet at the sound.

I keep my eye on the window by the door. The blinds don't move. The cracks between the blinds are dark.

I knock again, harder.

I lean, listen, pull hard with my ear. Either I'll hear them whisper to each other inside, or I'll pull hard enough to suck a bullet through the door. The *elation* it would bring. The final spark in my mind would express, *Aaaaahhh...* and I'd slump into the bush, feel the leaves rattle and scratch on my skin. And hopefully my awareness would remain long enough to hear the crickets when they calm and start again.

I knock even harder.

I wish I could see them through the wall as blobs of heat pacing from room to room, crouching at the corners of windows upstairs. Maybe grabbing weapons from the closets.

I bang on the door.

Calling the police. That's probably what's happening. Had they seen me from a window? At such an angle to notice the hammer jutting up under my jacket? The police are noting that the caller's address is next-door to the strange person who requested assistance very early this morning.

I knock again, and resent that it's weaker than the last. They're safe behind their locked door and drawn blinds. They've always had the advantage.

A clicking sound comes down the street—a dog's claws on the sidewalk. An older man walks with the dog. If he isn't already one of them, this guy would probably still report me.

"Hey, guys?" I say through the door.

I turn and go back down the walkway. I don't look at the man. But I do shove my hand into my pocket, as if stowing my keys. *Walk like you're leaving your own house.*

But he's going the same direction as me; I can't just turn up the stairs of my building and go to my apartment, or he'll know something was up. Everyone's going around looking for something to care about, their chance to be a hero. Would he see this as his chance? And if so, would he take it?

I turn down the alley. *Walk like your car is parked on the next block.* I shake my head, thinking, *Damn street sweeping, had to park all the way—*

As I walk I look up at their house and see the light on in the window. Blinds drawn. Is someone parting them with a finger to watch me go? To make sure I don't climb the wall into their backyard? Call the cops, get me with trespassing—who knows what kind of trouble the hammer in my back pocket would add. Have me put away.

The clicking claws turn into the alley, god damn it, and now the man is pulling out his gun, or his chloroform, nodding and giving a hand sign to the eyes in the window. Once again they've tricked me into leaving my apartment, and when I had the chance to go home, turning away seemed like the safer option. Fucking moron.

I look for reflections out the corner of my eye, in the windshields of cars parked in the carports. I only turn far enough to see myself in them. No hands reaching for my throat. If I turn further it'll be too obvious. Almost the end of the alley.

I don't have the energy to walk for two hours again, to outsmart shifting shadows, so I turn to wind around the block to my building.

The man turns the other way back into the neighborhood. Exactly as he would if he were an old guy walking his dog in the evening. A fine performance.

I just have to turn right at the next corner, then up the stairs, and I'll be home.

Cars whoosh by and shout over their own noise, pointing me out to each other. *That's the crazy guy. I saw him staring at a little kid's ass in the grocery store. Then he gave an awful look to a Black woman in the parking lot. If there hadn't been anyone else around, he would've raped her. It's obvious he's the type; look at him. What's in his pocket? A gun or a knife? Why'd he circle around the block? He was knocking on his neighbor's door a few minutes ago. A hammer? Is he going back to try again? If he turns right, he's definitely going back. Yeah, if he turns we should call the police. That guy's dangerous. Probably a serial killer on top of being a rapist. He's walking around the neighborhood with a hammer in his pocket. It's only a matter of time. Fucking watch.*

"Yellow, green, red, blue."

Correct. I shuffle.

"Red, yellow, blue, green. You fuck."

Correct again.

This test of my new security system isn't going well.

I had lined up four mugs, each with some water and a drop of food coloring. Then I tore a notecard into four strips and dipped each strip into a different mug, dyeing the end. They drank the mixture eagerly, and I dabbed them with paper towel and laid them on a plate to let them dry.

Handling them has stained my fingers a deep purple separating into layered colors around the edges. When I turn the flashlight off and look at my hand, my fingers look like bitten-off stubs in the dark. I'm becoming night, starting with my fingertips.

Now that they're dry I shuffle and fan the strips, but the observers guess the order every time.

"Green, yellow, blue, red."

Correct.

"Kinda fun, isn't it?"

"Yeah, but what is he doing?"

Even when I lean into the dark alcove of my stovetop, they can see.

"Blue, green, red, yellow."

Correct.

"Hey Alex, what the fuck kinda game is this?"

"Yeah, and haven't we won yet? Are we winning? How many points do we have?"

I hunch over the stove again, shuffle the strips without looking. I hold them up with my eyes closed, head turned away.

Quiet.

It's either a trick or they really can't see, except through my eyes.

"Hey, what colors?" I ask.

"What are you doing?"

"Tell me the colors, or I dunk the smoke detector."

"You do that, and we'll murder you."

"I WISH YOU WOULD!" My voice rings in the space. Everyone in the other apartments heard it, if they're home. "Tell me the colors."

"We don't know the fucking colors."

I hold up the fan of strips, still not looking at it myself, and turn it left and right. "See it?"

"No."

I let go of the strips, and they spin to the floor while I take the smoke detector from the cupboard.

"Alex, if you do that—"

"I know," I say. "Come on over with your guns or knives or cat-o'-nine-tails or whatever the fuck you wanna use. Or come empty-handed, and you can improvise with stuff I've got here. But come over! Let's do this NOW!"

I drop the smoke detector in the kitchen sink. A small piece of plastic shoots off the edge.

"Ah, fuck! What are you doing?"

I pick it up and throw it into the sink again. More bits of plastic explode from it, one hits my forehead.

"God damn it, my ears!"

I lift the broken thing, curl my fingertips into the seam. Dyed near-black with rainbow edges, my fingers look like demon hands prying apart an underworld artifact. I pull, the thing rattles in my shaking hands, the plastic creaks and bursts apart.

"No, fuck! You're fucking dead, Alex!"

I toss the shell aside and stare at the innards. It has a circular circuit board with several little capacitors and resistors, plus two cylinders—one of which is plastic, looks like a voice box you'd find in a stuffed animal, and the other is larger, metal, lined with slits on its sides and capped with a yellow sticker that says, "Warning: radioactive material." Aside from the two cylinders, nothing else looks like a microphone or speaker.

As they shout, I lift the thing to my ear. The sound of their voices doesn't change. They only scream in my head now. But if they do have a microphone in this device, it's hidden in the part labeled dangerous. I go to the window and hold it in a sliver of streetlight. I shine the flashlight through it. The slits are too slanted to see through.

I snap the two cylinders from the circuit board, then crack the board in half.

"No! No, fuck, no!"

Everything goes in the sink. I put the stopper in the drain and open the faucet, let it fill.

"Fuck! God damn it, fuck!"

When the pieces float, I push them back down. I rotate the cylinders, watch them exhale their final bubbling breaths.

I say, "You're in deep water, fellas."

They brood in silence.

I light a cigarette and think, staring at the colored strips of paper on the floor.

Then I collect the strips along with Scotch tape, an X-Acto knife, and another notecard.

I pull the pots and pans from the low cupboard, climb inside, and close the door with my foot. Boxed again in darkness and the warm smell of wood.

"What the fuck is he doing?"

"I don't see him."

I drop the strips on the floor of the cupboard and shuffle them around.

"Listen... Hear that?"

I collect them, careful to feel around and get all four, and shuffle them again. The water-warped texture helps me discern the colored ends.

"Alex, how are you gonna know—"

"Shut up," the other says. "Listen."

In the dark I take the notecard and tape from my pocket. Feeling the warped end of a strip, I tear off a tiny corner. Then I take a bit of tape from the roll and stick the torn-off bit onto the notecard. Then I tear a bit from the next strip, and tape that bit below the first.

I do this until all four colors are accounted for, their stacked order copied onto the notecard. Then I fold the notecard and put it in my pocket. I keep the strips stacked in my fist.

I slide out of the cupboard and replace the pots and pans with my free hand.

"What the fuck did he do in there?"

"It's just to scare us."

"I don't like it."

I take my phone, put the flashlight and hammer in my back pockets, the wet smoke detector cylinders in my front pocket, put on my coat, and go out the door.

Looking down at my feet, I reach for an improbable spot up high and close the door on the fanned strips.

"God damn it. I can't believe he did it."

Chills. I have done it.

I grin at the white ends of the strips sticking out from the doorjamb. I use the X-acto knife to slice those ends off as close as possible to the wood. They become imperceptible from the outside, untouchable. My own secret code against trespassers hidden in the seam of my front door, and its cipher hidden in my pocket, unknown even to myself.

If they enter my apartment while I'm gone, I'll know.

A RED CAR PASSES me on the freeway. Could be them.

My office shares a wall with the sign printing company next door. That's probably where they're rushing to, to get their equipment ready to receive the direct feed from my chip. To watch my heat map blob through the wall as I sit and type, go to the restroom, make coffee, repeat. To watch my computer screen through my eyes.

Near the office I turn on my phone.

"He has his phone with him?"

There are a couple more missed calls from Dad's number.

There's also a text message from a number I don't recognize. It says, *Hey. You should come over again soon. ;)*

It's timestamped just after I went to the neighbors' house. I'm surprised they hadn't tried to mess with me in text messages before this. Maybe they didn't bother because I was ignoring my phone. I'm also surprised they didn't have their shit together to grab me when I knocked earlier, and now they hope I'll come back.

Many possible responses come to mind, but since I'm driving I keep it short: *FUCK OFF.*

Then I call the office.

My supervisor answers. He sounds tired.

I explain that I'm still sick and that I thought I'd feel better by now, but I don't.

"What the fuck? He's not going to work."

My supervisor recommends that I see a doctor in the morning, in case it's serious.

I tell him I'll definitely do that, and drive past the office. No cars parked at the sign company. Maybe they parked somewhere else.

"Shut all this down, we've gotta follow him! Quick!"

I power my phone off as I turn onto the arterial. The next light is red, so I turn right to keep moving.

Yellow streetlight beams wipe the minivan's interior and make me feel like I'm gaining speed. I'm not, of course. With my luck I'd get pulled over by the two goons who came to my place last night.

I rejoin the freeway going northwest. No one follows me up the ramp, nobody changes lanes near me, I merge left and join a preexisting flow of strangers like I've been driving this freeway all day, all my life.

I let five exits go by before I unroll the passenger window and toss the smoke detector cylinders over the center divide. I'd love to see them dance through traffic to get their shit back.

"He dropped the bug."

"Fuck it, stay on him."

That car? Or that car? None look like the red car that passed me before, but it probably wasn't them anyway. I should've looked at the license plate.

Neighborhoods gather and disperse like clusters of stars seen through a wormhole, a futuristic superhighway paved and dotted with pools of cold, white light.

They're silent for a while. I'm a dot moving on a map. Their own dot is somewhere behind me, hopefully with distance growing between us.

I hum to see if they comment.

When they say nothing, I sing. Softly at first. "Hello... my baby..."

I wait.

"Hello... my honey..."

Still nothing.

"Hello, my rag... time... gal..."

"He's fucking singing."

I grin and sing louder. "Send me a kiss by wire... Baby... my heart's on fire..."

"That crazy fuck."

"If you refuse me... honey, you'll lose me... Then you'll be left alone, oh, baby..."

"Where the fuck are you going, Alex?"

"Telephone... and tell me I'm your own!"

"He's lost it."

Then as loud as I can, "Hel-lo, my baby! Hel-lo, my honey! Hello, my ragtime gal!" They're somewhere out there. "Send me a kiss by wire! Baby, my heart's on fire!"

"His heart is racing."

I press my fingers to my throat. They're right. "If you refuse me, honey, you'll lose me..."

Signs sweep by for San Fernando.

Then I'm out of San Fernando and heading toward Santa Clarita.

The office buildings and warehouses thin out. Neighborhoods huddle with little lights through curtained windows. Large, slow hills of rock and brush grow around me. The wormhole road tilts up, weaves serpentine ever skyward.

Metal nets cling to rock faces stretching up into the dark. If they want to stop me they could cut those nets and send boulders down to block my path or crush me.

I pass other cars on the upward grade. They can slither across the whole continent with no concerns, stop for gas or food and take their time. Everyone else in the world can take their time everywhere, and spit on the sidewalk without shame.

The road levels, tilts down, and the milky orange grid of Santa Clarita rises into view. The van sinks back toward Earth.

Still, I feel I've passed through a membrane they didn't expect me to pierce. Like a tuna who braved a stretch of open sea with sharks on my tail, and now before me swirls a glinting new school in which to hide.

"You need to stop for gas, Alex."

Had they seen the gauge out the corner of my eye? Or did they plant a sensor in the van somewhere?

"You don't want to know."

You know what I'm thinking, don't you?

"Yes, of course we do, you fucking moron! You still seem to think this is fucking amateur hour! We're the real deal!"

Rumbling tension blooms at the back of my skull. I pray that isn't where the chip was planted. I picture a latex-gloved hand holding a melon baller.

"You want us to tell you where it is?"

Anything you tell me will be bullshit.

"Yup. Or the truth disguised as bullshit!"

Exactly.

Suddenly I'm tired again.

"Gonna just drive till you run out of gas?"

I say nothing, try to think nothing.

"Hungry, too?"

It's an unfamiliar feeling. I'd mistaken the emptiness in me for agility, like how birds have hollow bones. But now a void expands in me. My dyed demon fingers are cold and stiff. Somehow this needs to be resolved before the gnawing darkness on the outside meets the expanding nothing on the inside. I suddenly understand animals who take their food somewhere hidden to eat.

An exit appears, but at the last second I swerve left and surprise a car on that side. It honks.

If I act before impulses become ideas, my thoughts might remain unreadable, my actions unpredictable.

"Sure Alex, you could kill yourself, too! That works just as well for us!"

If there's an accident, they'd arrive at the scene before any paramedics. Haul my body away to dig out the chip and dispose of me. Maybe they'd rip off my jaw and leave it in the car, spray the car with government-grade accelerant and set the car ablaze. The jaw would match my dental records, and investigators would assume the rest of me had burned away.

Next exit passes.

I could call the paramedics to report an accident, wait until their lights appear in the distance, then—on purpose—ram myself into a wall. The paramedics would be there to take over immediately, and I'd be put under hospital care. They'd do X-rays and find the chip.

"First of all, it won't show up in an X-ray. Second, we own the hospitals."

"Yeah, what makes you think we couldn't just send our own doctors to look at you? Give you a pill or a needle and then do whatever the fuck we wanted?"

There's one more exit before the end of Santa Clarita and the beginning of empty hills for miles.

"Yeah, Alex, we could drug you up and throw you in a giant maze."

"You think you'd be good at a maze?"

Freeway dividers and guardrails, plastic bumps and painted lines, and the rest is rough impassable landscape. I'm already in a maze.

"I think he'd try to climb the walls and tire himself out."

"Yeah, you're not good at following rules and staying inside the lines, are you, Alex?"

To the left a silhouette of scrubby hill moves aside to reveal the lit ribbons of a roller coaster bunched on the horizon. Magic Mountain.

"Or he might chew off his feet."

On an impulse I check my mirrors, look out the windows, and veer right.

"What's he doing?"

"Whoa, whoa, he's getting off!"

Acting in advance of my thoughts will take practice.

"That's what we mean by coloring in the lines, Alex. You're so far outside the lines you're drawin' on the fuckin' table!"

At the bottom of the exit ramp, I turn right.

The parkway is a seven-lane field of concrete.

The next light is red. I wait.

"Aw, you're no fun, Alex! What happened to the chase?"

How's that for following the rules?

Two pairs of headlights appear and grow in my rear-view mirror. One changes lanes to slide up on my left—an older man in a dark blue Mercedes. The other—an SUV—slows to a stop far enough behind me that their headlights smear my back window.

I watch my left, expecting to see a gun. He shifts in his seat as if readying to draw. Or maybe he heard me think that and is anxious because he thinks I'm the one who's armed.

I watch the right too, to make sure no surprises have crept up from the SUV.

The light turns green. We three move at the same time.

The guy on the left goes faster then slower, eyes ever-forward. A consummate naturalist performance. He's probably running the dialogue, *Look, I'm just a guy, it's late, and I'm just trying to get home*, over and over behind his eyes.

I'm playing that game too, while the SUV's headlights blast my rear-view mirror.

"Too bright for ya?"

The preliminary bubble of a response rises in me, but I sink the thought back down with a word written in extruded lead: *NOTHING*.

"What the fuck does that mean? Hey, did you hear me, Alex? I said are we makin' you nervous, you fucking pussy?"

NOTHING.

I slow and watch if the guy on the left turns his head or speaks into his collar. The SUV honks to scare me.

But it doesn't work, because I think *NOTHING* and change lanes behind the man.

He glances at me in his mirror.

I turn left, leaving the other vehicles to their straight-line inertia. Their taillight eyes watch helplessly, shrink, and are gone.

***

The vast, empty parking lot is like a rest stop for the freeway wormhole, spotted with the same pools of cold light. I park in a pool at the center. Dark sentinel trees edge the lot. No movement out on the road.

Light drapes a circle of protection over the minivan. The hood and windshield glint and flare.

The lot is for a Target store. The lit bull's-eye logo on the building rises like a red sun in my mirror and stares. Another circle of protection? An evil eye?

I climb over the seats to the very back, where there's a duffel bag containing jumper cables, tools, bottles of water, a box of expired protein bars, and a first-aid kit. I take the first-aid kit, a protein bar, and a screwdriver back to the front seat.

The protein bar is supposed to be vanilla flavor, but it just tastes chalky and thick. Sticks in my teeth. My cheeks sting and salivate.

I use the screwdriver to remove the passenger-side visor, which has a mirror in it. I tilt it next to my ear to catch its reflection in the rear-view mirror, but can't get the angle to work.

I push my pinky finger into each ear canal, careful for the poke of a foreign body, maybe the amplified rustle of my finger brushing the mic.

With the flashlight on the dash, pointed at my face, I peel open the pink valleys between my lips and my gums. I look into my throat where my tonsils cower and pulsate. I search my molars for signs that one is artificial, maybe replaced years ago when I had my wisdom teeth pulled. I tap each tooth with the tip of the screwdriver, listening for a false note. I clamp the flashlight between my legs, flare my nostrils, and search the tangle of nose hairs for a glint of metal. I peel my eyelids up and down, roll my eyeballs to see if the edge of something peeks out behind them.

Dread hardens in my chest—if it's not accessible through one of my orifices, it must be surgically embedded somewhere. Maybe it's a piece of nanotech they put in my food that, once inside, jabbed a neat little path through my organs to wedge itself between my clavicle and vocal cords. Or it could be plugged directly into my spinal column. My hand massages the vertebral hump at the base of my neck.

Strange contours of bone, muscle, and fat shift against each other beneath my skin. Tendons stretch like twine down my arms and legs and spider out in the backs of my hands. For nearly three decades organic material has ballooned, stretched, congealed, and accreted in various spindles and bulbs to make my personal geometry.

That thing could be anywhere, concealed in my weave of lumpy, knotted fibers.

If I find it, should I try to cut it out right here in the van? And then drive to the emergency room? Or will I feel it, pinch its contours to make sure—yes, it's a tube, or a disk, or a square, or whatever intrusive shape—and then drive to the hospital in ecstatic terror, with one hand still pinching the thing beneath my skin to make sure it doesn't move?

"Where does he think it's gonna go?"

"He thinks it's some kind of robot that'll climb out of his mouth like a bug, or drill out of his skin and fly away. Check this out, he's imagining what it looks like."

"Lemme see... Whoa, you're right, that's wild! I wish we had shit like that!"

I massage the hunk of muscle in the arc of my jawbone. The glands at the top of my throat feel like giblets in a hairy leather bag.

"Alex, you should make movies or something. This insect robot idea is fucking crazy."

"You waste all this time yelling at us and having your paranoid freak-outs, when you could be writing this shit down."

"Fuck you." I slide my hands under my shirt, press on the flesh between my ribs. It might be somewhere behind the bone, or in my back where I can't reach.

"Yeah, you could be a writer or something, but all you do is smoke weed and go to your bullshit job. You called in sick, so you've got all this free time right now, and what are you doing? You drove to fucking Santa Clarita in the middle of the night to sit in an empty parking lot and shine a fuckin' flashlight up your nose!"

"Fuck you!" My voice is close and loud in the van.

"See how easy it is for us to fool and manipulate you? You've got no integrity! No volition! You're already dead!"

"Shut the fuck up!" I watch my mouth stretch open in the mirror, cavernous, hoping I can shout loud enough to hurt their ears. "You fucks, shut the fuck up! Get the fuck outta my head! Shut up!" Of course, they knew I'd yell, so they probably turned the volume down.

The quieter I imagine they hear me, the less air I feel in my lungs. I take heaving breaths between sentences. "Leave me alone!... You fucks!... I'll fucking kill you!..." My volume lowers, thick quilt after thick quilt settles over my head. I recline my seat and close my eyes, "...shit..." my heart's footsteps are loud in my ears as it runs right off the edge of the cliff.

***

A shadow to my left reaches in through the window and shines a light in my face. It has just asked a question. The upholstered cave of the minivan is still full of its booming voice, but I can't remember what it said. If I don't answer fast, something bad will happen.

I raise my hands, quick at first, then slow when I remember the figure might have a gun, and I say, "Uh-uh"—my voice moans in my skull—and I shake my head to communicate, *I am not a threat.*

"What was that?" the figure's voice booms again in the small space.

I squint against the light and push up on my elbows. My eyes adjust and see that it's my own flashlight still perched on the dashboard and pointing at my face. The window is still up, the door is still shut and locked. The red eye stares unblinking in my mirror. Time has not moved.

"Rise and shine. Have a nice nap?"

I turn to look behind me in the dark van.

"It's been weeks, Alex... Months, even. You were asleep forever."

I crawl through the van with the flashlight, search behind and under all the seats to make sure no one has gotten in with me. I look in all directions at all times to catch anyone ready to pounce over a seat, or an arm reaching underneath to slice my Achilles tendon.

Beneath the passenger seat I find a refrigerator magnet from the auto shop that tuned up the minivan when I bought it from my parents. That was long before any of this. I was a different person then.

They mutter something. I think I hear one say "magnet."

I turn off the flashlight and lie across the bench seat in the back. I remove my shoes and socks, then my pants. I press the magnet against the pads of my toes, slide it around the edge of my foot and across my toenails.

Still quiet, "Did he hear us?"

The magnet continues under the ball of my foot and around to the top, across the instep, and down into the arch.

"We whispered."

"I think he fucking heard us."

I continue the spiral around my foot, up my leg, pressing the magnet against my skin until I get to my haunch, then I repeat on the toes of my other foot.

"Why didn't you turn our fucking mics off?"

"I didn't think he'd actually do that!"

I smile and slide the magnet incrementally, touch every square centimeter up the leg.

Then come my crotch and buttocks—difficult shapes to traverse with a flat rectangle, but I'm almost positive nothing is hidden there anyway.

I crane my neck to see that there isn't a police car approaching, since it's the wee hours and I'm in an empty parking lot rubbing a refrigerator magnet in my butt crack.

History of mental illness in your family?

I pull my pants back on and take off my shirt to pass the magnet around my hips, across my back and stomach, push in on my belly button to get closer to anything deep inside. I suck in my stomach to shift things around and do an extra round.

The magnet isn't big enough to pass from one hand to the other behind my back, so I press against the seat and rub like a bear against a tree until I can reach it.

I slide it under my arms. Odor wafts.

"What's gonna happen when he finds it?"

"Can't say. Maybe nothing."

"We'd better hope so, or we're fucked!"

Nothing in my arms. Along my clavicle, circling the base of my neck.

"Fuck, man!"

"Shut up. Let's just see what happens."

Around my neck, over the bump of my Adam's apple, up under my chin, pressing against the giblet glands, the firm squish of my under-tongue, the contour of my jaw, over my mouth, smelling the stink it absorbed from my armpits and nether regions. I slide it under my hair, against my skull, and when I reach my ear I hold it there a moment and press harder to warp it toward the canal.

A high-pitched tone sounds in my ear. It's quiet and electric like the sound of a muted CRT TV.

"Ah, fuck, what's that?"

"I think he got it."

"Are you fucking serious?"

I hold the magnet there to sense any pull. There's no attraction, unless it's very weak. But something's happened, because the tone is constant and they're screaming.

"God dammit, that's so loud!"

"Turn it off!"

"I'm trying!"

"Take off your headphones, assholes," I offer. "It's that simple."

"The whole thing's fucked up, shithead! That sound's coming from the fucking computer itself!"

"God damn, my fuckin' ears!"

If they give up now, I'll savor the silence all the way home. Then I'll sleep. Tomorrow I'll get an X-ray and relish the moment when the technician squints at the white fleck in my ear and asks, "What the hell is that?"

"It's a long story," I'll say, "and I still don't know the half of it!"

Based on its size and placement, the doctor might be able to tell me something about its installation, and maybe even how it works. He might deduce from the wax buildup how long it was in my ear. Then he'll put it in a small baggie or jar for me, and my next stop will be the police station.

The Cherub and the Strategist probably start work sometime in the evening, so when I show the chip to a day-shift detective

I'll say, "You let Officer McCormick and his little buddy know that I've solved the case, no thanks to them."

The tone is gratefully quiet in my ear, but the observers are still shouting. If someone were here, like if a cop rolled up right now, and I asked him to lean in close to my ear, would he hear it?

"Tune it out, just tune it out."

"It's fucking *loud*, man!"

"We can't stop listening, he's gonna bust us!"

I press the magnet against my other ear.

And lo, a tone sounds in this ear to match the first. High-pitched, yes, but soft. Like the sound of the cold, white photons streaming down onto the minivan and the circle of pavement around it—the hum of my circle of protection.

"Fuck, it's louder! What the fuck!"

"He must've got the other one, too!"

"God dammit, why'd we use two of them?!"

"That was your idea!"

"I didn't think he'd put a fucking *magnet* on his head! Who does that?"

"Alex! Alex, please, can you hear us?"

I drop the magnet and fold my hands in my lap. I smile and watch the empty road through the trees.

Dark SUVs screech, spitting out foot soldiers with guns to "apprehend the subject." A chopper rises over the tree-lined perimeter, shines a spot and shoots out my tires. Each of these things manifests in a blind corner, but dissolves into quiet dark as soon as I turn to look.

"God damn it, Alex, please, please, you gotta help us, please!"

"Yes?" I say.

"Look, you won! This is all fucked up now! You broke our stuff, and this sound is driving us crazy! You gotta stop it!"

"How do you expect me to do that?"

"Tweezers! There's gotta be tweezers in that first-aid kit! Right?!

The other one adds, "Please say there's tweezers!"

I find tweezers.

"Okay, take the tweezers, and you're gonna go straight into the ear canal, and there's—fuck, it hurts!—there's a little tab on the chip..."

I look in the mirror and aim the tweezers into my ear, slowly, like a docking maneuver in space. I can only see myself head-on, so it's hard to aim. The corner of the tweezers scrapes the skin in my canal. I adjust. "How far in?"

"Not far."

The tweezers are about a half-inch into my ear. I slowly close them, waiting to catch, readying to hear the loud rumble when they bump into the chip. How far can I go before I touch my eardrum?

"You'll hit the chip before you get too far, don't worry."

My fingertips hold my ear to avoid slipping as I push further.

I make small, slow circles. Nothing but sensitive flesh all around.

I remove the tweezers and eyeball the length to my fingertips—they were almost an inch into my head.

"Come on, you were so close!"

"Maybe I should let a medical professional handle this. I'm not stabbing out my eardrums to relieve you fuckheads of your own stupid mistake."

"Yes! Yes, it was a mistake! This was all so stupid, and we've been assholes to you, and we're sorry! We're so sorry! Just please, you gotta help us now!"

"Can't you just turn it all off yourselves?"

"No, there's a whole chain of backups! We'd have to destroy *everything* to get this to stop!"

"Then I guess that's your solution."

"No! God dammit! That would be destroying the evidence, Alex! You don't want us to do that, you deserve justice! The government should pay for what it's done to you! We never wanted to do this, but it's our job! We're sorry, we feel terrible and we know this is what we deserve, but please turn those things off!"

"I'm sorry," I say with a smile, "you're breaking up."

"What? Oh, god, no! Alex! Alex, can you hear me now? How about now? Alex!"

I say, "It's hard to— over the— and— saying..."

"Oh, fuck! Hello? It's cutting out! Alex, hello! You can't leave us like this! Please! Hello!"

Over the treble drone, their panicked voices tickle in the back of my head like the quake of a jackpotting slot machine, sirens and lights, rush of coins onto the floor.

I stifle a laugh. "Hello? Hello? I ca— hear—"

"Alex, for the love of god, please, hello! We're here! It's cutting out, can you hear us? The sound hasn't stopped! Please, Alex! Hello!"

"Hell-o..." I say, slowly and clearly.

"Alex! You're back!"

"My baby... Hello, my honey..."

"Oh, god damn it, FUCK!"

"Hello, my ragtime gal!" I pull my shirt on. "Send me a kiss by wire! Baby, my heart's on fire!" I put my shoes back on.

"Alex! Please, you gotta—"

I carry the magnet and flashlight back to the front seat. "If you refuse me, honey, you lose me, then you'll be left alone, oh... bay-bee..." I sing slow and loud, buckling my seatbelt.

"No! Alex, no!"

"Tel-le-phone..." I let the final words linger as I start the engine. "...aaand tell meeeee... I'm... your ooooooooooown!"

LILI SAID SHE LEAVES for work early in the morning. There's a single parking spot available on the whole street, waiting for me.

The sky lightens over the houses, birds are noisy in scattered trees.

The observers say their ears are bleeding.

A few people come out of her building. An old woman with a big dog. Across the street a man wearing a reflector vest and carrying a lunchbox leaves a house and drives away.

I hope she uses this door. Maybe there's another door I can't see. I could go around the block to check, but then I might miss her coming out the front door. So I stay put, knowing she might be somewhere else.

There she is.

She looks like a stranger. I realize I've never seen her like this. The first moment I saw her, when she walked down the sidewalk to my apartment—and even before that, in her photo—she was looking at me. She existed in relation to me.

Here, though, she's just a stranger walking. A figure painted on the veil. Opaque.

She doesn't seem concerned that someone might be watching her.

Why can't I look this way to others? What does she have that I lack? Or is the problem something *I have*—this parasite gnawing at my brain?

I almost let her keep walking, just to see the natural way she'd walk down the street to her car. How she'd get in and attach her seatbelt, start the car, maybe take a moment to find music on the radio or put on a CD. I don't know which car is hers. I wonder what it smells like. Especially now—overnight upholstery odor eclipsed by the smell of her clean morning body, icy tea-tree hair, breath of coffee or orange juice or toothpaste.

I only know her white wine breath.

My hand opens the door. The overhead light goes on like a game show podium.

"There he goes," say people watching from windows. "He's going after her now. Get my phone in case he tries something."

She doesn't look my way. She doesn't know to look, because she doesn't expect me. She's walking away when I shut the door and press the key fob, locking the van with a honk. Her head turns slightly.

"Lili."

She stops. I see the moment she recognizes me, a look different than the one she gave when approaching my place, different than in the photo. This look knows who I am but isn't happy to see me, is confused and possibly frightened of me.

I wonder if "old whiteboy" Eric ever did anything like this. I don't like thinking he might have.

She ignored it when I touched her hair while she held me in her mouth. And despite that, she still smiled at me and invited me into her apartment, into her body. But now, standing outside her apartment building at this time of day, uninvited, this is a transgression.

I agree with the look on her face. I'm the creep they always wanted me to be.

"I'm sorry," I say, holding my hands up. Purple fingers. "I know this is weird. I don't mean anything by it."

She holds the strap of her purse and shifts her stance. "Why are you here?"

"We met under strange circumstances. At least strange for me. I wasn't expecting to meet anyone on the site, actually." I hope her eavesdropping neighbors can't infer what I mean by "site." But if they can, at least they'll know I'm not some predator who picked her at random; we have a history.

"Then why did you sign up?"

"Well, I *wanted* to meet someone, but I didn't think it would happen like it did. It's bad timing, because something's been happening with me, and I don't want to bring you into it. But I like you, and—"

She frowns. "Then why'd you tell me to fuck off?"

"What? When?"

"The text."

A horrible tickle crawls through me.

The unknown number.

"I meant that for someone else." I sound far away.

She just stares.

"I'm sorry, I—"

"I have to go, Alex." My name is cold in her mouth. The way she'll say it when she tells other people about this.

She goes, still turning to look at me as I climb into my van. She sits in her car, probably waiting for me to go first so I won't follow her. Maybe she'll memorize my license plate.

My parking job was so snug and I'm so distracted that I have to shift back and forth a few times to free myself. Then I come to the end of the block, stop at the sign, and wave to her.

She stares, stone-faced.

I turn and quickly reach the speed limit to show I'm really going.

Even at 7:30 a.m., my hash brown patty has the outer chew and inner squish of something day-old reheated. I sit on a plastic bench in a small alcove off the main dining room. The phrase "dining room" makes me think the cobalt sky I see through the sticker ads on the window should be a gray-orange sunset, and I should be eating a burger and fries on my way home, where I'd go to sleep like everyone else.

Sleep...

They'd stopped screaming before I ordered my meal, but the tone still hums in my head. I picture them lying on the floor of their room. One monitor shows my sad, hunched form on the bench; another looks through my eyes at the single bite I've taken from my McMuffin; another shows the regular peaks of my heartbeat, calm now; and the air in their room is thick with feedback, the computer's breathless scream.

They may not be human. There may not be a chip. They could have rays that read human thought and bodily functions, and laser-focused megaphones that project their human voice facsimiles into my ears alone.

I remember *Flatland*, a book narrated by a square who, like his fellow Flatlanders, lives in a world with only two dimensions. When a sphere visits Flatland, the square perceives only a 2D slice of it—a circle.

My point of contact with these beings is in the limited plane of my conscious thought.

One of them was assigned to follow me, and it performs transdimensional acrobatics like a jellyfish forever turning inside-out while its tendrils keep a tight hold on my mind. It speaks to me in voices I recognize and understand. It can move and act in ways I cannot—its opposable thumbs have opposable thumbs. I'm a paper doll in its voluminous clutches.

Maybe we've always seen and felt these beings slipping into our dimension, but we've mislabeled them. Our trees are their antennae sending and receiving signals. Or the clouds are their thoughts made visible in our atmosphere. Or the cotton of our clothes is their hair, and we pick it, spin it into fabric, and unwittingly drag these things tethered to us like balloons on the wrists of children.

Maybe the mental rumbling I feel as more people enter the restaurant and spill out to the tables around me—more eyes with whom to avoid contact, for whom to act casual, I am tired of pretending, all the world's a fucking goddamn stage—maybe this rumble comes from the interdimensional being attached to the back of my head.

The thing might feel the rubbery shard of hash brown lodged between my back teeth, and the scrape along my tongue as I try to dislodge it.

It seems to have a deep interest in human shame. Shame is its music or its food.

A woman appears with a tray at the edge of my vision. I think she looks at me briefly before sitting at the window.

I'm hunched over my tray like a ghoul, so I sit up, and my arms rise automatically to conceal my straightening as a stretch. Just in case she's in on this, and the observers are informing her with an earpiece or hand signals from the parking lot. Or maybe she can read my thoughts because the tentacles of her being are commingling with those of my being.

Because she was dim in my peripheral vision, I initially assumed she was Black, but when I pretend to look at something out the window and see that she isn't, I feel a chill of relief.

For the moment, "racist" is off the observers' list of possible accusations.

A male voice from around the corner says, "He wishes she was Black, I heard it."

No, I hoped she wasn't, so you couldn't—

"He's relieved she's white because he only wants to sit by white people," says a female voice.

Where are they watching from? Is it that woman with her toddler?

"Oh, so he's cool with *fucking* a Black person, but he won't *sit by* them?"

"That's what it sounds like." The mother doesn't seem to mind the man's strong language around her child.

Staring down at the word search printed on my placemat—seeing *MILKSHAKE* and *BIGMAC* and *FRENCHFRIES* glow among the gridded nonsense, finding that the letters around the edges of the grid are anagrams for *KILL* and *RAPE* and *RACIST*, and a cartoon cat points at a letter W, which I follow in a meandering zig-zag through the middle of the grid to spell *WE SEE ALL*—my hackles tell me that the woman seated near me suspects my casual act. She's tense.

Of course she is, considering this chatter from the other customers.

She's possibly my age, maybe a bit younger. I avoided getting a good look. Could be having breakfast before work. She's in a fitted purple jacket with the sleeves rolled up. Her straight brown hair hangs freshly washed and combed down her back, and her jeans hug her butt in an upside-down heart on the stool. Stop looking.

"He's thinking about it."

I'm not looking.

"Those jeans are so tight, Alex," an observer says, "you know she's looking to fuck."

The other adds, "Why'd she come into this tiny corner of the restaurant unless she's fishin' for you?"

"Hey!" the first screams. "The guy behind you is staring at your ass!"

I worry that holding my jaw shut will amplify their sound in my teeth for her to hear, but opening my mouth might create a better resonance chamber, so I clamp my lips between my teeth as a damper.

"He's a deviant! Watch out!"

She's on her phone. I can hear the little clicks as she types. Reporting to them.

"I don't know why she's taking the risk," the concerned mother says, "she really should move."

"There's too many people around for him to try anything sexual, thank god," says the guy.

"Still, he's clearly been pushed to the edge."

Pushed to the edge—is this empathy? Does she know this, or is she reading a wildness in my eyes?

"Alex, reach around and grab her tit."

"She's already wet for you, dude, we can tell. She's got a chip in her too."

My heart trips on its rhythm. I hadn't considered that this could be happening to strangers around me. How many do they have going right now, just in Los Angeles?

"Not many for now," one says, "but a strange side effect is that chips gravitate toward other chips."

"Yeah, somehow—we still don't know how—they find each other."

Are you talking to her right now, too? Are we just a couple of dolls you're knocking together?

"Nah, she's got other people working on her. We know them, though. We could talk to them for you, if you want. Put in a good word. But I'm telling you, you don't need our help."

"She found you, Alex. Go to her."

I imagine us escaping together into the woods.

Or atop a mountain with nothing but rocky cliffs on all sides, and we'd use a pulley system to get to our house. While at home, we'd pull up the ropes so no one else could use them. If the house ever caught fire, we'd just sit and watch it burn, knowing that even the fire department couldn't reach us. That's the price we'd pay for living as free as we could. Then we'd move on to somewhere equally remote.

We'd visit town maybe once a month for supplies. And knowing our chips were back in reception range, we'd train ourselves to keep our minds on a set list of things—no personal information or anything that could provide them a way back into our lives. We'd add a few jokes to play on the observers, like thoughts of moving to impossible parts of the globe. They'd think they got a hot lead, and scramble for transport to Siberia—but then we'd go nowhere.

I smile down at the word search, where I've found a path in the mess of letters that spells *EXIT*.

"That plan wouldn't work now, 'cause you just told us about it. You gotta wait till *after* you move to the mountaintop to think about that kind o' shit. Now grab her fucking tits!"

Maybe I'd run errands in town while think-repeating a word or phrase, for old time's sake. *Annoying, annoying, annoying...*

After some time together, this woman and I might be intimately close. But I would also train myself to never, ever think of her naked while we were within range of the observers.

"What a fucking gentleman. I guess chivalry isn't dead. Are you gonna do something about that boner, or what?"

I don't have a boner. She's not here for me. Please don't do anything to this girl. It's a goddamn miracle she hasn't already seen me and screamed.

"Yank her off the stool by her hair, then get on top of her and put your dick in her mouth."

My heart is fast, my palms are hot.

"Alex, her hair looks so soft. Probably smells amazing. What do you guess? Almond? Coconut? I think something fruity, judging by the look of her ass."

"He's not listening to us anymore. Our man's on a mission. Grab her hair, Alex. Pull her head back far enough to bury your face in her tits."

"Wait, no, see if you can get your dick in her mouth *and* your face in her tits at the same time."

"Oh, that would be amazing. Alex, do that!"

The mental images are so strong, I can feel her hair in my fist. Like the zing of lemon juice before it hits your tongue. I close my eyes. But I worry I'll open them to find the lapels of her jacket against my face, her smell in my nose, her screams in my ears.

"She won't scream as much with your dick in her mouth."

"You'll miss your chance."

Get the fuck out of my head! I don't want to do any of these things!

"You popped a boner, dude. That's intent."

Intent to do what? She's attractive. That just happens sometimes.

"No, you popped a boner in a restaurant, you sick fuck. While we were feeding you rapey ideas."

That's not why. Fuck you, that's not why.

"Your body doesn't lie."

My muscles hold tight. I want to squeeze myself so small that I fit through a hole into the other dimension. Rip the tendrils from the back of my skull. I'd like to see the truth now, please. I've been so patient.

A tapeworm can travel through a person's bloodstream to the brain and lay its eggs there, where they're attacked by the person's immune system and never hatch; they become cysts that cause seizures and lesions. It's a horrible mistake of the natural world that benefits neither the tapeworm nor the human. Yes, the Lord works in mysterious ways.

All of this could be explained by my mind lacquering parasite eggs in a protective shell, like pearls in an oyster. Maybe this has nothing to do with shame. Maybe my shame and fear are side-effects, like when a lesion or a tumor or a ruptured blood vessel in the brain changes someone's personality. A tossed pebble creates ripples upon waves upon currents upon tides.

I crumple the greasy paper on the tray and finish my burnt coffee, staring into the cup, watching the dark water disappear into me. I look at the pastel-stripe wallpaper as I stand and go to the trashcan. I ask a cashier for the restroom key while averting my eyes.

As I walk away, she tells a guy at the soda machine, "He's gonna go jerk it now."

"Fucking pervert," the guy says. "Got an eyeful of that girl, and now he can't help himself."

"Place your bets!" says the man in the dining room.

Someone laughs.

Another shushes.

"Pull her hair! Grab her tits! Do it now!"

Halfway to the bathroom, I stop and loudly say, "No."

The woman at the window turns her head to listen. She knows this is our moment. I'll speak for both of us.

"Can we say the jig is up?" I ask the people at the far tables. "Call a truce?"

They look at me.

"What does the end of this look like?" I walk toward their section.

The employees at the register are watching me too.

"What do I have to do? Shrivel up and disappear? Attack someone? What will satisfy you?"

They look surprised. Some point their phone cameras at me.

"Or are you all just day players? Extras? Do you even know what this is?"

A fryer beeps. Even the employees in the back are watching through the heated shelves of food.

"Sir, do you need something?" says the cashier.

Her calling me "sir" makes my neck go cold. It's almost more insulting than any of the alternatives.

I turn to her and say, "Stop!" My voice rings in the space. "Just stop everything now! That's what I need. What do I have to say to get you all to stop? I don't know what they're paying you, but it's *blood money*!"

Another employee says, "Sir, please leave."

The cashier tells him quietly, "He's got the bathroom key."

I hold up my hands. "I've said my piece." I turn to the customers. "I won't bother you anymore. I *beg* you to do the same for me." I motion to the woman by the window. "And the rest of us."

She's got her phone aimed at me too. Maybe she's just another plant after all. Or she's recording this for herself, to watch when this is over and shiver with sense-memory adrenaline from our moment of liberation.

When I walk back to our section, she shifts on her stool and holds her phone tighter with both hands.

I smile. "You know I'm not the one you have to worry about." I continue to the bathroom door. "Good luck."

I use the sticky key to enter a cream-colored space with a mirror and sink on one wall, a toilet and urinal on the other. The door locks behind me, and for a moment I'm safe. My whole body pounds and vibrates. The light is harshly real. I could stay here forever.

But they'd call the police, bust in, plant a gun or a bomb and lock me up. They're probably calling the police now. I shouldn't stay longer than it would take to pee and wash my hands—quick enough that they can't claim I masturbated.

I look in the mirror, and my face pulls into an expression that I hope inspires empathy in whoever or whatever is watching. I stare into my eyes—into their eyes.

Maybe they're gone. Maybe they've finally pulled the plug.

I try to see into my ear canal until my eyes hurt.

I wonder if this room is the inside of a hollow pearl lodged in the mind of a greater being. And that being is dragging a magnet across its flesh, desperate to remove me, the parasite. When the magnet nears the pearl, the air will turn deafening.

I SENT PLEAS INTO the air all the way to Gavin's apartment. They consisted only of the word itself, "please," because thinking directly about Gavin would give away my impulse to go to him. As soon as his face flashed in my mind I pretended he didn't exist, and I pictured a hardware store a few neighborhoods away to throw them off the scent. I made a mental shopping list of raw materials for weapons, traps, and reinforcements. I imagined tripwires in my doorways, buckets of corrosive solution poised to fall, strips of clear tape holding nails point-up on my floor. All while saying, "Please, please, please..." and driving to Gavin's instead.

Outside his building I stopped pleading aloud to avoid looking crazy, but I still shaped my breath into the word, a silent seamless mantra—someone would hear it only if they put their ear to my lips.

Now I stand at his door clutching a rolled copy of the *PennySaver*, mustering the courage to knock, imagining that after I knock he might not answer, and I imagine all the ways I might find him "silenced"—whole or in pieces, cut or blown apart, hung or suffocated or poisoned to look like a suicide.

He opens the door, travel mug in hand, and screams.

"I need your help, please." The expression on my face feels much worse than what I saw in the restroom mirror. "Please, can you help?"

He pats his heart. "Jesus Christ. Of course, sure, what's going on?" He steps aside, and I enter.

"I need to lock myself somewhere. Can I hole up here?" I squeeze the *PennySaver*, willing him to shut and lock the door. "No one's been here since I was here yesterday, right?"

"No—what? I mean, yeah, I had a date over last night."

"Do you trust her?"

"What?"

"How long have you known her? Did she leave anything here?"

"Sit down. What the fuck are you talking about? Do you need water or something?" He stays by the door, still holding his mug and keys. "Hey, breathe. You gotta slow your breathing down."

He looks at my purple-dyed fingers, and I'm embarrassed. They make me look like I put my hand in something strange.

I speak softly so my voice doesn't carry. "Shut the door, please. Lock it. I'm really sorry. I didn't want to bring this here. I just can't do it myself anymore."

He shuts and locks the door. But there are still the windows. There are still ducts and vents and spaces between the studs in the walls. Closed cupboard doors, crevices under the boards under the carpet, apartments under the floor, rooms behind me, rooms around corners, entire streets and cities of stacked-up, closed-box buildings. So much of the world is invisible all the time, infinite places for them to hide.

I sit against the wall under a window, which conceals me on that side, and out the other window is empty blue sky.

"What's going on?"

"Close those blinds, please." A drone painted sky-blue would be invisible beyond a certain distance, and able to zoom in on me through the window. A red dot could appear between my eyes.

Gavin draws the vertical blinds, which sway and reveal scissoring slices of blue, then settle. He says, "You gotta tell me. What."

I make him promise that he's my friend. That no one ever approached him about me or any kind of test or observation. I have to believe we were set up as college dorm roommates by luck of the draw, not within the parameters of some grand experiment. I have to believe that during our years living together, he wasn't keeping notebooks or videotapes.

He promises that he knows nothing about anything like that, and that he's my friend.

I ask what he knows about Lili.

"Who's Lili?"

"Gavin, I have something inside me that monitors everything I do. And I think it could control me completely if I let it. Thoughts, actions, everything."

"You mean... your brain?" He's not joking.

I feel safe enough in the spotlight of his incredulous stare to relax my own vigilance, if only a little. The muscles loosen in my neck and my knees. "Do you have a flashlight and tweezers?"

"Yes... Why?"

***

I sit on the lid of the toilet. Gavin stands over me, shines a penlight down into my ear canal and takes pictures with his phone. He shows me each image as it's taken. At first glance, the glint of a hair or the shadow of a hump always looks like metal.

Something about having someone I trust shine a flashlight on me—into me—puts me in another circle of protection.

While he searches, I narrate a tangled version of important points from the past two weeks, starting after our camping trip. He's impressed to hear about the sex site, says he never thought I'd do something like that, and he's proud of me for taking such a leap into the unknown. I don't like hearing this, because it means my actions were somehow extraordinary, which makes me a good candidate for observation.

He wiggles his eyebrows and asks if "Lili" is someone I met on the site. I tell him she was the Skype scammer, and that I haven't met anyone from the site in person. I don't know why; it feels easier.

After we've confirmed and reconfirmed that there's nothing in either ear, nor in my nostrils, nor at the back of my throat, he says, "I think you're good."

He's probably worried I'll make him look in my ass. I hesitate, but there's no way to do a thorough search without special tools. And he's already been gracious enough to take his day off to search my head.

He gives me a sleeping pill and insists he'll stay home with the door locked while I sleep.

His couch is an L, so I lie on the long part and he sits at the short end. He flips channels. I've got a pillow from his bed with a clean pillowcase from his closet. He has cedar chips in his closet, and the combined smell of cedar and closet must on the pillowcase teleports me into my kitchen cupboard. Then when I open my eyes I'm back in Gavin's living room. Both are places of relative comfort.

As I sink into sleep, a familiar voice says, "You thought you could get rid of me. Well, you should know I'm here to stay, baby."

The slow wave of sleep breaks against a rock wall. I open my eyes.

On TV a woman in a torn jogging suit, with dirt smudges on her cheeks and forehead and a few leaves in her carefully-mussed hair, points a gun at a man with spiky gelled hair and a jutting chin of contoured stubble.

"Posey," the man says, "it wasn't my idea! I love you!"

Gavin's phone rings. He takes it from the coffee table and goes to turn off the TV.

"No, it's cool," I say, "leave it on."

He takes the phone into his bedroom and shuts the door. I get up and creep closer to hear what he says. It's work-related.

"Don't lie to me, Clayton," says Posey on TV. "You and the Scartellos always wanted to get rid of me."

I take my *PennySaver* from the coffee table, slip it into my pillowcase and lie back on the couch.

"But I haven't been involved with the Scartellos since Dorothy came out of her coma! And they were only using me to find out what I knew about Mayor Branding's reelection campaign!"

The show is a soap opera called *Time and Again*. I remember captioning this episode.

After the long, backstory-infused argument they're having now, Posey shoots Clayton in the leg. He falls, knocks his head on the desk, and passes out. Then Posey ties him up and enlists the help of Dorothy's father—Reverend Jonathan Millsmith—to put Clayton in a burlap sack with several raw steaks, and they hang it from a tree in the woods far outside of town.

Posey won't find out for another three episodes that it wasn't Clayton or the Scartellos who drugged her post-workout smoothie and buried her alive, but her own brother Hank, come for revenge after their parents died and left their entire estate to Posey.

Still, after ditching Clayton in the woods she worries that he's innocent. She tries to relax in a bubble bath but is tortured by flashbacks from being buried alive, plus visions of a ghostly, judgmental Clayton with dark circles around his eyes and clumpy white makeup in his stubble.

Meanwhile, a well-trained bear walks onto the soundstage set of fake trees drenched in blue nighttime light, and the bear takes an interest in the hanging sack.

A guilt-ridden Posey jumps in her car and speeds out to the woods. When she arrives, the bear attacks her car and pops two of the tires. She finally scares it away by flashing her headlights and honking the horn.

Then she unties the sack and frees Clayton. She apologizes profusely, and he is strangely understanding. He's a skilled ER surgeon, so he uses strips from the burlap sack to bandage the gunshot wound in his leg.

Posey's cell phone is dead, and Clayton strikes two rocks together to make a fire to keep them warm through the night. In the car trunk they find a leftover bottle of wine from her parents' funeral. She splits it with Clayton to dull his pain, and they take the steaks from the burlap sack to cook over the fire.

The last shot of the episode is them kissing by the fire, seen through a tangle of leaves. Her brother Hank watches from the bushes.

But this time I only see as far as the end of the argument, when Clayton is shot and knocked out, before the tide in me swells over the rocks and spills across my consciousness.

I drift as Posey wipes the tears from her eyes and Reverend Millsmith consoles her. "This son of a bitch will never hurt you again, Posey. We'll make sure of that."

I HEAR A VOICE. The room is dark except streetlight through the open door, and Gavin is talking to someone. My heart speeds up.

"Thanks," Gavin says quietly. He closes and locks the door.

I shift my elbows under myself, planning a route backwards off the couch and through the apartment. If we weren't on the second floor, I could dive out his bedroom window.

He stops in the dark when he realizes I'm awake. "Oh, hey."

He turns on the light, and when my eyes adjust I see he's holding two pizza boxes.

"Hungry?"

***

One is pepperoni, the other is sausage and mushrooms. After the pill-induced sleep, my brain feels like it's emerged from a steamy shower into cool air. But I pretend I'm still groggy and not ready to eat, until Gavin takes the first slice. Sausage.

He bites it. Chews. Swallows. Nothing happens.

Then I take a slice of sausage, trying to randomize where I take it from—not quite my side of the pie, but also not right next to where Gavin's slice was. Despite this tactical thinking, I acknowledge that getting poisoned or drugged would mean discovering the truth. And if my best friend is involved, what's the point of living, anyway?

"So," Gavin says, "when I got off the phone you were out and snoring, but I'm embarrassed to admit I watched the rest of that show."

"I captioned that one. Fun episode."

"So you know about the bear."

"A real fuckin' bear." I shake my head.

"They put the dude in a sack, hung it from a tree—in a soundstage, sure—but then they got a *real bear* to show up and knock the sack around. And the guy's definitely still in it! It's not just a bunch of pillows or whatever."

"Yeah, you can see him moving."

"I guess they trimmed the bear's claws? And it's trained, of course. But what if the sack swung the wrong way and hit him in the nose or something, and he got pissed?"

"Movie bear. Doesn't get pissed, I guess."

Next he takes a slice of pepperoni, which means I can try it too. I take a slice next to his to maintain unpredictability.

"Speaking of your work," he says, "are you gonna go tonight?"

I sit back in the chair and stare at the pizzas, both missing slices like countdown clocks. This is yet another moment that I wish could last forever. Actually, not this moment but a few minutes back, when we were talking about the soap opera bear and eating pizza on the couch in Gavin's living room. All the familiar objects on the shelves around us. There's the weed dragon Kobayashi curled around its glass spire next to a stack of Gavin's books about various climbers who overcame obstacles and/or died on mountains all over the world. Gavin's shoes by the door. Mine are there too.

A feeling surges down my back like scales pushing from my skin. "I don't know if they'll be there tonight."

Gavin looks at the stub of his crust. "Have they been there before?"

"Close. Outside, in the parking lot. Maybe the building next door."

"So they've got full coverage on your life? All the places?"

"All the places." I tap my temple.

"When you told me this morning, I didn't know what to say. It's... really a crazy thing."

The external acknowledgment makes my chest tremble. Part of me has started to acclimate after so many false alarms and false victories. Maybe that's the experiment. For the observers' presence to accrete onto my life.

I say, "Yeah, I wish I knew..."

"I don't mean anything by this, and I know you're not fucking around..." He stares at the bitten end of his crust. "But do you think it's possible you're... imagining them?"

"Like just voices in my head?"

He shrugs and nods.

"It's..." A shiver moves through me.

"Maybe you could talk to someone."

The resigned part of me pushes out its tendrils, wants to pull itself apart, wishes it didn't have to exist, is encouraged by his words.

"It's possible, I guess, and I've wondered about it. But I never let myself stop to seriously consider it." My eyes sting. I remove my glasses. "Because if it's *real*, and I let my guard down for one second... that's when..." I put the slice down and hold my palms over my eyes. My mouth grimaces. A warm line slides down my chin.

Alarm bells sound in my brain, orders zap to my muscles to bend my face back into neutrality, or to hide my face in my arms and hold my breath to squelch vulnerable sounds. Be still until it passes. Don't let them win.

Is this the result they want? Why not let them win? Maybe telling another person is the end condition of the test. To see how long I'd keep this weird secret to myself. They could be coming up the stairs right now.

They know. My heart rate tells them I'm crying. And the ringing in my ears. The muffled head-down sobs in my arms. The way my torso convulses. Part of me hopes the shifting pressure in my head is the chip self-destructing, releasing me from their stare and dissolving like they never existed.

But even with my chip gone, if they got to Gavin—maybe something in the pizza, maybe something else a long time ago—they have a front-row seat through *his* eyes and ears, filling their hard drives and copying to numerous backup drives at several megabytes per second.

Fans whir, tower lights flash.

AT MY DESK I feel like a different person.

Gavin lent me one of his T-shirts, since I'd stunk up my own by cleaning the mess in my apartment, driving miles through the night, sleeping all day on his couch, and anxiously sweating throughout. I showered with his soap, dried off with one of his towels, and brushed my teeth with his toothpaste on my finger—not as good as a toothbrush, but it gave me the fresh taste of having slept, and it chilled my teeth in the night air when I left.

The smallish collar sits higher on my throat than my own shirts. I hook a finger, careful not to stretch it as I pull it away from my neck. The shirt is red and has a logo of jagged yellow letters: RZT. I don't know what it means, but I never thought to ask until now, since I'm wearing it. The shirt had spent months draped over the back of Gavin's chair in our dorm room, where it wasn't a shirt but part of the environment, a piece of his presence in our shared space. Now it's like a talisman from that time—an invisibility cloak.

I wonder if my wardrobe change fooled the observers.

Seeing red at the bottom of my view, I think about how I don't have any red shirts. Nothing so bright in any color, really.

When I emerged from his apartment tonight, for a delicious moment they may have kept their eyes fixed on his door or his window, still waiting for a glimpse of my sorry face, when I had in fact already slipped away.

***

The clattering of keyboards fades down the dark hall and laps at the bright chamber of the kitchen.

As I wash the coffeepot in the sink, a voice says, "Alexssssss..."

I close the tap and hear laughter. "Hello?"

"You wanna be someone else now? You think wearing your friend's clothes will make us go away?"

"I thought fucking up the chip with the magnet made you go away," I say.

"Yeah, you fell for it, you stupid piece of shit! Like every other time. Hey, I want to show you something. Listen to this..."

A tone fades up in the background—the feedback tone that had supposedly hurt their ears so badly the night before.

"It's a fuckin' keyboard, Alex! Gotcha again!"

The pitch of the feedback jumps around, plays *Mary Had a Little Lamb*, then blurts some dissonant chords punched with a fist.

My body becomes heavy, and I walk differently back to the coffee machine. "I didn't come rushing to your house, did I?"

"No. You were gonna let us sit here in torture."

"Of course I was, because fuck you."

"Machine acting up?" A different voice, not tinny and muffled.

"Huh?" I turn.

Aaron stands in the doorway.

"Yeah, I couldn't get the—but there it goes." I push the pot into place below the nozzle.

Aaron goes to the sink. "Feeling better?"

"Yeah, it was a food thing probably, or flu, I don't know. But yeah, way better."

"Keith said there's a package for you." Keith is the day shift supervisor. "He would've put it on your desk, but he saw it on his way out. It should still be at the front door."

"Great, thanks." A package? Direct communication? The grand finale?

While the coffee trickles into the pot, I walk past reception to the front door, a door we night shifters never use because the parking lot is in the back. Through the glass door I see a box out in the cold night air next to the standing ashtray, as if it's taking a break. Written on it are Matt's name and return address. It's the router he configured.

I'm touched he went to the trouble, but I stare at it the way the ghost of a person who starved to death might look at a bowl of hot soup left at the feet of their corpse.

I don't know how long the box has been here. Even if it was originally from Matt, it's been outside where anybody could grab it, open it, tamper with or replace its contents. Maybe I'll open it to find the router smashed and a Post-It note saying, *gotcha again!* Or they used Matt's box to conceal a bomb or toxic gas. Maybe opening it will trigger a burst of glitter with a card on a spring reading: *FAGGOT.*

But the worst-case scenario is to open the box and find an internet router, normal in appearance, and to plug it in and find it in working order. Because that could mean yet another parasite that I won't discover until later, possibly never.

I'll have to get on the phone with Matt before I use it so he and I can compare the configurations he made with its current settings. Unless the observers made it lie about its settings...

I'm tired again. Like cresting a massive sand dune only to find that the land ahead rolls up and down similar dunes into the horizon, past the curve of the planet, on and on.

I open the door—watch the street, the bushes, the dark shapes of parked cars—and use my foot to nudge the package into the building like a stray cat that might bite, or have fleas, or shed flakes of mange, or shit writhing tapeworm segments everywhere. And I take the box to my desk, turning it over in my hands, examining the tape for signs of having been opened and re-taped. I wait to hear hissing gas or see smoke. Check the labels to see if they were pulled from another box. At any second, it could explode in my face. Then I slide it under the far corner of my desk and walk back down the hall to the bathroom.

It's bright. White walls. No cameras, unless the fire sprinkler in the ceiling has an eye. Maybe one behind the grate of the heat vent. Or in the floor drain. The sink and mirror are on the wall shared with the sign company next door. I look at the mirror. Knock on it. Would be easy to cut through the wall and make this a two-way mirror.

One of them could be standing on the other side in the dark, staring back at me. So close. If I stare long enough, maybe I'll catch the shine of a computer screen, I'll see part of their face or some of the room. I could thrust my fist into the mirror and grab them by the neck, pull them through the jagged hole and kill them with my bare hands.

Then I'd have proof—a parasite successfully extracted, crumpled and dead on the floor. The others would stand framed in broken glass, horrified, then flee to burrow somewhere else. I'd turn the dead one over to the authorities. Those two cops. They'd see. They'd analyze the body to identify it. Maybe it would have no identity. A drone, animated and spoken through by something else, something bigger.

"Can you see us?" The voice is low in timbre now. Calm. Confident, but curious.

"Show me." I speak quietly because there's no lock on the bathroom door, and I don't want someone to walk in on me talking to myself again. "Shine a light on your side."

"There is no light on our side."

They feel almost tangible behind my reflection. What do they mean, no light on their side? Are they not in the building next door, but inside the wall? Or between here and another place? If I could see them, would I only see pieces of them, shifting in and out of my world from somewhere else? What would those pieces look like?

I look at my own form and imagine it straddling dimensions.

***

Against my better judgment, I check my email. There's a two-day-old message from Dad. It says:

Hey, it's me.

I tried calling, but it keeps going straight to voicemail. If your phone is turned off and you're still having trouble with it, could you just respond to this so mom and I know you're okay?

Matt told me about your router, apparently someone did something to it? Probably just to leech free internet off of you. He said he's sending you a new one he's configuring himself. I think that's a good idea. He said it should arrive in the next couple of days, so hopefully that will do the trick.

He said you thought your phone might be hacked, but he told me that's not really something just anyone can do. It's more for the government to find terrorists and things like that.

That isn't to say I don't believe you. You know more about what's happening than I do. But do you ever wonder if maybe the router problem got you thinking, and now you're imagining the worst case scenario? You've always had a powerful imagination. It's one of your strengths. I know I have trouble shutting my brain off once I start thinking about something. You probably got that from me. If that's the case, I'm sorry about that.

We love you, and we're proud of you.

Love,

Dad

"Alex, as one of the government scientists being paid to watch you shit and jerk off, I'd like to say we're proud of you too."

I open a reply and write, *I'm sorry I didn't respond. I'm fine.*

"Ha, fine. You think you're fine?"

I've had my phone turned off this whole time. I don't know if Matt told you, but I called him from a pay phone just in case. He was very helpful, and I'm eager to get the router and have a clean connection.

Of course, I'm not sure I should even take it home.

I'm writing this on my work computer because I'm still offline at home. I'm tired of feeling like they're seeing everything.

"You didn't believe us when we told you—we see *every*thing."

The router is a good start. And I've got another idea that I won't mention here in case they see this.

"Can't wait to find out what that is."

"Are you getting any of it?"

"It's too fuzzy to make out. We'll have to wait until he focuses on it."

"He's probably bluffing anyway."

But everything is fine.

"The witnesses at McDonald's submitted their videos to the police. The girl you almost raped agreed to testify. They traced your license plate and found where you work."

I'll call you once this is over.

"They're waiting for you outside."

I love you too.

-Alex

WHEN I ARRIVE AT Gavin's in the morning, he mentions the camping trip.

"If you're up for it, we'll go tonight when Eli and I get off work."

"I'm definitely up for it," I say.

"You're sure? We can totally call it off and stay here instead. I didn't tell Eli anything, but he'd understand."

"No, I'd like to get away a bit."

"Cool. You can go pack your stuff today and be here when I get back?"

Right, what was I thinking? He doesn't have an extra pair of boots in my size, nor an extra pack. I have to go home to get my own things.

"Sure," I say, "Absolutely." Then I think about it. "When're you packing?"

He points at his pack leaned against the wall. "Done last night while you were at work. I knew you'd say yes." He winks and hands me his apartment key. "Lock up when you go."

"Don't worry. I'll be very careful."

***

Climbing the stairs to my apartment I've got the hammer at my side, gripped tight but swinging, casual, as if on its way back to the toolbox.

I stare at the door like an actor in the wings. This is my cue, don't miss it. My neighbors watch through their windows like stagehands gripping the curtain ropes, waiting to pull.

I unlock the door and push. But the door doesn't make its familiar unsticking sound.

A slideshow of reasons flickers by—they forced the door, so now it doesn't close the same; they replaced the door with one that looks exactly like mine, but it's packed with audiovisual sensors or an amplifier for the signal from my chip; they booby-trapped the door with something wedged in the frame, triggered by— But a booby trap has gone off, a tiny explosion: four strips of paper, each dyed a different color—red, yellow, green, blue—spin and swoop and settle on the floor.

"Some trap, ya fuckin' idiot!"

"What the fuck did you think was gonna happen?"

I hadn't thought it through.

"Hope you kept that card you made, you fucking psycho, so you can check your super-duper secret code!"

The card is in my pocket. But now that the strips have fallen it's impossible to know whether they were still in the correct order. They could have come here, but I'll never know.

"Yeah, check the colors! Are they in the right order, Alex, you stupid fuck?"

But I know they've been here, because everything looks as I left it—in a suspicious way, as if all the objects in the room are holding their breath, hoping I won't notice that something's amiss.

I hold my breath too, and listen for the thump of footsteps or the swish of socks. The place is small; I'll only hear a couple of steps before they reach me. I raise the hammer.

Behind the coat closet door I find coats. I plunge the hammer into them to make sure. Then I close and lock the front door.

Had I left the blinds open that much? I would've closed them. They probably cracked them to signal to each other between our windows. In the strips of daylight I see a sprinkle of sugar I missed around the base of the couch. There are bits of broken plastic on the floor and the kitchen counter. The carcass of the smoke detector still lies in the sink.

Footsteps keep almost rushing in from the bedroom and bathroom.

I push the bathroom door until the knob hits the wall. I peer into the tub. Nobody crouches there. They'll knock me into the tub. It's the ideal place to beat me to death, because the blood will rinse down the drain.

I anticipate them charging from the bedroom now, over and over again, hands held high or low, lunging headfirst, brandishing a gun or a bat, face snarling, face screaming, face laughing, the face I recognize from next door, a face I've never seen, a face I maybe saw but couldn't remember where, a face smeared by a nylon stocking. My hammer hand twitches.

Did I hear the front door open and close? Are they waiting in the entryway to slip out? If they have a key, they can lock it behind them and I'll never know.

But I have to check the bedroom first because they're probably hiding in there, praying I'll have these exact thoughts and go re-check the front door. Instead, I'm closing in.

"We've been doing this a long time," one says quietly, not to me. "I'm exhausted, Alex is exhausted, and I can tell you're exhausted. Let's just stop."

"Stop? And lose all our progress? Are you nuts?"

I push the bedroom door until it hits the wall.

"What progress? He's terrified of leaving his apartment, and terrified of staying home. What more can we do? We're just gonna keep this up forever?"

"That's what we agreed."

The dim morning bedroom looks like someone else's room. The foil is silent because the window is closed. On my desk, the origami stars are still in their chaotic constellation around my laptop.

"No, that's just what we told him. I had no intention of doing this forever."

I crouch to look under the bed, listening for the closet to open, anticipating the flash of a gunshot from under the bed into an ankle or foot. Then my eye. Only vague dust bunnies in the dark.

"Shut up," the other says. "Now."

I open the closet from the side.

"Alex, can you hear us?"

Nobody rushes out. I lean forward, search for swatches of unfamiliar fabric between my own hanging clothes. I thrust the hammer in, ready for the dull thud of a ribcage or the squish of a stomach.

Or the flash and crack of a gun into my body or face.

"Alex. Can you hear us."

I say, "What did you do here? Poison my food? Plant a gas bomb?"

"We did all of those things. And we're doing the same at your friend Gavin's place. Better hope you trigger our trap before he does. Wouldn't you feel terrible if you caused the death of your best friend?"

I check the rooms for footprints, anything. But everything is dubiously inconspicuous. And I'd been so distracted before I left, I don't have memories to compare.

Quiet again, not to me: "We have to stop."

"We will never stop."

"So this is the rest of our lives? Shouting at him while he tries to ignore us? At work? At home? On dates? At his wedding we'll make him fuck up his vows or trip while he's dancing?"

"You think someone'll *marry* this sick fuck?"

"Will we mock the births of his children? Make him say inappropriate things in PTA meetings? Do you realize that when we go to his kid's high school graduation, we might be *fifty* fucking years old? Still in this goddamn house?"

"He'll move at some point. We'll move too."

They might see that this conversation is making my heart race. I ache for such elegant timing, to have their sticky web tear apart just before I go on a weekend camping trip, leave them to bicker and blame each other, while far away I immerse myself in silence, wind, birds, rustling leaves...

"And then what? We keep going? If his wife dies first, do we laugh through his eulogy? Do we do this until *he* dies?"

"Yes. And we bring popcorn to his fucking funeral."

Crickets. Tonight I'll fall asleep to crickets.

"But you know he'll be gone before any of that can happen. He can't go to the grocery store without ogling babies or doing racist shit. You think he's gonna have a fucking kid?"

"Ogling babies? He's barely looked at anyone for a week! This is the end. It's over."

"This is only the beginning."

"I've got other shit to do."

Well said. So do I. I take my pack from the closet and lay it on the bed. I dig through the tarp, first aid kit, poncho, sunscreen...

"If you go, you jeopardize everything we've built."

"What is our ultimate purpose?"

"You know we can't say. He'll hear us."

"It's been so long, you don't even remember anymore."

"If you really want out, it can be arranged."

"Thank you."

I almost gasp out loud. One down, one to go. I wonder how long before the stubborn one gives up too.

"Why are you locking the door? He's not coming over here, he's going camping."

"I'm locking it for you."

"But you said I could leave."

I unscrew the nozzle on my air mattress and roll it tight on the wood floor, squish it under my knees, and listen.

"No, I said your exit from the experiment can be arranged. But I'm not finished, and you're not gonna fuck it up!"

"Where did you get a gun?"

"I've had it the whole time, in case you tried something."

I assumed they were *both* armed, but by now I'm used to being wrong.

"Me? I'm your fucking *partner*! Alex is the one you've gotta worry about! He's gonna get us for this—we've already had too many close calls! I want out."

A tinny thump, a crash.

"Ow! What the fuck are you doing?! Alex! Alex, can you hear me?"

I gather boxers, hiking socks, T-shirts, hoodie, fold them, roll them...

"He's duct-taping me to the chair! Alex, help!"

Tape rips in my ears.

"Alex, I'm sorry for everything! This was all a huge mistake! Please, he's gonna murder me!"

If one murders the other, that's one fewer observer to worry about. And the remaining one would be so busy covering up the murder he'd have no time to watch me. He'd probably destroy his equipment and fade into obscurity, on the lam in his own paranoid nightmare.

But if he's well-connected enough to kill his partner and make the evidence disappear...

Or if—a big if—I'm to entertain the idea that the observers aren't human, are somehow beyond human, the "two" I perceive might actually be one, and this power struggle is just a Punch and Judy show, a trap, a predator mimicking the call of a human in distress.

Or this is another test. A morality test—does the tortured come to the rescue when one of his torturers is put in harm's way? I wonder if this twist was triggered by something I've done. Described in their documentation as something like: *When the subject seeks refuge beyond their primary residence, allow time for security and confidence to strengthen in them. Then, at the first sign of this feeling's inevitable plateau and decline, one observer is to turn against the other. Coordinate with your partner ahead of time to decide which role you will take. The "victimized" observer is to request the subject's help. It is imperative that the subject's response to the scenario be carefully detailed in your report—time elapsed before initial reaction, reaction modes (apathetic, nihilistic, pleased, ecstatic, angry, furious, violent, et cetera), as well as the subject's actions and comportment following the scene's arrival.*

"You've gotta help me, Alex!"

Or it could be genuine dissent.

"If I survive, I'll explain everything!"

I search the cabinets and dark fridge, collect ramen noodles, cheese, bagels...

"Alex, he's lying about the gun and the chair. He's just sitting here next to the open door. Actually, I'd *love* for him to leave, but he thinks this act will get you to come over so we can tape *you* to a chair. I told him you're not stupid enough to fall for it."

I pause, holding the sack of bagels. *But I heard you say he couldn't leave.*

"Of course I did, to follow his lead. If there's no continuity, you wouldn't believe a thing we say."

"Alex, if he kills me, he'll eventually kill *you*!"

"Bullshit. I'm the nice one."

"You're the nice one? You taped me to a chair and have a fucking gun on me!"

"I've got a girlfriend, Alex. The guy claiming to be the victim here is single, because *he's* the unstable one."

"Fuck yourself. You haven't seen your girlfriend in months."

"And when he did have a girlfriend, he *hit* her."

"That's a fucking lie!"

I push the smoke detector pieces aside in the sink, fill my water bottles and slip them into the pack. Then I carry the pack to the door.

"You can't just leave! Look out your window. See our blinds?" I hear the metallic rustle of cheap Venetian blinds. "Look at our blinds! You gotta believe me, Alex, see our blinds?!"

"Stop it!"

I go to the window and peer across the alley. No movement.

"Did you see, Alex? Please, did you see?"

No.

"I was moving the blinds with my head! But he pushed my chair to the other side of the room. You gotta believe me!"

I pick up the hammer and go back to the door.

"Alex, please, I can tell you how to get in."

"If you come here, Alex, I'll shoot both of you."

I wedge my hiking-booted foot behind the door and open it a little to look outside before leaving.

"There's a key under the back doormat."

"Shut the fuck up!"

"Just jump over the—mmph!"

I pause halfway down the stairs. Sure, many people probably keep a spare key under a doormat. And many of those people probably leave it at the back door, where it's less likely someone will stumble upon it.

But if I jump the wall in the alley, and if I *happen* to see a doormat at the back door, and if that doormat *happens* to have a key underneath it...

"Yes! Please, god, Alex, do that!"

I'd have proof. I'd go back out to the sidewalk to call the police in the open. For once I'd want people to see me. As many eyes as possible. And while explaining the situation, I might see a flash in one of the windows and hear a muffled crack. Or the front door might blow open and the guy might come pounding toward me, eyes dumb as orange navels.

I'd stand my ground, and the gun barrel would stare me in the face before spitting clean through it.

I light a cigarette and find the most chaotic music on the radio, then dial a bit past it to distort the signal. The complaints in my skull become muddy buzzing.

"Xxs, xxsxsx! Xsxxxx, ss x xxxs xxx x xsxxxs xx sxxx, xxxss xxx xxsx sx?"

"Sxx, xss xxsxxsx, xxxsxx xx ss!"

The buzz continues all the way to Gavin's. When I park and turn off the car, it becomes clear again.

"Xx xxs sxxx xs xxssxxxsx, xxs gonna kill both of us! Come back, Alex!"

After the radio noise, the cul-de-sac's air rushes in like a quiet sandstorm under the faraway whine of his voice.

"Don't worry, your friend's apartment is safe."

"That's a lie, Alex, he's not even here anymore! He's talking on a headset! He's out there with you!"

"Shut the fuck up!"

How did he arrive before me?

"We know a back road that's faster. He's already in the apartment waiting for you!"

I keep my actions as fluid as possible—no hesitation: enter the building, ready the key going up the stairs, unlock the door, expect nothing as I open it, there will be nobody here, even though somebody here would mean the end, so I'm not afraid of somebody here, but there will be nobody, step inside, close the door, lock it.

I drop my pack on the couch and walk from room to room.

No tripwires, no gas bombs, nothing happens.

There's no more screaming, either. Maybe they cut their mics. My cavalier attitude could be pride before the fall.

But there is something from below, vibrating through the carpet, a familiar vocal pattern of complaint. I focus and make out: "What's he doing up there?"

It's a smoother voice, possibly female.

"Just pacing around. Thump, thump, thump, all over the place."

Gavin's downstairs neighbor hears my footsteps. I kneel and put my ear to the floor.

"Driving me nuts!"

I remove my boots. Then I lie on the couch, still waiting for someone to rush in from every direction. Kicks against the door. Shots through the window.

But I've done it. My bag is packed and ready, retrieved from ground zero.

I remember the pizza in the fridge, so I take a couple slices—their countdown clocks advance that many ticks—and put them in the microwave.

"Now what's he doing up there? That's the loudest microwave I've ever heard!"

I'm listening too closely to notice the cycle end, and it beeps long, loud notes. Even opening the door doesn't stop it.

"That beeping is like ice picks in my ears! We have to tell him to get a new microwave! What's his name, again? It's written on his mailbox."

I'll warn Gavin about an incoming angry message from his downstairs neighbor. I'm still too buzzy with adrenaline to go down there and apologize myself.

Instead I pad into the living room, sit carefully on the couch and turn on the TV, which is loud at first—

"Now the TV!" she says, "There's no *peace* in this place! Isn't he supposed to be at work right now? These are the only quiet hours of my day. He probably got fired. I knew he was nothing but a lazy stoner!"

Gavin, I'm sorry I made your neighbor hate you.

I turn the TV volume down to where it's just audible above the pizza chewing in my head and the muffled complaints from below.

Later, I creep back to the kitchen for more pizza...

"Clattering cardboard boxes now! He must be *high*!"

...and I eat it cold.

Then I turn off the TV, carefully lower my plate into the sink, and ball damp toilet paper in my ears. But the couch cushions creak every time I roll over, and the floor always has something to say about it.

WHEN VOICES COME UP the stairs, I run on tiptoe to the bathroom, but the downstairs neighbor hears me anyway.

"Running now," she says. "It's like a pack of elephants!"

I listen through the cracked door as keys jingle and ratchet in the lock. They enter laughing about something, and a heavy pack thumps on the floor. Thudding boots.

"Yo, Alex," Gavin says from the living room.

Boots approach the bathroom. I silently close the door, then flush the toilet and wash my hands.

"Hey," Eli calls through the door, "I hope that was a one, not a two."

I dry my hands and open the door.

Eli leans against the doorframe with his arms folded—no weapons.

***

While Eli is in the bathroom, Gavin asks how things went at my place.

"Fine. Got everything."

"Good. How are you feeling?"

"I'm good."

"Good." He seems to want to ask more, but isn't sure what or how.

When Eli returns, we open our packs and go over our collective supplies. Gavin adds things from his cupboards.

We finish the pizzas. We all use the microwave, but I wait by it to open the door before it beeps.

Eli lets it beep while he messes with his pack. He also keeps his hiking boots on, and the floor grumbles, "What is it, a three-ring circus up there?"

Gavin and Eli don't seem to hear her. Or if they do, they ignore it.

***

Gavin and Eli pass a pipe between them in the car.

I opt for a cigarette instead.

As traffic gathers they blow pot smoke out their windows in billows, and a woman in the next lane says, "You can't smoke on the freeway! Fucking potheads, I'll report you!"

I lock eyes on a passing building and pretend to read its sign while my eyes sweep back, but I only catch the front of her car.

"I see you with that cigarette. You're not fooling anyone, you stoner piece of shit!"

I say, "You should probably put the piece away. Someone over there is freaking out."

Eli lowers the pipe to his lap. "Who?"

"To the right, a little behind us."

Eli reaches out his window and pivots the side mirror. "That guy?"

"Sounded like a woman, but I guess it could be a guy."

"If anything, *he'd* be complaining he can't partake with us."

The other lane gains on ours, and the car creeps into view.

It is a guy. He's driving a brown El Camino with primer spots on it. He has long hair pulled into a sloppy bun, and his arm has tattoos of screaming skulls on it. The woman must be behind us, or on the other side? Or nowhere?

The guy notices me looking, and I smile, squinting my eyes tight enough that for a second I leave the car, disappear from under his stare. But a smile-at-a-stranger length of time later, my eyes reopen and there he is, still looking at me, so I find a building to look at. I pretend to be interested in the differing qualities of light in the windows. *Some clearly incandescent, some fluorescent...* Is it enough to pull off seeming like an electrician? Would he believe that's why I was looking his way?

Now he watches the road. Loose wisps of his hair twist in the breeze like snakes. His lane advances, so I get to see the El Camino's flatbed where there's a plastic laundry basket of children's toys and a large collapsible dog cage.

I drag my cigarette and stew.

Everyone who looks in the back of this guy's car—if they think *anything* about what they see—probably assumes he's just a grungy family man. Or maybe they think he's dropping off or picking things up at his baby mama's place.

But when *I* see a basket of children's toys plus a dog cage, I think: *that guy locks up children.*

Forget seeing kids in the grocery store, or passing them on the sidewalk, or being in the same building as them... The mere combination of objects in the back of his car—even in the absence of a child—is sinister.

Actually, with no kid around, the effect is worse. Is he "finished" with these items? Is he driving somewhere to set up his dungeon? Or is he making a contribution to someone else's basement or warehouse full of whimpering children in cages? They each get one toy from the basket, shoved between the bars.

Now I don't have to pretend to be an electrician; I'm staring at him as a responsible citizen.

"That guy may be a stoner," I say, "but check out his other hobby."

"What do you mean?" Eli asks.

"Look in the back."

He laughs. "What? Oh wow, that's a kiddie cage."

"Right? That's what I was thinking!"

Gavin looks and laughs too.

A wave of calm surges through my body, and I lean back in the seat. I stare hard at the messy bun on the back of his head, burn laser beams into his arm powerful enough to remove the tattoos. *He's the one you want. Follow him. Put a chip in his head. You could take down a whole pedophile ring.* I glare at his license plate, repeat the letters and digits in my mind, mouth them silently, willing the observers to write them down.

Do you see this?

"We do. So?"

Are you gonna do something about it?

"What are we supposed to do? It's a guy in a car."

"Alex, he's still got me taped up! Get your friends to drive to our place. Call the cops! I'm in the back room, when you go in the door it's—"

Shut up! You see this pedophile, right?

His lane slows and we catch up to him again. I stare my lasers into his cheek. If he looks, I'll give him a knowing grin and nod toward the cage.

"Pedophile? Takes one to know one?"

I'm fucking serious. Why the fuck would you follow someone like me who's done nothing wrong, when there are actual criminals to be dealt with?

"Actual criminals? You only think he's a criminal 'cause he's Mexican, you racist piece of shit."

How is it racist to point out that this guy is transporting children's toys and a fucking cage?

"I don't see any kids around. If he was drooling over a kid like you did in the grocery store, then I'd be concerned. But he's just a family man with a kid and a dog. *You're* the creep who paid a website to get someone to fuck you."

I lean between Gavin and Eli. "Hey, could you put on some music?"

"Sure, what do you want?"

I say, "Anything." But that sounds desperate and weird, so I add, "Something cool."

Gavin puts on a CD I don't know. Upbeat rock.

I let it play for several seconds before saying, "Turn it up."

He turns it up, but the music's undertones still buzz with accusations and epithets.

I faintly recognize this stretch of highway, but now it's evening and there's nothing reminiscent of a space wormhole. The pavement bathed in sunset light looks earthen. Primeval. Like clay smoothed into a vast plane by thousands of hands.

Two other cars are parked at the trailhead—a blue pickup and a brown hatchback. I wonder whose they are and how long they've been here.

The sky bruises as we tighten our laces, throw on our packs, and adjust the straps. The close hug of my heavy pack is comforting. It contains all I need for the next couple of days. If I were more skilled, it could be all I need for the rest of my life.

I once captioned episodes of a show that explained basic survival techniques. On the trail I see manzanita trees and think of all the uses for their peeling bark. Our boots clomp over rock shards I could sharpen into arrowheads. Our legs brush past the fleshy, pointed tongues of century plants, which I could saw from their bunches and strip into strong fibers.

Crunchy desert soil grinds on the faces of rock staring up at us. I listen to my breath, listen to the water bottle on my left side slosh because I drank some of it in the car, listen to the straps of our packs whine in time with our steps.

These are the only sounds.

The sun has gone and left a fading blue to the west. Everything else is deep purple. The trail is dark enough that I can only make out differing shades of rocks, dirt, and pockmarks. We turn on our headlamps, which shrink our awareness to bright, slanted circles, and all around us rise cutout silhouettes of pointed, twisted trees.

There are no walls here. I like knowing that if they've followed me, we occupy the same space. The only thing between us is air.

"We don't have to be there, Alex."

You're not here?

"It's not necessary."

Gavin is in front, then Eli, then me. A giant hand could reach down from the dark and pluck me away.

The headlamp moving over the ground before me is like a hole cut through to another place, a dimension where the air itself is solid dirt and rock. Like Lili's sunflower world, but in this dirt dimension I wouldn't breathe or see or move. And neither would anyone else, so even though I might suffocate there, I'd be safe.

They said they don't need to be here. *They* don't. Is that because Gavin and Eli are here? Are they my executioners?

Then is it hubris or stupidity to let me walk behind them? Possibly a strong bluff. A dare. The observers know I have a Swiss Army knife in my pocket. Of course, Gavin and Eli have knives too. And I don't know what else they have in their pockets. Pepper spray—for mountain lions, they might claim, and I'd have to accept that explanation. A taser hidden in one of their packs. Handcuffs. Rope. *Can't be too careful out here,* they'd say. *What if we run into a crazy person?*

I can't argue with that.

***

After two hours hiking, the chaparral is smaller and the terrain is rockier. Trees are dark and spindly with no leaves.

"Oh shit," Gavin says. "This is the edge of the fire zone."

I slide my finger along a branch of manzanita, guessing from its shape. It looks like a giant tumbleweed. The tip of my purple finger comes away slippery and soot-black in the light of my headlamp.

"We could probably backtrack into that woodsy part and find a spot."

They'd prefer not to do whatever they're planning in the open. I say, "I'd like to stay here. Where we can see the stars." I look at the land beyond my headlamp, the layers of hills against hills, differing shades of dark. Open space to run, plenty of folds to hide.

"Eli?"

"Honestly," Eli says, "I'm cool with the fire zone. Another fire's unlikely, since there's nothing to burn, and I kinda want to see this place in the daylight."

"Okay, I'm sold."

The creek trickles somewhere ahead.

When we gather wood, I move in unpredictable zig-zag paths disguised as meandering, and turn to face them before bending to pick up each piece.

The fire is warm but dim, because the wood is mostly charcoal and prefers to smolder. It lights the undersides of our faces a deep red.

Eli takes out a bottle of whiskey, which we pass around. They both drink first. I watch them handle the bottle.

It feels like we're in a closed room with black walls, and a floor made from stones and hard-packed sand brought from somewhere else. Only the breeze hints at our being outside. But it could come from a vent in a wall, in a dark corner of the room, *our* room, beyond the reach of the fire.

"Weird fire," Gavin says. "But it's kinda nice like this."

"I wish I had my hatchet." Eli rips a yucca stalk from the ground. "Or an axe."

I'm sure you've got something in that pack of yours.

He holds the head of the stalk against the embers, and yellow flames grow. He lifts it like a torch. "This is what fire's supposed to look like."

"You wouldn't be complaining if we had some meat to cook," Gavin says. "This fire's fucking perfect for that."

I wait for them to untuck bibs from their shirts, pull knives and forks from their pockets, sprout wolf snouts and stare, drooling, at me.

"Alex, you've got the animal tracks book, right?" Eli says, "Go catch us a rabbit."

"I wonder if all the bunnies around here burned up in the fire." Gavin looks at the air. "Poor little fellas. Or at least lost their homes."

"Gavin, you and Alex find some poop and track a food animal for us."

Is it us versus Eli? Are we supposed to walk off into the dark so he can shoot us both in the back of the head?

Gavin chuckles. "Food animal? Is that one of those survival phrases like 'wild edibles'?" He motions for the bottle. I give it to him. "Alex, always remember..."

I say, "You sweat..."

"You die," he says.

I know what the phrase means, but what does Gavin mean by it right now? Was the embedded message, "you die," the important part? Or was the whole phrase "you sweat, you die" his way of giving me a friendly reminder—*be careful out there*—in case I have to flee? Does Gavin know Eli's an observer, and did he arrange this trip, where there are no buildings and the landscape isn't alive with agents, to give me a chance to escape with supplies on my back?

Eli drops the stalk curling with flame into the fire and reaches for the bottle. "What does that mean, 'you sweat, you die'? Is that some kind of code phrase for 'push Eli into the fire'?"

I look at the glints in his eyes and ask, "Do we have a reason to do that?"

Gavin says, "It's from a show. *Survivorman*. And good advice."

"Never seen it," Eli says. "My advice is: don't sweat the small stuff." He hands me the bottle.

"What is 'small stuff,' in your opinion?" I take a long pull. The sterile heat of the whiskey feels good, and my salivary glands squeeze in the backs of my cheeks.

He shrugs and rips another stalk from the ground. "Like when your neighbor saw you jerk off. So what? What're they gonna do? If they tell anyone, *they* look like the weirdos for watching you."

"That's true," Gavin says, staring at the fire.

I say, "They could record video and put it all over the internet."

Eli scoffs and holds the stalk in the fire. "Half the internet is people jerking off."

I say, "But what if the 'small stuff' turns out to be really big stuff?" He must know I'm onto him. I wait for him to swing the torch into my face. If I time it right I can roll back off my rock to dodge the flame and onto my feet to run.

"Like what kind of 'big stuff'?"

"They could watch me all the time, as part of some government test."

"What are they testing?"

"They—"

"What could they possibly learn from you that they don't already know? It's the *government*, Alex. They may be a bunch of shitbag hypocrites, but I still think they've got more important things to do than post videos of some nobody jerking off all over the internet."

"Maybe they want to see how I react."

Eli laughs. "They don't care how we react to stuff. They don't even listen when we fucking *vote*. This is America. As far as the government's concerned, we're on our own." He groans and tilts the torch to keep falling bits of flame from landing on his hand. "Okay, okay, I change my advice to: don't sweat. Period." He tosses the torch onto the fire and it flares. Then the flames lower like a demon sinking back underground.

The black hood of paranoia lifts from my head. My forehead relaxes in a way it hasn't for a long time, and its thin muscle buzzes, and I do feel like a nobody. The center of nothing. Orion, with his arrow trained between my eyes, is just stars and empty space. Eli is flesh-and-blood real, Gavin too, and me—the three of us are nobodies, animals, out here together. I shrink into an infinity of relief. The rest of the world, loud and chaotic, looking all directions, seeing everything and nothing, ends at my skin. I'm another rock, another tree, another star, a bat in a cave, an ant in a hill. I am a drop in a wave, a grain in a dune sculpted by an indifferent wind.

After a silence, Gavin says, "I mean, you could die from *not* sweating, too."

"Jesus! Okay, my final advice is: we're all gonna die! How's that?"

Gavin laughs, and so do I. Our shared mortality comforts me like the whiskey burn in my throat and the knowledge that I am nothing.

Eli sits on a rock and reaches toward me. "Gimme that."

I hand him the bottle.

We watch the slow inner flicker of the embers. Lights on in a house at night.

***

The campsite's large oak tree is mostly burnt, and some of its larger limbs have been amputated. My headlamp edges the velvet-black branches against the dark sky like ghosts in smoke. I can tell by the size of the tree that the root ball must be massive, reaching down into the dimension of solid dirt and rock beneath me.

"Gotta take a piss, Alex."

I turn. Eli looks asleep, and Gavin reads a book with his headlamp.

I realize it's me who has to pee; that was my own thought I heard.

"No, I have to pee too."

Why are you telling me?

"Because I'm still tied to a fucking chair. You left me like this."

"He's fine, Alex, he'll just piss himself."

"Fuck you."

I stand and walk, look over my shoulder to see Gavin still reading and Eli turned away. Near the edge of the half-charred forest there's a cluster of boulders I hide behind, and I pee as quietly as I can, listening for the rustle of a sleeping bag, the soft crunch of footsteps. The paranoid hood slips down, and I have to pull harder to breathe as if something literally covers my face. My forehead hardens. If Gavin and Eli brought me out here to get rid of me, they already know I don't sleep much—this is the moment to catch me unawares.

As my tired eyes adjust to the dark, the fuzzy black holes between trees become grottos full of watchers, then tunnels of more trees between trees.

The urine sinks easily into the dry ground. When there's no more standing liquid I press my boot into it. Forensics will find it. *We did a comparison, and it doesn't match either of their boots. There was a third camper with them. And that print was too clean to be an accident—he left it for us; he knew he was in trouble.*

I sit against the rock and wait for the print to dry.

I open my eyes to a stiff neck, a sharp ache in my back, and the sound of steps from our camp. I watch the spaces between the trees to see that they haven't changed, while I silently unzip my pocket and remove my knife, unfold the blade.

"Alex," comes a whisper around the boulder. Why would he call to me before killing me?

The patch of ground is still dark, with my print in clear relief. If he sees it...

I grip the knife and lean against the rock to stand. Stinging fuzz swells in my feet. I wiggle my toes to move the blood, ready to run.

"Alex?" It's Gavin. Blinded by bias, I suspected the wrong friend. Keep your enemies closer...

"Yeah, I'm here."

"Okay. Just checking." A pause. "You taking a shit?"

In a second he'll come around and I'll swing the knife. If they're working together, Eli might be ready on the other side, so I'll have to be quick. "Yeah, whiskey shits. You know."

If I plant it in Gavin's ribs, it might get stuck. I should aim for the throat.

"Okay, gotcha. You were gone a while. Had to make sure you weren't eaten by something."

What is he waiting for? "Nope, just doing this."

He laughs. "No worries. Take your time." Footsteps crackle back to camp, a sleeping bag swishes.

He didn't step into view out of respect for my privacy. My privacy, out here in the wild where anything can happen and no one has to know.

Why is my knife out, ready to plunge into the throat of the one person who still respects my privacy?

We exist in another triangle constellation. But this triangle is skewed, fragile. I'm the far point, stretched and separated from the other two by a wall of rock.

I'd almost gone much further. I could still be walking. Constant steps from the night I was followed a week ago, only stopping to eat and sleep, and I'd be in Las Vegas by now. Or Tijuana. Or withering somewhere in Death Valley.

If I break from this triangle and flee into the forest, I'd become a lone point in a tangle of possible constellations. But if I walk back to camp, our triangle will regain its strong, equilateral dimensions, and point outward at encroaching threats rather than stab inward at itself.

An equilateral triangle fits neatly inside a circle of protection.

I fold my knife and put it in my pocket.

My boot print is still intact, well-formed. If anything happens to us, it will signal our presence. It's up to me to protect us.

At camp, Eli snores. Gavin reads. The land is quiet.

I get into my sleeping bag and imagine the observers, far away in their room lit with glowing screens, sitting up through the night to watch us.

"Heart rate's down. He'll sleep soon."

I want my body to be a closed-off secret again, like everyone else's. I fantasize jamming a fork into an electrical outlet to fry the chip.

"Great idea. Short yourself out like your apartment. Solve all your problems."

In my fantasy, the shock kills the chip but also sends a surge to their computer, and the entire array blinks out.

"Whoa, wait."

"You saw that?"

"Yeah, what happened?"

"You've got this all in surge protectors, right?"

"Yeah, but that screen just—"

"There it went again... What the fuck?"

My heart speeds up. I close my eyes and concentrate on the screen displaying my heart rate.

"Dude, there's a problem."

"Holy shit. Is he doing that?"

I imagine a flare from the screen's power cord.

"It's on fucking fire! Put it out!"

"Jesus Christ, it's melting!"

I hear the foamy bursts of a fire extinguisher.

Then I focus on their computer tower, and imagine it explodes in sparks.

"Unplug it! The whole thing's gonna go!"

"Alex, fucking stop! Stop! Oh my go—"

I hear Gavin turn a page. Breeze skitters sand across stone. The creek is distant and barely audible, but there.

Power sizzles through my nerves to my fingertips and toes. It buzzes in my head. My breathing deepens.

Gavin or Eli swishes in a sleeping bag.

I turn off my headlamp and lie in the dark.

Fire-brittle branches rattle in the wind.

AFTER BREAKFAST THE THREE of us pump water from the creek and wade in barefoot, slipping on rocks and making "yip" and "yoo" noises about the cold water.

We leave camp with just our day packs, carrying water, snacks, some pot, and my book on animal tracks. Along the riverbank I find a walking stick and use my knife to scrape away the burnt bark.

Someone says, "Up and running?"

I look to the hillside where Eli says he may have seen an animal.

"Yeah, feed's up."

"Look at that, heart's going already. You think he can hear us?"

"Alex, can you hear us?"

Yes, I hear me loud and clear.

"That's a yes."

"Look, fuckhead, you cost us a lot of fucking money with that shit you pulled!"

"You're lucky we have this backup!"

What's this "we" stuff? Isn't one of you taped to a chair?

"Not anymore! Ha! Surprise, motherfucker!"

Nothing's a surprise at this point. You were never a hostage, and there never was a chair. You're right here with me.

"We'll murder you and your friends if you do anything like that again."

"Yeah, we're watching *all* of you now."

Oh yeah? You put chips in my friends, or what?

"Drones, idiot."

Wouldn't we hear them?

"Not these ones. From a distance we can zoom way in. We could read a fucking book over your shoulder, and you'd have no idea."

Interesting. I look around. *But what if we see them?*

"Painted blue. And it really is a beautiful day, isn't it? Not a cloud in the sky!"

Yes, it's beautiful. I concentrate on a patch of sky in my mind. There's a hint of something hovering. I can almost hear its buzz, like a mosquito, in my jaw.

"Dude, number four's bugging out."

"We're out here with you now. Close enough that if you pull any shit, we're gonna cut your friends' throats while they're asleep and make you disappear."

"Hey, there's some poop over here!"

"Alex, get the animal tracks book!"

An explosion vibrates softly in my jaw, like popping my ears underwater.

"Four's dead!"

The sky is clear. No flash, no puff of smoke, no tinkling of shrapnel on wood and rock.

"God dammit, you fuck! Stop doing that!"

"Coyote, would you say?"

"Or bobcat."

"Now seven's going."

"But seven's looking right at them. They're not doing anything, just looking at shit on the ground."

"What shit?"

"Literal shit! On the ground!"

I hold back a laugh.

"Bobcat or mountain lion?" Eli asks. "They're not the same thing, are they?"

"Check the book."

"Alex, you got the book?"

"Listen to seven's audio."

"How the fuck is he doing that? He's doing something!"

"No, he's just standing there too."

I pull the book from my pack, plant my walking stick with each step as I approach Gavin and Eli, and I feel like a fucking wizard. I bestow the book upon them like a grimoire to summon the creature's spirit from the poop.

Gavin looks at me. "Why are you smiling like that? Do you know what it is?"

Eli makes a face, "Don't tell me it's human."

"There's no way that's human."

Another one pops in my ears and rings in my jaw. I can't help grinning bigger.

"Shit, there goes seven!"

"FUCK YOU FUCKING FAGGOT FUCK, FUCKING STOP! FUCKING STOP NOW!"

I laugh.

"Did I step in some?" Gavin looks at the soles of his boots. "What's so funny?"

Eli examines my face, then the poop. "Something we're not seeing."

I laugh harder.

And I focus again and imagine their computer sends a signal blast to all the drones. I picture each of them hovering like jellyfish above the shallow valley around us, and one by one they pop into tiny fireballs and sprinkle debris like pinches of pepper from the sky.

Distant fireworks.

I sit on a rock and watch the guys pry the poop apart with a stick.

"Some fur."

"There's our rabbit."

"You think that's a rabbit?"

"Prairie dog?"

The blackened trees dotting the valley around us stick up through new grass and wildflowers like frozen explosions. Mines gone off and paused midair. Parasitic blisters beneath the flesh of the earth bursting in the sun. I hear each of them blow as I look, one by one and simultaneously. The landscape explodes everywhere.

And they scream. So much that I think they're dying.

***

I have an hour of peace, just the three of us tracking what we think is a mountain lion—"Gimme the book; this is a paw print," or, "Broken branches. Something pushed through those bushes up the hill," or, "Look, the top layer of dirt is scratched away."

But they come back.

"Alex, say goodbye to your friends. We're gonna murder you now."

I'd love to see how you'll do that. I've blown up your imaginary drones and two computer towers at this point. Time to send in the transparent tanks to blast us with ambient-temperature napalm?

"Look, fuck. Your implant chip is next to a nerve. If we send an impulse strong enough, you'll have a heart attack and die. The chip is made to dissolve when it goes inactive, so no one will find it; no one will ever know we existed. And you'll be dead."

There's a war on, but of the three of us in the war zone, I'm the only one who knows.

"Whether you believe us or not, you're gonna die in the next hoar-waouwah."

I sit on a rock looking out over the valley. Light glitters on the creek below.

"I mean, the next half-wshimawoa."

"What's going on?"

"I daou knwou!"

I focus on a phrase. I imagine it as immense block letters floating over the dust and dead trees, dragging heavy shadows.

"I yam aw fuhkring cowaid..."

"Dude, what's wrong with you?"

"Ay caw mahe yeyw fukx sai woteyer I wanets! Lukit mee, I ame a peesh of shit and use my own insecurities to prey on others. But as a result, my life amounts to nothing! I want you to shove this microphone down my throat!" I feel him struggle back. "Nnooo dohn—yyyyess pleess do it! If you don't feed it to me, I'll eeet eyt meesailf! No, no, fucking donets do eyt! Pleayse do it, feeed mee! No! No, down't!"

I take the observers in my hands like clay men and contort them to my will.

"Oh, fuck! Oh, my god!" I make him take a shotgun mic from the desk. "Oh-opennn wide!" He pries open the other's jaw.

The eater's voice gets louder as the mic enters his mouth, and I make him sing: "Hello, my bAAYbee! Hell-HOH, hy HAAARRhin! HEH-hoh, hy HAY-HIYE HAAAAA!"

The feeder's arm is sunk to the elbow in the eater's mouth. He struggles to remove it as he joins the song: "Send me a kiss by wire! Baby, my heart's on fire!" Then he rips the mic back out, trailing snagged intestines like cable. "Telephoooone, and tell me I'm your ooooown!"

I turn them by their shoulders like corkscrews and watch through my mind's eye as their torsos twist into tight hourglasses, their organs constricting and displacing into their chests. Involuntary moans push from their lungs, and their spines pop, one after the other.

Small sounds, like chicken bone cartilage.

Gavin is on his hands and knees searching tiny ground-out pockets in the rock. He crawls sideways like a crab to get close without disturbing possible tracks. He has an extra pair of hiking socks tied around his knees to lessen the discomfort of crawling on grit.

Eli stands by huddled boulders searching the crevices for a lizard he saw.

The observers are quiet now. They're wrung-out messes on the floor. A blood-spattered screen shows my heart rate, which is back down to a calm, even pace.

"I got something. Here's a paw print!"

"A real one?"

"Come and see."

Eli still stares into the boulders.

I squat by Gavin.

"Look," he says. "There, there, there..." He glides his finger, zig-zagging where the front and back paws hit the ground. The steps vanish over a stretch of rock, then reappear across a patch of packed dirt and sand, clear enough that he finds the animal's path up a slanted rock face to some dry grass that, despite the erasing effort of the wind, still looks parted from the animal's passage. "What do you think? That's it, isn't it?"

I grin. "That's gotta be it. Good eye."

Eli turns with his hands cupped together. "I caught my guy, here." He comes and opens his hands just enough for us to see. A lizard's tiny flat head stares out at us. The rest of its body curls in a black S in the cave of Eli's hands.

"You gonna name him?"

"Yeah. This is Walter."

Walter shoots out, turning in the air like a spindly star on his way down, then scuttles across the ground with Eli after him and disappears into a crack.

***

We find a rabbit in the tangled shadow of a black tree. Its throat is open, its body hollowed out. Skin lies deflated over what's left of its abdomen. Ants drink at its eye open wide in frozen surprise.

"Didn't leave much for us," Eli says. "You think rabbit eyes are any good? Like, on a bagel?"

Gavin snaps a charred branch from the tree and uses it to lift the pouch of skin. "Probably happened this morning."

"We're on the hunt for a ruthless killer." I smile.

Gavin says, "Mountain lion's just doing what it has to do. Can't go around picking berries."

"True. No basket." Eli looks for his own prodding stick.

Gavin pushes the skin back as far as he can, revealing the spine and the cavern of the rib cage. "Mountain lion's got no fingers for picking. Or weaving a basket."

"What about a mountain lion with human hands?" I say.

"That's terrifying," Gavin says.

"Climbing up trees."

"Yeesh."

Eli examines residue on the end of his stick. "They say there are still like five million undiscovered species." He stares at the horizon. "Something like that could be out there somewhere."

"How do they know it's five million if they're undiscovered?" I ask.

Gavin sits on a rock, pulls out the pipe and weed and packs a bowl. "Undiscovered mammals, though?"

Eli tosses the stick down the hill we climbed. "No, they're mostly insects. And a bunch of fish and invertebrates. They think there're only about a dozen mammals left to discover."

Gavin puffs on the pipe.

I say, "But what if one of those insects happens to be gigantic, and it *looks like* a mountain lion with human hands?"

Holding smoke, Gavin grunts. "When I wake up screaming tonight because I think one of those things is chasing me, I'm blaming you." He exhales and gives me the pipe.

I pass it directly to Eli. "Imagine tumbling into a nest of those things, made out of mud and spit and tree fiber. Full of eggs. Some are hatching—little mountain lions pushing open their shells with human hands."

Eli stares. "Something wrong with you, dude. You're not even high."

***

We prepare the fire early, while orange light still splashes the hills over a rising flood of dark in the valley. I walk through the dry grass collecting hunks of wood, and I hear them.

"Thought you could get rid of us?"

I was wondering where you assholes went. Good thing you had backup bodies ready, huh?

"Nah, we were just pretending to get hurt."

"You can't do shit to us, man, telekinesis isn't real. Fuckin' idiot."

"Ow, what the fuck?" He wipes a trickle of blood from his ear.

Sounds real to me.

"Shut up, faggot FUCK! God dammit!"

"We're gonna fuck you up so bad tonight, Alex. When you and your faggot friends are asleep, we're gonna tie you all up and pull your nails out with pliers!"

Fingers or toes?

"Both. But we'll let you choose which we do first."

"Yeah, then we'll cut a slit in your stomach and shove a hungry rat into it!"

Too cliché.

"How 'bout we shove a glass rod into your urethra, and then snap it?"

That's a bit more creative. But didn't the Nazis do something like that? Unoriginal.

"Then we'll..."

I make it a game: I have to find and pick up a piece of wood before they finish each violent description. With time, the descriptions become slower and more elaborate.

"And we'll—we'll, uh, take your arms and attach them behind your back, and we'll use a rope to lift them up until they pop out of your shoulders!"

"Yeah, then we'll cut 'em off and use 'em to beat you to death!"

And quieter. Like a radio on somewhere, listing torture techniques in an empty room.

As our fire grows I make each crackle the sound of something happening to their bodies. Bones snap, joints pop out of place, skin stretches. The bigger the sound, the more severe the result. They become fleshy gargoyles of bends, breaks, and bulges.

But I like the small pops best. Little bubbling movements under the skin that scare them more than anything. And I like ignoring their pleas for mercy while we talk around the fire.

I make them sing, and I hum along with them.

"What's that?" Gavin asks.

I hum louder, drowning out their screams.

Eli says, "That's that dancing frog song, right?"

I hum more, and we all sing.

By the end of the words we know, we're alone again.

HIKING OUT, WHILE ELI tromps among the boulders to find a spot to pee, I ask Gavin if I can stay at his place a few more days.

"Of course. How has it been?"

"Interesting. In a good way. But I need a bit more time."

"Take as much time as you need."

"Thank you." I want to hug him, but Eli is coming back.

I'd brought the *PennySaver* in my pack, and I flip through it in the car. One apartment listing catches my eye. They call it a "micro-studio," and it's two-thirds the rent of my place. Plus it probably isn't haunted.

***

They tell me that while I was gone, they went door to door warning everyone that I'm a sex offender and a racist, and to look out for me because I have a series of aliases across several states and am currently on the lam from recent rape and murder charges.

"The FBI, Alex. We weren't supposed to intervene—that's one of the rules of our experiment—but you have to be stopped before you do real damage."

"You've got a problem, Alex."

I agree. A mind that creates people like you is sick.

"You've got it all wrong, Alex. We're here to help you." As he speaks, his voice slowly rises in pitch. "You need us to keep you in *line*." Rising. "You're a hair's breadth from *madness* and *violence*, and we've come to show you the *sharp edges* of yourself." Still rising. "God damn it, Alex, we *are* you!" The pitch holds at chipmunk level, slow but manic. "If you can't trust us, it means you can't trust yourself! If you can't trust yourself, then you're fucking *broken*!"

I don't interrupt. The string of reproaches grows longer and longer, segmented like a centipede, and the segments break out in clustering tumors with little rasping heads of their own that in turn grow their own clusters of rasping heads.

I step lightly in Gavin's apartment, and caution Gavin to do the same, explaining that I heard his downstairs neighbor complain.

"The apartment below mine?"

"Yeah. An older lady, I think."

He stares at me. "That one's empty. Two guys our age moved outta there in August."

***

I shower before work, periodically turning the water off and back on—the voices seem more distinct with the rush of water. They carve shapes from white noise as if from bars of soap.

They follow me to work that night. And the subsequent nights. They sit partially-formed in the sign company next door and toss transdimensional popcorn kernels through the wall that burst at the back of my head.

On my second night back to work, I take my 4 a.m. meal break to drive to a 24-hour copy shop and use a computer to make an appointment with a psychiatrist. I hope he's good, because my insurance won't cover it and I only have enough money to see him once.

From my seat I can watch the copy shop's front door, but behind me are floor-to-ceiling windows. Eyeballs traveling the street sweep light across my back.

***

Counting the days to the appointment, I become a prolific serial murderer. It has to be done every two hours or so. Sometimes it takes three or four tries.

I flatten them against the ceiling and/or floor. I have them strip the wires from their equipment and thread them through their bodies from anus to mouth, then plug them in. I shrink the room until they squeeze out the tiny window like toothpaste.

By Wednesday I'm out of interesting methods.

While I try to sleep on Gavin's couch Wednesday afternoon, they take turns slapping each other in the face. I make them do this until their swollen hands flop on broken wrists and their cheeks are black and heavy with blood. I count the slaps like sheep. But they won't die, so I finally make them shoot each other in the face. It takes a lot of time and fiddling to manipulate the guns, since their hands are shattered and virtually useless. But it works.

I still don't get to sleep.

DR. JAMES DEVNET IS bald like someone pulled a large hank of white hair from the top of his head. He's wearing a sweater of horizontal zig-zags in terra-cotta tones and deep greens. To me it represents my heart rate on the observers' monitor, and the electrical signals surging all around me. But the earthy colors signify that I'm grounding myself.

When I get to the part of my story about the observers hacking my computer, he says he hopes his name "Devnet" doesn't make me nervous, since it sounds like the name of a dystopian computer corporation.

His sense of humor puts me at ease.

After listening carefully to my story—including the ill-fated video call with the scammer, my dates with Lili, my long walks and drives, and finally the ways I've discovered to temporarily destroy the observers—he diagrams a flow chart on his white board showing how each situation can inspire changes in my beliefs, emotions, physical feelings, and behaviors, and how those all interact to enhance and augment each other.

He says, "You have a thought: 'that person is frowning at me.' And they may not be, in fact they're probably thinking about something else. But with no proof that you are the cause, you conduct yourself *as if* you were the cause. And once you've gone down the road of 'no proof, but just in case,' anything is possible. You could live the rest of your life at the mercy of that person's frown, while they don't even remember you were there." He waves his hands at this, dissipating an imaginary cloud of dust.

Specks of that imaginary dust settle and sting in my eyes.

"Do you think about the simulation theory?" he asks.

"Of course."

"Me too." He squints at the ground.

I expect him to tear open the zig-zag pattern of his sweater to reveal that the background state of the universe is solid noise, a sea of zig-zag lines combining infinitely into bigger and bigger waves.

But instead he looks at me. "If that is the reality of the world—that we're plugged into some pod, or in a basement being fed drugs to imagine all of this, or we're just microprocessors in some vast, dreaming computer..."

"Or vestigial growths on some massive interdimensional being..."

He marvels. "Yes, what a beautiful idea." Then he points the dry-erase marker at me. "If *that* is reality, what do we do?"

"Well, we can't prove that it is, because we're trapped."

"Exactly! It is fascinating to ponder, and we should feel free to ponder, of course. I can see that's what you're good at, this pondering. And do it! Ponder! Imagine fantastic tales!"

Did I mention the observers had told me to write? How does he know? I can't remember. My recap is already a blur.

"But even if we surrender ourselves completely to this scenario, with no concrete proof, we still exist in this reality with food and laundry and sex and taxes..." He counts these on thick fingers. "And so we begin to juggle ourselves between these multiple realities. Which, admittedly, is fun for a while." He shrugs and smiles.

The phrase "fun for a while" gives me the same shiver I got holding the hammer on my neighbor's front doorstep. My neighbor with the cardboard-hole eyes who, while thickheaded, was most likely 100% innocent.

"But this juggling can only last for so long before it gets *fucking exhausting*." He drops his arms and sags his shoulders. The zig-zags on his sweater curl into layered frowns.

My eyes sting. "Yes. Exhausting."

I float in the ring of a life preserver, the only circle on a sea of jagged lines, tied to a cleat on Dr. Devnet's boat. He drags a massive shape from the deep onto the deck of his boat in a net labeled "stuffs."

"Whenever a situation triggers 'stuffs,' conduct a reality check. Don't get lost in the hypothetical, examine only what you can *prove*."

He cuts open the net, and the dark shape breaks apart into piles of glinting, gasping minnows.

Lastly, he prescribes a low dose of risperidone, an antipsychotic that he says should help "get my head above water." I hadn't expressed my oceanic metaphor aloud; he somehow felt it. This is the first time the idea of someone seeing into my head brings comfort.

"As long as it's okay with your friend, stay with him. But also fix that fuse and turn the lights on in your apartment. Light is good. Change the lock if that will help you feel better. That place is going to be 'haunted' for a bit, while you get your footing."

Haunted. He really can see into my thoughts. But he handles them like porcelain.

***

At the pharmacy someone in the next aisle says the pharmacist is swapping my risperidone prescription with sleeping pills.

Another says, "Then while he's asleep, we'll take him out."

***

But I walk the dim rooms of my apartment with fresh courage. The observers scramble to synchronize their commentary with my actions. They threaten to jump out of the coat closet—no, shoot me in the kitchen—no, strangle me in the bathroo—set me on fire in the bedr—and it sounds silly all mashed together like that, debunked and revised every few seconds.

While I change the locks on my open front door, daring the world to rush in, they tell me, "Dr. Devnet's full of shit, and he's working for us."

If he's working for you, why would you say he's full of shit?

"To see your reaction! You still haven't figured it out, have you?"

"You changed your mind so fucking fast. 'Oh, I guess I'm crazy!' What a gullible shithead you are."

The stepladder I bought creaks open and lifts me high enough to touch my head to the ceiling. My fingers bat the hanging wires, fearing a bite from them, but when the wires prove dead I pull more slack, strip their tips, and secure them to the replacement smoke detector with shiny new screws.

I change the fuse and flip the switch on the panel. The lights blink on. My fridge hums to life. It's almost like time travel.

The walls still radiate hostility, and I stare out the window as I open the blinds to let sunlight mix with the electric light, smiling but feeling closed-in and now only 50% sure that the neighbors are innocent. Because all of this could've been part of the plan.

I unplug my old router, wrap it in its cords, and shove it onto the top shelf of the closet.

I seek out every stray shard of the smoke detector on the counter and floor. I move the furniture to sweep up the last of the sugar and rice.

It feels like cleaning up a child's tantrum years after the child has gone.

THE DAY I VISIT the micro-studio is the day I start to feel side effects from the risperidone. I know it wasn't switched with sleeping pills, because I still can't sleep more than a few hours at a time. When I close my eyes for longer than a blink they dart around in their sockets, watching an invisible tennis match at 100x speed. My thighs ache.

The voices threatened to cancel my visit. Said they'll pretend to be the landlord and I'll never know. That could be true.

How do we know that the biggest crowd we've ever seen isn't actually all the people that exist in the world, and each person we see over the course of our lives isn't just someone from that group playing a different part?

They say it's a small world.

***

I walk onto the lot where the micro-studios stand in a row—a single building divided into a linear hive—and I shake the landlord's hand.

The voices tell me, "He's got a boxcutter in his pocket." I don't look, half out of stubborn trust of this stranger, and half out of dread that they're right. Maybe I already saw it, unconsciously, and that's how they knew to mention it. So of course I would look down, and lo and behold there would be a blade.

"He's gonna use that boxcutter to get our chip back."

"Hi, I'm Alex." I smile into the man's eyes and feel the calloused edges of his hand.

His eyes smile back. His name is Lawrence. He's a Black man in his late fifties or early sixties. His gut pushes at the buttons of his plaid shirt, and he has suspenders clipped on his jeans.

The unit is the second-to-last in the row, which means it shares walls on both sides.

Lawrence wipes his feet on the mat before climbing the two wooden steps into the front door. I do the same. Our shoes on the vinyl floor are loud and close in the small space. There's a window next to the front door, and about five paces from it is the back window. Stretching my arms at my sides, the fingers of each hand are only a foot from the side walls. The ceiling is just a bit higher than I can reach with flat feet.

"Yeah, it's a small place." Lawrence says. "Something to get used to, not for everybody. But the rent's cheap."

The chemical stink of fresh paint lingers. Everything is L.A.-apartment beige.

Through the walls come muffled voices and sounds—on the right a TV plays, on the left someone talks on the phone.

Lawrence notices me listening. "Once you've got furniture in here it'll dampen sound from the others a bit."

"Oh, I actually don't mind." I realize I'm smiling. "The place I'm in now is actually worse."

If I put my desk at the window it might just clear the doorframe. A narrow bed could go along the wall behind that. A single shelf about a foot and a half deep crowns the entirety of the room, even above the front door.

It's like a tomb. The burial chamber of a pyramid, full of the mummy's possessions. Everything they'll need in the afterlife.

When Lawrence turns to show me the back of the unit, I do a quick squat to stretch my aching thighs. I wonder if that gesture would still be possible with furniture in the room.

The back is divided into two spaces. Straight ahead is the kitchen, with a waist-height counter and a tiny sink beneath the back window. It looks like the sink in an airplane toilet. The whole kitchen has the standing room of a phone booth.

Lawrence moves to its center, sucking in his gut, and says, "Room for microwave, toaster, what-have-you," with flicks of his hand as if to conjure each device. "Got a mini fridge down there, comes with the unit, but we can store it if you've got your own."

I crane my neck to see the fridge behind his legs. It cowers in the corner next to where the trash can would probably hide, by a metal dish towel hook that's lumpy with the ubiquitous beige paint.

"And then the bathroom." Lawrence has nowhere to go with me standing outside the kitchen, so he just nods at the dividing wall.

I back up to look. He flips a switch in the kitchen that illuminates a plastic dome light in the bathroom. Another phone booth, with a plastic floor and a toilet in the center. A wall-mounted shower head points down at the toilet. The floor slopes toward a drain in the back corner.

At least in this place, the debate about shitting before or after showering is over.

"You'd probably want to keep your TP in here." Lawrence pats the kitchen counter, which is within reach of the toilet. "Just to keep it dry when you shower." He pulls the shower curtain from behind the dividing wall, closing off the bathroom. Then opens it again. "It takes some practice showering sitting down, but I know some people prefer it."

"Sounds relaxing."

Lawrence chuckles.

"Watch that boxcutter, Alex," they say.

"He's about to push you onto that toilet and cut the chip out of your head."

Behind the row of units is tenant parking, next to an old wooden shed that's divided into coffin-sized segments, each with a padlock-able door.

"This is extra storage, comes with the unit. Keep anything you want in here. Put your own lock on it."

My own lock. My own space. Living sandwiched between other real people. Real sounds, ambient sounds, innocuous sounds. The human equivalent of cricket chatter.

A place with no hidden corners. Micro-studio surveillance only requires a turn of my head. I'll be like a snail in my home built for one.

***

When Gavin helps me move in he adds, "But you're like a snail that can't go anywhere."

I hope my new neighbors don't hear him say it. A couple of units have their windows open. Someone is typing.

I'd asked Gavin to keep the router from Matt hidden in his kitchen cupboard until I moved. Now I put it up on the shelf and make a mental note to call Matt to check the settings before I use it. I'll do that at the office again, since my new neighbors can probably hear everything I say, including router settings, SSIDs, and passwords.

But knowing they can hear me feels better than wondering if they can.

I'm CLOSER TO THE river than my previous apartment, but also further downstream, where the runoff channels combine in a concrete trough the size of a freeway, and castaway plant matter grows in gooey aggregate islands.

I try to run along the river each morning after my shift. Running is good for endorphins and dopamine, aggression relief, and to deepen my sleep, but mostly I'm trying to get my legs to relax.

The risperidone tightens my thigh muscles so much that sitting feels like holding a stretch. My legs bounce constantly during my work shifts to keep themselves occupied. One night a coworker complains that my desk is rattling.

Dr. Devnet responds to my email and says an antihistamine can reduce the side effects. I try it once, and it makes my brain feel like cork.

I go on 3 a.m. jog breaks around the office block but feel no change. My legs crave either a run to the end of the world or a nap for the rest of time. No matter my level of fatigue, when I lie down to sleep my eyes jerk around watching pitch-black fireworks.

I threw away the aluminum foil shade when I moved because my new apartment has small curtains. Daylight bleeds in at the edges.

When I do sleep, it's still only for a few hours. Mostly I listen to the neighbors shuffle around in their own tiny boxes, and I feel a throb of comfort when I can tell they aren't talking about me.

I've met one of them. Her name is Shannon. Her usual look is a messy blonde bun and a sweatsuit with a logo across the breasts and butt in sequins or rhinestones. She smokes long, thin cigarettes. She says she's thirty-two, but I'm convinced she's almost forty. I hear her repeating one-sided conversations; I think she's practicing lines.

She sometimes has sex with a guy in his fifties who speaks with a vague Eastern European accent and wears an old black leather jacket rubbed soft at the seams.

Coming home from work one morning, I see him sitting on the curb a block from our apartments with a bloody nose. After I park, I walk back and pull him to his feet, almost falling over myself. He's drunk, can barely stand, and leans so far into me that we almost hug. I don't know if he recognizes me as Shannon's neighbor.

I still haven't met the guy on the other side. I've waved, and he's nodded.

He's maybe in his early forties, very tall, and his knobby legs make every pair of shorts look like swim trunks. He has close-shaven black hair and intense eyes, and he often moves things back and forth between his locker and his unit.

The voices try to tell me he's another chip victim who's further along in the process.

***

Lawrence and I cross paths occasionally. The voices rattle off lists of things they want me to say. They've placed bets on how long it'll take to get me to offend him.

I'm winning, for now.

I'm embarrassed to admit that exchanging niceties with Lawrence triggers a little buzz in me, a ding on a karmic scoreboard. The higher that number goes, the more I'm somehow absolved of the awkwardness I inflicted upon Lili.

Before my move I sent her a message saying, *Hey, I'm sorry I got weird. I was having a tough time, and it had nothing to do with you. No hard feelings?*

She hasn't responded.

I know she has no idea what's happening in my life, and probably doesn't care. She doesn't know where I'm living. She doesn't know Lawrence. She and Lawrence don't convene for secret meetings to consult the karmic scoreboards and share their evolving opinions of me and other white people in their lives.

So why after a polite moment with Lawrence do I hope that Lili can feel it too, wherever she is?

Do I win points for having good intentions? Or do I lose points for secretly hoping that people take notice of my cordiality and label me "one of the good ones"?

Maybe thinking of human interaction as a test means that I am, in fact, failing the test.

ON MY WAY TO buy groceries I see a sign in the window of a pet food store, and just like in a movie, I walk in, apply, and get the job. The pay will be less than what I've been making, but I prefer this job.

The day I give my resignation at the closed-captioning office also happens to be the day I decide to start easing off the risperidone. In the office bathroom I take a quiet moment to stare into the mirror—through the mirror—to bid farewell to the gargoyles hunched on the other side.

It takes them about a week to follow me to the new job, but by that time I've settled in.

The owner of the pet food store is a Korean man named Peter. He pays no attention to how he puts on his socks—I often see the gray or yellow heel patches bunched up under the tongues of his sneakers.

I answer directly to Paul, also Korean, who is the warehouse manager. Our "warehouse" is twice the size of my micro-studio, piled with forty-pound bags of dog and cat kibble and stacked with shelves of smaller bags and flats of cans.

Answering to Paul alongside me is a Mexican guy a little younger than me named Fernie, which is short for Fernando. Through Paul's accent, his name is "Funnie."

When deliveries arrive, Paul smokes Marlboros on the loading ramp and watches us unpack the pallet. Fernie always hands me the invoice because his favorite part is running in circles to remove the plastic wrap. He says things like, "I'm going as fast as I can, Alex, jeez! Such a taskmaster! Paul, you see the way this guy treats me?"

Paul laughs smoke and says, "Funnie, you treat youself."

When bags arrive damaged, Fernie samples the food. I've heard him give customers recommendations based on his personal taste for one food over another. Peter told him to stop doing that, in case secret shoppers come through and hear him brag about eating dog food.

Fernie keeps asking how much I'd pay him to eat a bully stick, but I refuse to answer. Bully sticks are dried bull penises, also known as "pizzles." Dogs love them.

During a lunch break on the loading ramp, Fernie tells me he used to smoke meth. Before the pet food store he worked at a pizza parlor owned by his cousin, but he got fired when they caught him stealing bags of pizza dough. On another lunch break he tells me his girlfriend is pregnant and he's looking for a second job. He thinks he might beg his cousin to give him back the pizza job.

Sometimes customers bring their dogs, and they pee or poop in the aisles. It makes Peter mad, but I don't mind cleaning it up. I find it funny that someone's allowed to get away with doing that in a store, even if they aren't human.

When it's busy, I work a register. It's a series of forced eye-contact interactions for which I've found a comfortable script. I smile, and most people smile back. A lot of our regulars stop on their way home from work just to buy a bully stick for their dog. I ask if they'd like a bag, and they all make the same joke: "No, thanks, I'll eat it on the way home!"

I wonder how many of them know what a bully stick is.

The voices say they've planted bombs among the cans of cat food I'm stacking, or that they'll meet me out back when I close. They're still anticipating the perfect opportunity to throw me into the trunk of a car. I'm often told my lunch is poisoned.

The store's speakers play an adult contemporary radio station that shuffles through the same hundred songs. I appreciate the constant music. If I focus, I can make the voices sing backup to whatever's playing.

After repeated listens, the lyrics of songs like "In the Air Tonight," "Rocketman," and "Margaritaville" shed humorous light on my experience with the voices. For the most part, the radio is on my side.

***

Fernie got his job back at his cousin's pizzeria part-time, alternating days with the pet food store. He uses me for one-sided conversations about how he's never doing meth again now that he's got everything figured out, and how ridiculous it was to steal from his cousin. He says he's a different person now. Family is everything now. He's got dark bags under his eyes and he moves slower than before, but he keeps up the high-energy act, like a birthday clown desperate for tips. His baby is due soon.

His tenacity inspires me.

On the street I try to smile at people, but I rarely get smiles in return. I think people in Los Angeles don't like being looked at when it's not on their terms. After a while of not getting smiles back, the voices start suggesting reasons why, and I take a break from direct eye contact.

I've made a weird compromise where I still smile at strangers but my eyes scrunch closed to avoid seeing their reactions. I tell myself that their reaction is their business. Giving them a smile is like free money—if they decide to snarl in response, it's got nothing to do with me.

But I don't like my squinty smile. It feels like curling into the fetal position. From the outside it probably looks like I'm saying, "Please don't hurt me," which, if I'm honest, is *exactly* what I'm saying, but projecting that message could invite trouble.

When the voices get too distracting, I murder them. Rarely as creatively as before, now it's simple maintenance, and they only take about fifteen minutes to reconstitute. I'm meditating every day to try to increase that time. They find that hilarious.

I see Gavin about once a week, either at his place or mine. He smokes weed, and I stick to cigarettes.

Some people moved into the apartment below his. He says I should've moved in there, but I couldn't even afford that place when I was captioning.

I'm self-conscious talking about my meditation with him, but only because I'm convinced I'll slip and say "masturbation" instead. Talking to Gavin is good for reality checks. Things I believed in silence sound ridiculous when spoken aloud to a friend.

On one of his visits, he hands his phone to me with a YouTube video open.

"I hesitated to tell you about this, but you should probably see it."

The paused image is of me shouting. The video is titled: *VEGAN FREAKOUT IN MCDONALD'S.*

"Oh, shit," I say. "But why 'vegan'?"

Gavin chews his lip.

"You watched it already?"

"Yeah, sorry. I wasn't sure whether I should tell you."

The video has almost two million views.

My skin vibrates like it did that day.

I play the video. The framing is vertical, shot from the corner of the dining room, and starts zoomed out. I see the other customers—the woman with her kid, the man, others. Beyond them I see myself standing by the registers.

"What does the end of this look like?" I hear myself ask.

The shot zooms onto me from the torso up. My stance curls forward, and my shoulders are raised almost to my ears—not shrugging, it's more like I'm trying to pull my head into myself like a turtle. My eyes are white glints inside dark purple sockets. My fingers are dyed a similar purple.

"What do I have to do? Shrivel up and disappear? Attack someone? What will satisfy you? Or are you all just day players? Extras? Do you even know what this is?"

The fryer beeps.

"Sir, do you need something?"

Gavin says, "Wait for it..."

I scream at the cashier, *"Stop! Just stop everything now! That's what I need. What do I have to say to get you all to stop? I don't know what they're paying you, but it's blood money!"*

"There it is," Gavin says.

"Oh, my god."

"I didn't know you were vegan."

"Sir, please leave."

I should be having a panic attack right now.

I start the video again. It's like performance art. None of the people in the video—nor any of the two million others who've watched and shared it online—have any idea what they're actually seeing.

I play it again, and I can't breathe. I'm laughing too hard.

Gavin laughs too. "The comments mostly point out that their 'blood money' is minimum wage and you should give them a break. But the vegans are rooting for you."

The laughter in my gut swirls around a pinprick black hole, the ultimate confirmation that I can't control how I'm perceived. This feels like dread, but is it freedom?

***

On another visit I let him listen to the recordings I made with his microphone. Part of me still hopes he'll hear them and I'll finally have my proof. But he only hears me. Both of us only hear me. He says it's like listening to a recording of a ghost.

***

I called my parents soon after I moved, and sent pictures of my new place. Mom called it a "storage unit." I told her it's temporary. I make just enough money at the pet food store to stay afloat in my little lifeboat.

I also called Matt—from Gavin's place—and confirmed all the settings on the router he sent. Finally plugging it in at home felt like injecting snot into my arm, but if I can't bring myself to trust it I don't know what else to do.

I could still be walking, weeks after the night ethereal henchmen first followed me through the streets. By now I'd be halfway across the country, turning the great gear of the earth with disintegrating shoes and raw feet, always looking over my shoulder, a stranger to the kindness of strangers.

But I choose to live as if the observers never existed. I can't reach beyond my own perception, so I put the burden of proof on them. I'm tired of pulling curtains aside only to find more curtains.

I still aspire to look my fellow humans in the eye, and to not be ashamed of looking. Because they see me too. Standing before each other, like it or not, we are unabashedly tangible.

***

I can masturbate in the shower. Having the toilet to sit on is convenient, but I have to be quick or the neighbors will get wise.

At night I can close the curtain and masturbate in bed, in the dark, to the movies in my mind. In these moments I can take my time.

Then, drowsy, I open the curtain and let the streetlight in. It ripples through leaves, and I imagine I'm below deck in a boat, watching orange moonlight splash through a porthole onto my wall, reflected off the choppy waters of a vast, black sea.

afterword

This book is based on my personal experience with auditory hallucinations.

It's not a memoir. Some aspects of my story had to be altered in translation—the truth was bent in order to more effectively convey the truth. Characters were combined or omitted, events shifted in time, but rest assured, everything in Alex's imagination happened exactly as described.

Here I must acknowledge the biggest change, to give credit where credit is due and allow for some further discussion of my recovery.

At the time of my "unmooring" I was in a long-distance relationship with a woman in Paris, France. Her name is Louise. We're married now. The long-distance portion of our relationship lasted for a year and a half, and I started hearing voices smack-dab in the middle of that period.

She appears nowhere in the novel.

Why would I exclude such a monumental change in my life—a move across the world for love; a change which, it could be argued, contributed to my break from reality because for the first time in my life I had something to lose?

Well, the novel takes place in the mind of an unreliable narrator, and a handful of the characters are imaginary. In our post-postmodern world the inclusion of a "long-distance Parisian girlfriend" would sound alarm bells for most readers, who'd spend the duration of the book waiting for the obligatory reveal that the *girlfriend herself* is imaginary and the "move to Paris" at the end is simply a delusional euphemism for Alex's institutionalization.

Or the reader might accept the Parisian girlfriend as real but feel she's an outlandish plot device inserted to save Alex by whisking him off to France at the end.

The fact is, both of those natural and understandable assumptions are wrong. Louise is indeed very real, and moving to France *didn't* solve my problems.

So I excised the "French connection" from the novel entirely, and replaced it with my brief online dating experience. This had the added benefit of opening the book up to deeper exploration of the sexual and racial aspects of Alex's troubled mind, which were equally important to my real-life episode.

Now the other big omission—my recovery. Clawing my way back to reality took several years of focused effort, which would make for a tedious ending to a novel, so I'll condense it for you here.

While I cut myself off from online/phone communication with Louise and my family, they had their own long-distance chats about my increasingly strange situation. A psychologist family friend had instructed them to question the suspicions and delusions I presented as "facts," to avoid reinforcing the paranoid wall I was building around myself.

During a rare moment of reconnection, Louise finally suggested to me that my tormentors might be imaginary.

Had the idea come from my parents, I might've brushed them off as not understanding or appreciating the gravity of the situation. It would've felt belittling, like assurance at twenty-seven years old that there's no monster under my bed.

Even hearing it from Louise, the person I trusted most in the world, made me bristle. There's an inevitable tinge of betrayal when someone suggests you're imagining things, especially someone who's not physically present for the experience. How did *she* know the observers weren't real? She hadn't seen the dumb surprise on my neighbor's face when I confronted him. She hadn't sat from sunset to sunrise deflecting and returning their taunts through the smoke detector. She didn't know as much as I did about America and its history—data that lends disturbing credibility to my most outlandish ideas.

The quest to expose my observers had cultivated in me a powerful gambling addiction. I thought if I put my chips on the right spot and waited through *just one more* spin of the wheel, I'd hit the jackpot!

But when playing against opponents from one's own subconscious, "house advantage" takes on a deeper meaning...

The one thing I still hadn't tried was acting as if they were imaginary.

So I made a conscious and very difficult decision to pocket the few chips I had left and walk away.

On the recommendation of the aforementioned psychologist friend, I had a session with a doctor much like Dr. Devnet in the book. This doctor was in my hometown of Seattle, and my parents flew me up to see him.

I probably would have benefited greatly from continued therapy beyond that single session, but the doctor couldn't refer me to anyone in L.A., so I would've had to do the legwork to find someone myself. Not to mention my insurance didn't cover therapy, the American healthcare system (especially for psychological care) is an expensive mess, and I was broke and saving up to move to France. But the one appointment gave me some tools to sort concrete versus imagined evidence, and the doctor had given me a short-term prescription for an antipsychotic (risperidone) to help me "get my head above water."

In my case, I feel the pills didn't do much beyond unpleasant side effects. This isn't to discredit medication as a possible solution for others, but I believe my particular psychosis was behavioral rather than neurological. Over the years, strange weeds had grown in my mental garden. Some were protective.

Some I hadn't noticed. Some I kept because they were pretty. Then changes in the weather made those weeds flourish and overtake the other plants.

I cannot emphasize this point enough: one's ability to observe changes in the weather and tend one's personal mental garden is *power*.

While I was in Seattle identifying the weeds (seeing the psychiatrist), Louise dove into research. She sent me articles on auditory hallucinations, which we discussed during daily video chats. My strongest weapon against the voices was talk—with real people. Voicing my thoughts and experiences externalized them, which shed objective light on the stories I was telling myself. As Alex says at the end of the book, things I believed in silence sounded ridiculous when spoken aloud.

Louise was the most empathetic and least judgmental listener I could've asked for, but this wasn't an automatic solution. I had to consciously strip away layers of defensiveness and doubt, and I still felt a nagging suspicion that she wasn't getting the full picture from her vantage point on the other side of the world.

When I finally moved into her tiny studio apartment in the middle of Paris, the distraction of being in a new place made the voices disappear for a week or two.

Then they returned, talking to me through the ceiling. Louise tried to convince me they couldn't be real because they spoke English while we lived among French people.

This logic helped for a few days, until we found out the apartment above ours had become an Airbnb hosting an endless parade of English-speaking tourists who were, as I heard through the ceiling, unanimously annoyed by the "noise" of my existence and occasionally replaced with my "government spies" come to check up on me.

Later we moved to a neighborhood where English was less ubiquitous.

I continued my captioning/transcription work for U.S. companies at a distance, and fought my agoraphobia by taking long walks in the area. Universal healthcare exists in France, but without a French social security number I still couldn't afford to see a therapist, so this self-imposed "walking therapy" was all I had. My system was: any time the thought of leaving the apartment turned my stomach, I made it an exercise. I smiled at every stranger I passed. Not in a weird way (I hoped), but in a way calculated to convey: *Hi. We both exist, and that's nice.*

Unlike in Los Angeles, many of my smiles were returned. Some of the smiles even led to conversations with strangers on buses, on benches, in restaurants, at the grocery store. It felt so good to see and be seen, and to have tangible proof that the world didn't hate me. Other people were as curious to know me as I was to know them.

Meanwhile I took French classes, and the voices through the walls dropped their English and morphed into a French couple. As my French improved I caught the voices making the same grammatical mistakes I frequently made. Every shard of evidence chipped away at the voices' credibility.

A friend gave me a Tibetan singing bowl for my birthday, which helped drown out the voices' laughter at my continued attempts to meditate. When ignoring them became less of a struggle, I swapped the singing bowl for a loop of meditation beads that I used to count my breaths.

I kept all this up for over two years, until at one point I noticed I'd gone most of a day without asking myself, *Do I hear them now?*

This was a triggering question. As soon as I wondered, *Do I hear them now?* they'd burst into my ear like clowns through a paper hoop. *YES!* my brain would shout back, *WE'VE BEEN HERE THE WHOLE TIME!*

They'd pipe up when I was tired, stressed, or feeling insecure, and often take the form of family or friends when we visited each other. After I changed jobs for a company in France, I sometimes thought I heard my coworkers discussing a mistake I'd made or a weird look I'd accidentally given someone.

Still, I maintained my rule that unless someone says something to my face, I have nothing to worry about. Most of the time that's enough.

I continue to experience social anxiety, and am susceptible to worry that I've been misunderstood or hurt someone's feelings. On the rare occasion that I butt heads with someone, my mind plays out scenarios wherein I defend my position, or tell them off, or give a witty retort that shrinks their argument to nothing. But this is the sort of mental garden maintenance that most people have to do, and I'm now better equipped to recognize these digressions and guide myself back to a place of mindfulness before I get lost in the weeds. It's not always easy, but it's never as bad as it was before.

I'm grateful for this journey. If things hadn't come to a head, I might never have learned to manage my neuroses and defense mechanisms.

Plus it gave me this wild story to share with you.

As you know, I didn't go it alone. Louise was my anchor from across the world. I'm grateful for her trust and support, and I love her more than anything. My parents provided empathy and a safe space when I needed it. Other family and friends helped along the way. My thanks to the (real) people who took part in my adventure, knowingly or unknowingly.

Thank you to every stranger who smiled back. You have no idea what it meant to me.

Thank you to family and friends who read drafts of this book and shared their thoughts. Thank you to my beta readers on Critique Circle, whose feedback was so insightful, and who proved that my story could resonate with complete strangers.

Thank you to Eliott Blue, whose cover art beautifully encapsulates the novel's themes and atmosphere.

And thank *you* for reading.

If you're struggling with auditory hallucinations, you might feel utterly alone. The best thing you can do is find someone you trust and talk to them about what's going on. They could be a family member, a friend, a mental health professional, or another voice hearer.

Two of the best online resources I've found are:

intervoiceonline.org

hearing-voices.org

My final message to fellow voice hearers is possibly as terrifying as it is reassuring:

You are not alone!

May you find serenity and live like nobody's watching.

Bois-le-Roi
July 21st, 2023

Thank you for reading.

To further support this book and its author,
please write a review and spread the word.

For more fiction and related news
visit ZacharyDillon.com

Made in United States
Troutdale, OR
09/06/2023

12692344R00181